Mason—
Welcome
hunt! Enjy!

The Star Hunters:
Unbroken
Light

K. N. Salustro

Mason -
Welcome to the
hunt! Enjoy!

Copyright © 2015 Kristen Salustro

Cover Image: Adam Burn.

ISBN: 1517735157
ISBN-13: 978-1517735159

DEDICATION

For Mom, Dad, Jacki and Ben.
Your support means the world to me,
and your love gives me the courage
to keep dreaming.

ACKNOWLEDGMENTS

Thank you everyone who helped make this book a reality by contributing to the Kickstarter campaign, or otherwise supported its creation, publication, and distribution. Even if you were just cheering it on with kind words of encouragement, your support was invaluable.

CONTENTS

CHAPTER 1: DAWN

Sunlight sliced the clouds, cutting clean, unbroken paths through the sky. The light slammed across the planet, carving out the thick forests spread across the surface. The darkness retreated before the dawn, shadows fleeing and scattering a million different ways before the light could wash them out. There were some shards of the night that were not quick enough, and the trees snared them, holding fast. These bits and pieces of darkness sat huddled on the ground, clinging to each other as they tried to survive the day. As the sun rose, the shadows shrank back, cowering before the light, but they silently watched and waited for the night to return.

Indifferent to the hopes of the shadows, the sun continued to rise, and its light choked off the last traces of the night. Nothing could hide from the strengthening light, and the dawn finally found the hard, bulky hull of the stolen shuttle. Running along the edges of the shuttle, the light traced out the pale Star Federation insignia blazed across the metal surface, caressing the abstract shape of wings poised at the height of a beat and encircled by a ring, a symbol that invoked thoughts of power and freedom across a wide variety of species. The insignia was meant to inspire awe and unification, though in recent times, it had become more of a herald of brute force. The light danced playfully across the insignia, showcasing its own strength far more than that of the galactic military before moving on to wink off the thick, unbreakable glass of the shuttle's cockpit. Inside the cockpit, Lance Ashburn raised his uninjured arm to shield his eyes against the glare of the light, and with the dawn came the reminder that he was running out of time.

As his eyes adjusted to the strengthening light, Lance looked out at the towering trees that made up the Phanite forest. His last visit to this planet had been only four sidereal days ago, but on that day, rain and darkness had soaked the world. This clean, bright green forest was alien to him.

He could not believe that it had only been four days. He had spent most of that time onboard a Star Federation starship, drifting somewhere between unconsciousness and a waking dream as Captain Anderson had interrogated him, trying to pry more information out of him about the Neo-Andromedan organization known as the Seventh Sun.

Lance had not been able to give her much, or so Captain Stone had claimed. The more distance between Lance and his part-release, part-escape, part-desertion from the Star Federation, the more he wondered if Stone had released him as a form of manipulation. Recent events had smeared Lance's credibility, and now that the drug-fog of sedation and painkillers had begun to lift from his mind, doubt had crept in to fill the void. Perhaps the Star Federation had purposefully turned Lance loose with the intention of tracking him to whatever hideaway or rendezvous a traitor might slink off to. They were going to be sorely disappointed if that was the case.

But when he had released Lance, Jason Stone had been withholding knowledge of some process called an Awakening and the true threat the Nandros posed. He had claimed that he had not shared that information with Captain Anderson for fear of sparking a purge, and Stone had said that while plenty of unpleasant things came to mind when he thought of Lance, "traitor" was not one of them.

Lance had to trust Captain Stone. Not that he had much of a choice.

After the attack at Ametria and the unwitting betrayal of Captain Backélo, there was no one left for him to trust. When he had escaped the Star Federation ship, his superiors had been questioning his loyalties, and his subordinates had been leery of his motives. The only person who could say for certain what his motives were and where his loyalties lay was an Alpha Class bounty hunter known to the galaxy as the Shadow, and to him as Lissa.

She was not his first choice of ally.

But Lance owed her his life, and far more than that, for his hope of saving the galaxy from the looming storm rested with her. She knew things about the Seventh Sun that the Star Federation could only guess at, and with her help, the Star Federation might have a chance at rooting out the Seventh Sun before the Nandro organization had the chance to strike.

The old mantra echoed in Lance's mind: *Stand and Protect.*

But find her first.

It had only been four sidereal days since the Seventh Sun had ambushed Lance and Lissa on Phan and captured her, but that was more than enough time for the Neo-Andromedan agents to hide themselves somewhere between the stars. Lance was about to begin the hunt for them, and he could feel the crushing weight of that task bearing down on his shoulders. He had the arkins, but for the first time in a very long time, the Star Federation was not behind him. He had been under suspension and arrest before escaping the starship, and if the Star Federation ever caught up with him, he had doomed himself to court-martialing at the very least, and only if he was very lucky.

More likely, he'd be facing capital punishment: death, or the rest of his life on one of the isolated prison planets, however long or short that turned out to be.

He tried not to dwell on those possibilities, but when he wasn't imagining the consequences of his actions, he was thinking about the massive gap behind him that the Star Federation had filled for so many years.

Now, in place of the soldiers, the familiar technology, and

the vast resources, there was only the cold, hard knowledge that his life outside of the military had been nothing short of a disaster. The only comfort to him was that he had managed to pick Orion out of that mess and get them both back to the Star Federation. Maybe he could get a little good out of this chaos, too.

Lance did not expect to be forgiven for his desertion, but if he could track down one of the deadliest bounty hunters in the galaxy—*again*—and deliver whatever information she had on the Seventh Sun to the Star Federation, then maybe there would be a little leniency for him.

He did not consider the possibility of not going back. He knew what would be waiting for him when he did, but outside of the Star Federation, there was nothing. There never had been. There never would be. He had accepted that a long time ago.

With a groan, Lance pushed himself to his feet and began to gather his supplies. He tried to forget about his bleak future but his thoughts kept drifting back to it, and he moved too fast for his enerpulse injury. He gasped as the pain fired through his chest and down his arm.

I'll be lucky if I can get out of the damned shuttle without passing out.

Landing the thing had been hard enough. The enerpulse wound the Seventh Sun had given him had burned deep, and even though the Star Federation's medics had accelerated his healing, the wound would not fade quietly. Three times already, Lance had bitten back tears after he had moved too fast or reached too far, and Orion had whined in sympathy as Lance's breath had rasped through his throat.

Not for the first time, Lance found his hand dipping into the pocket that held the stimulators Captain Stone had given him before helping him escape. Lance let his fingertips brush along the hard capsules that contained the stims, but sighed off the hunger for relief and withdrew his hand.

Too much overlap between doses, and his heart would spin out of control. Then Jason Stone would find Lance's body in the middle of the Phanite forest, and that would be the end of everything.

As Lance waited for the pain to ebb back down to seething discomfort and for his mind to clear as much as the ever-weakening painkillers and the stims would allow, Orion stuck his head into the shuttle's cockpit and fixed a flat stare on Lance. His impatience stood out in sharp relief against the splash of black fur across his face.

The arkin was tired of being cooped up in the shuttle. There wasn't much room for him to move as it was, but with Blade taking up the rear of the shuttle and her depression seeping into the rest of the space, Orion was especially agitated. He was not going to be pleased once they landed and Lance told him that he had to stay with Blade to guard her and the shuttle.

Orion fidgeted as Lance stepped out of the cockpit and began to organize his supplies. The arkin tried to unfurl his wings, but they brushed the walls and roof of the shuttle and he snapped them closed with a frustrated grunt. He bent himself into a tight turn and skulked towards the back of the shuttle, and Lance got a good look at the patch of rough, dark gray fur on his left flank.

It was an old wound, and the fur had grown back a long time ago, but it had left its mark. Every time Lance looked at the dark patch, he remembered the way the arkin's scorched fur and flesh had smelled.

Lance had killed the man responsible for that wound a long time ago, a vicious gang leader that had gone by the name Red Jack. There were a lot of bad memories tied up with that man, and Lance had to give his head a hard shake to keep them scattered at the back of his mind.

But it was hard to look at Orion—gray and black and yellow-eyed Orion, with the burn mark on his left flank—and not remember.

So Lance looked away, found Blade's wing, and slowly picked out the full form of the black arkin.

Curled at the back of the shuttle and mostly hidden in the

gloom, Blade had her eyes shut and her limbs drawn in close, save for her injured wing, which she had spread out over the floor. The wing had been broken when Lissa had been forced to crash-land the starship *Resolution* in the middle of the Phanite forest, and though the injury had been treated while aboard the Star Federation ship, Lance worried that the arkin would not be able to fly again. Arkins were sturdy creatures, but broken wings were crippling.

As if Blade sensed him looking at her, she cracked open her eyes and stared back at Lance. Amber against shadow black. Usually bright and fierce, but dulled by pain and depression now.

"I'll find her," Lance promised for what must have been the hundredth time, but it was more for him than Blade by this point. He always felt better after he said the words.

Blade grunted and shut her eyes again, not opening them even when Lance opened the shuttle's airlock, letting the morning light spill inside. Lissa's abduction had hit her hard.

Orion tried to follow Lance out of the shuttle, but after some firm words, Lance managed to convince the arkin to stay with Blade. He left some food out for them, but they both eyed it with distaste, and from the way Orion looked out at the Phanite forest, Lance had the feeling that he would return to find a pile of bones left over from whatever unfortunate creature the arkin managed to catch. As long as both arkins were present when he got back, Lance would happily clean up whatever mess they left for him, but he knew that he was more likely to return to find the shuttle swarming with Star Federation soldiers.

Captain Anderson must have learned that he was missing by now. The scrambled shuttle signal would throw her off for a bit, but Phan was one of the first places she would look. Lance still had to see Aven before she sent her ship screaming after him. The visit would cut his time and bring him dangerously close to Anderson, and based on what Stone had told him, he did not doubt that Anderson would hand him directly over to Fleet Commander Keraun if she caught him.

Lance had to move fast.

Digital compass in hand, water and a little food in a pack slung over his good shoulder, and a hologram projector secured to his belt, Lance set off from the shuttle on foot.

He was glad that the clearing he'd found was not far from the city that held Aven's hospital, but that was more of a curse than a blessing. Anderson would find the clearing immediately once she had teased out his trail. Moving on foot, one slow step at a time, frustration boiling in his gut, Lance could almost feel her closing in, could almost hear the shriek of starships breaching the sky, but he forced himself to keep a steady pace. The forest floor was illuminated by golden streaks of sunlight, but tree roots and fallen branches were everywhere, and Lance was not certain that he could recover from a misstep.

The forest had not completely dried after the rainstorm, and the few patches of clear ground were soft and spongy under Lance's feet. The air was clear and crisp, but the scent of wet leaves and mud haunted the forest, although Lance was so grateful for the cool temperature that he would have endured almost any smell. While his enerpulse burns had been cleaned and dressed carefully, the cool air was a relief, and he lifted his shirt a little and let the light breezes play over his chest and side. The air could not touch the wound, but his skin felt hot outside of the bandaging and Lance welcomed the chill.

By the time he had reached the outskirts of the city, Lance was shivering a little, and was strongly tempted to take another dose of stimulators. Instead, he crouched behind the last row of trees and activated the hologram projector on his belt, letting the little machine envelop him in a disguise. It was a Star Federation standard-issue hologram projector, top-of-the-line as befitting Star Federation soldiers, but Lance hesitated long enough to raise his good arm and shift it around, watching the hologram react to the light and simulate shadow on fabric and skin. The settings were a little off, with too much contrast and not enough soft shading to pass as reality, and Lance took a few precious moments to adjust the levels. When he was finally satisfied, Lance peered out from the forest and checked for any unwanted observers.

There were mostly buildings and alleyways in front of Lance, but between them and the trees was a stretch of open land, a wide strip cleared away to divide the city from the forest. Judging by the uniform width of it, Lance thought that there might have been plans for a wall at some point, but they had been postponed or scrapped in favor of some other project.

Lance scanned the sky, took a step backwards as a small transport cruiser streaked over the outskirts of the city, steeled himself, then plunged into the clearing and stumbled across it as fast as he could. He made it to the closest alleyway and ducked into the gloom, pausing to catch his breath before setting off again at a slower pace and doing everything he could to conceal his injury. His hologram would not help him hide that.

It was still early morning, and a large part of the city had not come awake yet. There were, however, several figures marching across the overhead walkways, and as he drew closer, Lance heard the drone of the crowd from the main streets. When he emerged from the alley, he slipped into the thin pack without drawing more than a bored glance or two, and set off for the hospital. He let the crowd carry him along, but took care not to bump his bad shoulder against anyone. As the sun rose and the street swarms thickened, that task turned his easy walk into a strange, jolting dance, but by that point, he had almost reached the hospital and managed to avoid too much attention.

When he found the right building, he came up short, and someone jabbed him in the side and growled something nasty at him, but between the flare of pain and the surge of stress at seeing the group of Star Federation soldiers stationed outside the hospital, Lance did not hear it.

Ducking into a nearby alley, Lance forced himself to calm down and catch his breath. He peered out at the soldiers, awkwardly trying to keep himself in the shadows. He studied them for a quick moment, then pulled back, thinking.

The soldiers looked bored more than anything else. They must have been assigned to the hospital as a precautionary measure. Based on their lounging postures, they were not expecting anyone of special interest to pass their way. Lance weighed his options, but ultimately decided that his odds of sneaking past them were not good. Disinterested as they were, they were still trained soldiers, and they would notice that he was trying to hide an injury. If they stopped him, a hologram would not protect him from an identity scan. And even if he made it past them, there could be more soldiers inside the hospital, watching and waiting.

Lance moved away from the main street and threaded his way through the alleys, working out an indirect route towards the hospital. He'd been prepared to come up with some excuse to see Dr. Chhaya, but now he was hoping for an unguarded side entrance that he could force his way into. He knew that was about as likely as sneaking past the soldiers, but he was running out of options. If he could not find anything, he would have to risk the main entrance and hope the soldiers gave him little more than a passing glance.

When he reached the hospital and began to prowl around the perimeter, he felt his chances of success slipping further and further away. There were side access doors, but they either opened solely from the inside, or required identification scans to access. Lance could not bypass those.

Just about ready to give up, he turned one last corner and jerked to a halt when he saw the man standing in the alleyway. The man's eyes were closed, and his face was turned towards the sky as he spoke softly into the quiet. Sunlight had not yet slanted into the alley at this early hour, but through the gloom, Lance picked out the man's wiry gray hair, brown skin, settlements of extra weight around his middle, and soft age lines etched into his face.

Lance had never thought that he would be so thrilled to see Dr. Chhaya, but he held back and let the doctor finish.

Finally, Chhaya sighed and lowered his head. He withdrew something from his pocket, turned, and caught sight of Lance.

For a moment, the two men stood perfectly still, staring at each other. Then the doctor took a stumbling step back and turned to run.

"Dr. Chhaya!" Lance called out, as loudly as he dared.

The doctor hesitated, but kept edging away from Lance, throwing glances over his shoulder towards the main street where the group of Star Federation soldiers was stationed.

Lance held up his hands to show that he was unarmed, wincing a little when even that turned out to be too demanding for his wound. "Fleet Commander Ashburn," he said, then winced again, but not from motion. "Actually, just Ashburn now." He lowered his arms and touched the hologram projector on his belt, letting the disguise flicker.

Distrust lingered in the doctor's gaze, and the tension remained in his body.

Lance took a small step forward and thrust his chin towards the main street. He kept his voice low when he said, "Have the soldiers found him yet?"

Chhaya considered him for a long moment. "No," he finally said. "They're looking, but they don't seem to know what they're trying to find."

Lance breathed out his relief, though he knew it would not be much longer before the soldiers stormed Aven's room. "I need to speak with Aven." He took another small step forward and dropped his voice even lower. "It's about Lissa."

Something shifted behind the doctor's dark eyes, and he gave Lance a long, searching look. "They took her."

Lance swallowed. "Yes."

Pain flared across Chhaya's face, but he fought it back and quickly motioned Lance towards a door in the side of the building. Chhaya stood before the identity lock, allowed it to scan him, and then held the door open for Lance. When they had slipped inside, Chhaya snapped his hand on to Lance's bad shoulder, sending a fresh wave of pain down his arm.

Lance yelped softly, but even through the burning, he knew that the move was too calculated to have been an accident.

"I hope," Chhaya said softly, "that you're here for the right reason, Mr. Ashburn." His dark eyes drilled into Lance's.

Lance breathed through the pain, and nodded.

Chhaya released him and led the way through the halls. They bypassed security checkpoints without trouble, but paused at the decontamination ones. As one of the chambers sterilized them, Lance asked the doctor what he had been doing out in the alleyway.

The doctor looked at him sidelong. "I was praying."

"Really? I'm surprised."

Chhaya's eyes narrowed.

"I'm sorry," Lance said quickly. "That's just not something I expected from a doctor so far from Earth."

Chhaya said nothing until the sterilization process was complete and the chamber had hissed open. "If I were ruled purely by logic," he said as he led Lance through the hospital, "I would have given up on Aven a long time ago."

CHAPTER 2: MEMORY

Aven had been having a lot of trouble sifting reality from his fever-dreams, but there were six things that he knew for certain.

First, he knew that he was dying.

He had been dying for a long time now, though with the days melting into a uniform blur of hospital routines, he could not say for how long. When he had been healthy, he had been very powerful, very fast, and very, very dangerous. He had tried to maintain distant neutrality from the hunts at first, but towards the end of his time as the Shadow, he had begun to enjoy the work. Hunting had been thrilling. He had started to take on contracts more frequently, preferring to venture out on his own than lie dormant and try to blend with the rest of the galaxy. Then he had contracted the Banthan virus and the sickness had stolen his life. Now there was just the solid certainty of the hospital routine and the slow, steady trek towards death.

Second, Aven knew that he would welcome death.

He had wanted to die for almost as long as he had been dying. He had clung to life initially, believing that he would be healed and plunged back into the hunting field, but as the days melted into weeks and the weeks into months, he had given up. His doctor was a stubborn old human who refused to let him go, and his sister was more than just stubborn. She was afraid. Afraid to let him die, afraid to cut ties with him, afraid to face the galaxy on her own. Aven understood fear, but he had never let it get the better of him. Except maybe once, but he preferred not to think about that night on Terra-Six.

Third, Aven knew that the Seventh Sun had found him.

He had allowed himself the tiniest flicker of hope that the woman who had visited him—a day ago? Three days? A week?—had been another fever-dream, that her metallic eyes flecked with blue and the black collar studded with seven white stars around her throat had been nothing more than a waking nightmare.

Fourth, he knew better.

From the moment Lissa had dumped him in the hospital, Aven had known that the Seventh Sun would find him. Stuck on Phan, he could not hide, only sit and wait and wait and wait. And Lissa, stubborn idiot that she was, would keep returning to the planet, leaving a broader and deeper trail every time she did. He was really only surprised that the Sun had not found him sooner, and he had the feeling that the Seventh Sun felt the same way. The report of their agent would frustrate them even further. Aven was beyond their reach, too far past the realm of health to be any use as an Awakening candidate. Part of him was relieved, but a much larger part of him was depressed. An Awakening could have restored some of his strength, speed, and power, but as with his days as the Shadow, the time for that was long gone.

Fifth, Aven knew that there was something in the wall storage compartment of his room that might help him take down the Seventh Sun.

Well, not him, he hated to admit, but there were Star Feds running around the hospital.

That was the final thing that he knew, and if the Seventh Sun had found him, then the Star Feds couldn't be that far behind, although maybe he was giving them too much credit. They had yet to storm his room. Still, if and when the Star

Feds did come, he had something for them. Something that could lead them to the Sun.

And so, when the door to his room hissed open and Dr. Chhaya sauntered in with what could only have been a fresh nurse for him, Aven asked the new nurse to get the thing in the hidden storage compartment sunk into the wall. He couldn't remember what it was, but he knew that he needed it.

The nurse frowned, and threw a sideways glance at Chhaya.

"Aven," the doctor said, and something in his tone made Aven look at the new nurse a little more closely.

Not a nurse.

Dressed in traveler's clothes and not the hospital garments Aven had grown so accustomed to, the stranger was too lean and muscled to be a nurse. Too straight in the spine, too firm in the stance, though there were signs of pain and exhaustion that Aven had initially overlooked. There was a slump to the stranger's shoulders, and one of his arms was held a bit too far away from his body to be a natural resting point. There was an injury somewhere on the man's side, and it was sensitive. Prime target. That should have been the first thing Aven had picked out.

I would have seen that before, he thought. *I saw everything when I was the Shadow.*

He tried to peer closer at the stranger's face, but his vision swam and a violent coughing fit came on. He curved over as the coughs scraped through his chest and throat, and when he finally came out of it, he saw that the stranger had shrank back a step. Aven would have laughed if he weren't so disgusted with himself. He was helpless and weak, completely at the mercy of his illness and whatever drugs Chhaya and the nurses saw fit to give him, not to mention any prowling Seventh Sun agents, the Star Feds whenever they finally decided to show up, and whoever this stranger was.

He could not bring himself to care.

Closing his eyes, Aven wriggled a little further under his blankets, trying and failing to remember a time when he could breathe without his lungs burning in protest.

"I'll leave you to it," Chhaya said, his voice scattering Aven's mind all over again. "Wait for me outside."

"No security feed in here?" the stranger said.

There was no audible response, but Aven heard Chhaya's footfalls as he turned and left the room.

Maybe this man will kill me and I can finally get some rest.

Aven could no longer sleep for more than an hour without medication, and the drugs and the fevers often brought on strange dreams.

The previous night—or at least, he thought it was the previous night—had been filled with a dream so vivid. There had been a Seventh Sun agent standing over him, taunting him, and Aven had been unable to move or speak. He could only lie still and watch as the single agent became one hundred, and then they were doing something to Lissa but he couldn't see what. They had surrounded her in a swarm, and he had tried to call out to her, but either no sound had come from his throat, or she had not heard him. She had screamed and screamed until she had broken off into silence. The agents had dissolved away, leaving only her standing before Aven, tall and strong, her eyes blazing white, and she had whispered, "Welcome to the Light."

Or had that been him?

How many times had he been Awake? Two? Four? Seventeen? He couldn't remember if he had dreamed it all or not, and like all of his dreams, they were coating the world and making reality too slippery to hold.

"Aven?"

He opened his eyes to see the stranger looking down at him.

Not dead yet, and he's still here.

"I need to talk to you," the stranger said.

"I don't need to talk to you," Aven returned.

The stranger considered him for a moment, then activated—or deactivated, Aven realized—a hologram projector. The stranger's brown hair faded to dark blond, his blue eyes turned green, and his ruddy skin changed to pale olive. His jaw became squarer, his nose straighter, his shoulders a little narrower. The beard was replaced by patchy stubble, and the clothes became disheveled. The injury became clearer, with the clothing wrinkling and catching around the bandaging. Exhaustion pulled at the stranger's eyes, and he had the crazed scent of desperation clinging to him.

"I'm Lance Ashburn, a fleet commander—" the stranger began, but he fumbled the words a little and it took him a moment to get the rest out, "—of the Star Federation."

Aven eyed the officer. "You look awful."

Ashburn returned his stare. "You look worse."

In spite of himself, Aven felt his mouth curving into a smile. He found the strength to fight his way into sitting up, but even that left him breathless. Still, a fleet commander was far better than he had hoped for.

And then, even through his disease-nibbled mind, Aven realized that Ashburn had snuck into the hospital. That was wrong. "You needed Chhaya," Aven panted at the Star Fed, "to let you in. Why?"

"I am…" Ashburn searched for the right words. "Working under the radar. For the moment."

"Why?"

"It's a delicate operation."

"Don't trust your Fedlings?" Aven yawned.

"Not for this," Ashburn said, moving to cross his arms but wincing and dropping them instead.

Deep undercover, Aven thought. *Fascinating.* "So, what?" he said aloud. "You threaten Chhaya to get in?"

"Ambushed, I suppose. He stepped outside for some air and I was right there."

Aven coughed again, feeling something sticky in his lungs. "Lucky you."

Ashburn shifted anxiously, still keeping his arm away from his injured side. "Aven, I need your help."

Aven snorted, then sneezed violently. "With what?" He wiped the blanket across his nose. "And why do I care?"

"I'm trying to find your sister." Ashburn took a breath and swallowed. "She was taken by the Seventh Sun."

Aven froze.

He remembered now. Lissa had come and told him about the ambush. The Seventh Sun had tracked her down, and the Star Federation was on her trail, and she had no idea what to do. She'd been arrested by the Star Feds, by *Ashburn*, but then the Sun took her back and the dream of the agent standing over Aven and taunting him had not been a dream at all.

They took her. And if they have her, then they have her tracker.

He suddenly remembered the storage compartment.

Ashburn was saying something, but Aven cut across him. "Are you going after her?"

"I was hoping you could help me with that," Ashburn said. "I don't know where to look."

Aven raised a shaking arm and pointed to the wall. "Storage compartment," he told Ashburn. "Navi-sphere inside. Get it."

Ashburn threw a confused glance over his shoulder, but moved to the wall all the same. He began lightly tapping the wall with his knuckles until he found the right spot, and the storage compartment slipped open.

Aven knew what he'd find in there: a set of sterilized traveler's clothes that he'd insisted on keeping when Lissa had brought him in, spitting and hacking and cursing at her, and then not bothered getting rid of when the days had blurred into weeks into months into years; and nestled in the clothing, the black navigation sphere that doubled as a tracker. His sister carried its twin, and whenever they'd needed to find each other, they had always known where to look.

Not that looking had done much good when Aven had been stranded on Banth and Lissa had dawdled on Mezora, but it would serve him well enough now.

As Ashburn withdrew the navigation sphere, Aven reached for it hungrily.

"When did they take her?" Aven asked as Ashburn dropped it into his hand. It was heavier than he remembered, almost slipping through his fingers, or maybe he was just that much weaker since the last time he'd held it. *Pathetic.*

"About four and a half sidereal days ago."

That's too long, Aven realized. *He'll never find them.*

"I know it's a long shot," Ashburn said gently, "but I am going to do whatever I can to find your sister."

Aven sighed. *They're close to the base by now. Her tracker's signal is bound to be scrambled by whatever security they've got up. Although…*

If he sent the Star Federation to the main base, they would have the chance to eliminate the Sun. They were formidable enough of a force that they could find the base with a thorough search even without pinpoint coordinates, and if they kept quiet about it, they could catch the Sun unawares. Discovery of the main base would devastate them, and the Star Feds could wipe out the Seventh Sun with a few well-timed attacks.

For a brief but sweet moment, Aven saw the Seventh Sun's base swarmed by a Star Fed fleet, all firing pulse cannons in a solid stream of energy. He saw the base exploding in a burst of light, and then the dead debris drifting in the cold emptiness of space. Death of the Sun. No survivors.

Quickly, Aven activated the navigation sphere's special tracker, and sent it hounding after the signature left by the one Lissa carried, eagerly imagining the trail hers would blaze for the Star Feds to follow.

Aven's navi-sphere lit up and projected a hologram around itself, displaying nearby star systems. The hologram shivered around Phan for a few seconds, then leapt through space, rushing past stars and planets projected as blue, blurred pinpricks. Aven watched the trail unfold, but to his shock, it veered sharply away from where he had remembered the base to be.

Aven doubted that the Seventh Sun had moved their base. Situated just outside of the galaxy, they were well away from roaming starships and could never be stumbled upon. Had he remembered the exact location, he would have thrown away the navi-sphere and sent Ashburn and the rest of the Star Feds sprinting after them, but the years and the sickness had dulled his mind and he was no longer certain that he could properly remember how to hold an enerpulse pistol, let alone where to find the Seventh Sun's base.

There were some things, however, that he would never forget, and those things brought the rage boiling up his throat as the navi-sphere's tracker ground to a halt in a worthless little star system.

"That's the Paradise Void." Ashburn leaned in for a closer look. "Would they really have taken her there?"

"That's not where the main base is." Aven manipulated the navigation sphere, fumbling a little but eventually pulling the display away from the system and angling it towards the Andromeda Reach. "I can't give you a small search area. But put your Fedlings outside the Reach. Comb the outskirts. Tell them to sweep the void." He looked back at Ashburn, ready to say more, but the look on the commander's face stopped him cold.

"I'm avoiding Star Federation contact for a while," Ashburn said delicately.

Aven's eyes narrowed. "You can break cover for this."

Ashburn only shook his head.

"Why not?"

Ashburn considered Aven for a moment, then spread his hands helplessly, wincing a little.

Chest pain, Aven guessed. *From the wound. Very Sensitive.*

"I helped your sister, and I'm out of the Star Federation for it."

Aven felt a tiny spark of panic. "Then tip them. Send them to me. I'll tell them where to go."

"I can't do that. If they found you, they might kill you."

How many times do I have to tell them that I don't care about living or dying? He drew in a breath. "I don't care about—"

The rest was lost in a coughing fit.

Very aware of the pity on Ashburn's face, Aven felt the anger gather in his core, a heavy, familiar feeling. He was ready to let it melt through his veins and push him over the brink the way it had before, dulling the pain and bringing the pulse of the world into sharp focus. Aven let it boil, let it rage, and then it erupted out of him in another violent coughing fit.

When it had passed, his hand came away from his mouth wet and sticky, and he lost his grip on the anger. He crushed a corner of the blanket into his fist, grinding it between his fingers. He needed the Sun if he was ever going to taste an Awakening again, but he knew they would not take him. Not anymore.

"I'm sorry," Ashburn said gently. "I'll do everything I can to bring Lissa back. Now that I know where she is, I can—"

"I don't," Aven breathed, "care about her. Just the Sun."

The rogue Star Fed bristled in surprise. "You don't care?"

Aven looked at the man in disgust. "Can't you hear?"

"She's keeping you alive," Ashburn said quietly.

"Only because she's too scared to let me die." Aven deactivated the navigation sphere and sat glaring at the little black ball. It winked at him in the light. That brought the anger back, but it was cold this time, and Aven threw the navi-sphere at the wall.

The throw lacked any real force, but the delicate sphere cracked on contact and fell to the floor, spitting out a shining shard of black. Its guts of glittering circuits and small, tight coils of wire peeped through the small hole, taunting Aven further for his inability to shatter something so fragile.

Aven gripped the corner of the blanket tighter, and turned his face away from Ashburn, refusing to let the rogue Star Fed see the hard tears of frustration that pricked at his eyes.

There was a small silence, punctured only by Aven's heavy breathing. Then Ashburn's boots quietly traced a path to the fallen navi-sphere, then back to the door, and with a soft *whoosh* of the decontamination chamber, the rogue Star Fed was gone.

Whatever Ashburn did, the Seventh Sun would Awaken Lissa. She would slip into that bright, washed out world and run through it with raw power coursing through her body, and Aven would be on Phan, left to rot away in a hospital.

When Aven finally released the corner of the blanket, his hand left a dark red smear on the fabric: blood brought up from his lungs.

It was an eerily comforting sight.

CHAPTER 3: WOUNDS

"State your full name, please."

"Jason Mateos Stone."

"State your rank and district."

"Captain, third galactic sector."

"Your age?"

"Thirty-two."

"Good." Major Miyasato made a note on her datapad. "Can you tell me what planet you last visited?"

"Phan," Jason said with certainty, though his mouth felt fuzzy and words were harder to form than they should have been. He sat on a wall cot in the medical bay, machines monitoring his vitals and a dull throb beating against the inside of his skull.

"And what were you doing there?"

"Searching for Commander Ashburn." He thought for a moment. "We found him, but he escaped from this ship. He hit me with a tranquilizer."

Miyasato nodded, made another note, and checked the readout from a machine monitoring Jason's heart rate. She gently ran him through a few basic motor skills tests, asking him more questions as he proved that he could still control his arms and fingers. "How's the headache now?"

"Still there," Jason said groggily. "Not better, but not worse, either."

"And other than that, how do you feel?"

"Tired," Jason admitted. "Very tired."

Miyasato made a final note, then folded her arms over the datapad. "We're still not sure if that's from the tranquilizer or a concussion, but the good news is that neither one will keep you down for long. If it's a concussion, it's minor, and you should be fit within a few days at most." She frowned a little, and a faint line appeared between her thin eyebrows. "You do need to rest until then, however."

"Sure." Jason lightly rubbed his knuckles against his forehead. "Any word from Captain Anderson?"

Major Miyasato frowned again, and the line was deeper this time. "Captain Anderson has requested that you report to the control room once you are able to leave the medical bay."

"And am I able?"

Miyasato let out a hard breath. "I don't recommend it."

"But I'm able."

After a short pause, she nodded. "I will go with you."

"That's not necessary."

"Yes it is."

Ultimately, Jason found that he was glad for the major's assistance. Waves of dizziness washed over him when he tried to stand, and Miyasato steadied him while he waited for the medical bay to stop spinning. She helped him shrug his way back into the top half of his uniform, which had been removed during the initial physical examination, and gave his vision another quick check before walking slowly with him to the exit. When the door slid open to allow them into the hallway, Jason had to throw up his hands and shield his eyes. It was brighter in the hall than in the medical bay, and Jason's eyes took just a little too long to adjust. He stumbled when he stepped into the hallway, but Miyasato caught his arm and held him firm. She was stronger than she looked.

"Please don't push yourself, Captain Stone," she said as they made their way to the control room. "You need to take it easy before you can fully return to your duties."

"I know," Jason said, feeling a little better now that he was moving, though his stomach fluttered uncomfortably. He knew that had nothing to do with his possible concussion. "But if I don't see Captain Anderson now, I'll pay for it later."

Miyasato glanced at him. She had a round face with natural, friendly warmth set in to her features, heightened by the rosy undertones of her tawny skin. Her nose was smooth and delicate, and though there were lines at the corners of her mouth and eyes and faint touches of gray at her temples, she looked like she loved to laugh. But her eyes were fierce, narrow, sharp and dark, and Jason thought that he saw hidden knowledge in her gaze, the kind of knowledge that could threaten the security of his rank, though he was not certain if that was just paranoia tapping on his shoulder or not.

He was, after all, about to see Erica again.

When they reached the control room, Miyasato warned him against focusing on the instrument displays and data readings. Jason agreed, and they entered the control room.

There was a little too much noise for Jason's liking, and the flashes of holograms and screens made him feel dizzy all over again, but he took a few slow breaths and tried to focus elsewhere. Most of the soldiers were too absorbed in their tasks to glance his way, though there were a few that turned as he and Miyasato moved deeper into the room, and they fired off quick smiles and salutes from their seats. They used the more informal gesture, the right hand placed over the heart for a moment, then pulled across the chest and bunched into a fist in front of their shoulder. It was a salute traditionally reserved for wounded soldiers returning from combat. Jason returned the gestures when he saw them.

He heard Erica before he saw her. She fired off orders to the soldiers, anger ringing beneath the words, controlled but definitely present. From what Jason could tell, she had set the soldiers on a course for Phan, and now she was desperately searching for the signature of the missing shuttle that would confirm her instincts and tell her that Lance Ashburn had indeed sprinted back to that planet. She would find it. Jason could only hope that the delay between Ashburn's escape and the discovery of his unconscious self in the medical bay had given the fleet commander enough time.

Ex-fleet commander, he reminded himself.

After what had happened on the ship, on Phan, and even on Ametria, Lance Ashburn would be ejected from the Star Federation, if he had not been already. Jason doubted that he himself would fair much better, but he had to do what he could while he still had the chance. He started with Erica.

"Captain Anderson," he said, his voice undercutting hers. "You wanted to see me?"

Erica turned to him. She looked far more stressed than he'd ever seen her, but when her gaze locked with his, some of that stress gave way to anger. Her eyes, usually so soft, became stony brown, and she rolled the exhaustion off her shoulders and pushed herself up to her full height, which was still several inches shorter than Jason. She was about the same height as Miyasato, he realized, though Erica was clearly the combat soldier. She was thicker than the medical officer, hard with muscle, and her shoulders were broader and squarer. Her jaw had a stiffer set, and right now, her mouth was a hard line beneath her straight, narrow nose.

"We have a lot to discuss, Captain Stone." Erica clasped her hands behind her back, studying him. "I trust you're well enough to talk if you're up and walking?"

"Seems that way," Jason returned.

Erica did not smile. "Please wait for me in the hallway. I'll be there shortly." She turned back to the soldiers.

Jason looked at the back of her head for a long moment before turning away without a word. He found Miyasato looking at him again. That same flicker of dangerous knowledge was back in her eyes, and Jason forced himself to step away from her. She caught up to him quickly, and did not speak until they had slipped back into the hallway and moved away from the control room door.

"May I ask you something, Captain?" Miyasato said,

25

pulling up short and turning squarely to Jason.

"You may." He braced himself.

"When was the last time you had civilian contact?"

The question threw him, and Jason had to grope for the answer for a long time. "Back on Phan," he finally said. "As an officer. I'm not slated for leave for a while now."

"No, I meant correspondence." Miyasato cocked her head and considered him. "You have family, yes?"

Jason nodded gently, frowning. "You're worried that I'm going to have a mental break?"

"I worry that you're dealing with several sources of stress and could use more support than the Star Federation can give you." She looked at Jason with the familiar certainty of someone who had tried to skirt Star Federation regulations before, and possibly failed. "We don't want to lose you, Captain. Particularly not to circumstances within your control."

"I see," Jason said carefully.

Miyasato held his gaze for a long, silent moment. Then she raised her datapad and began entering notes again. "I can put in a recommendation for a video conference if you'd like, though written correspondence is more likely to be approved. However, given your current medical condition, I think I can nudge them in favor of verbal communication."

"Major, I don't think I need that at this point. I definitely don't have the time for it."

"Of course," Miyasato said, not unpleasantly. "If you change your mind, sir, let me know."

"Sure." Jason heard the control room door open and close. He took a deep breath. "Give me a moment with Captain Anderson."

Miyasato nodded and moved away as Erica came up behind him.

"Jason." Erica's voice was low and soft, and for a moment, Jason could pretend that there was no anger in the air. But only for a moment. "What the fuck is wrong with you?"

"Minor concussion," Jason said, turning to meet her flat stare. "That's what the medics told me, at least."

UNBROKEN LIGHT

Erica's eyes hardened. "This isn't a joke. You let a—no, you *helped* a prisoner escape."

Jason sighed and shook his head, spreading his hands in a defeated half-shrug. He could not tell Erica the truth. Not yet. "Ashburn got the jump on me."

Rage blazed across Erica's face, and she lost the quiet control. "Do you really expect me to believe that?" She forced herself to take a ragged breath and drop her voice low again. "I've watched the security footage over and over. I don't know what idiot killed the audio, but I know what I saw. You *let* him take you down, and then he somehow knew exactly where the arkins were, and which shuttle to take."

Jason held her gaze. "That's a pretty serious accusation, Captain Anderson."

Erica's pale face went even paler. She shook her head slowly. "If I have to report you to Keraun, I swear I will."

"Are you sure you have enough evidence for that?"

Erica erupted. "Do you think Keraun would care?" she snarled. "I don't need *any* fucking evidence, but I have enough!"

"Then why haven't you done it yet?" Jason asked calmly. Erica was standing only a few inches away from him now, her face turned up to his. They had stood like this before, playful laughter on their lips as they had slowly, teasingly closed the remaining distance between their mouths. This time, those few inches felt like several light-years, and as cold and empty as the space between the stars. But as Erica looked into his eyes, her anger slowly ebbed away.

"I can't believe you would have actually done this," she finally admitted. The hardness returned. "But maybe I don't know you as well as I thought I did." She turned away. "What did you say to him, Jason? What did he say to you?" She sighed tiredly. "Why did you let him go?"

Jason found himself looking at her hair again. It was straight and yellow, and Erica wore it short and pushed back from her face. It seemed held in place by the sheer force of her willpower, a straight sweep over the curve of her skull. He suddenly found himself remembering how he used to play with her hair in the exhausted aftermath of their explorations of each other. Sex had always seemed to leave her a bit more tired than him, and while she had rested, he had tried to curl and knot her hair, sometimes remembering the beautiful coils of another captain's thick, black hair, and sometimes forgetting. But no matter what he had done to her blonde hair, Erica had always stood up, run her fingers through it, and undone all the tangles.

It was the same with them. Jason was a minor snag in her life, something that she could smooth over with little to no effort. He knew that. He must have always known that, but he had hoped for more. Part of him still hoped for more. That part of him wanted to tell her about Dr. Chhaya's warnings of Nandro Awakenings and Ashburn's belief that the bounty hunter Shadow could help. The rest of him knew better.

He could not tell her. Not now. If Erica learned anything about Awakenings and the Nandros now, she'd turn straight to Keraun, and the Star Federation would initiate a purge. Not so long ago, he would not have called that a bad thing. But now there was something far more deadly lurking among the stars, and a purge would not help the Star Federation find it. A purge would only destroy those who were not linked to it.

Jason could not be a part of that.

He had thought that Erica couldn't be, either, but he wasn't certain anymore.

His voice was dry in his throat when he said, "I didn't let Ashburn go."

Erica whipped around. For a long time, she just looked at him in silence. Then she shook her head, and everything outside of her role as a soldier fell away. "Commander Keraun will meet us on Phan. You have until he arrives to tell me the truth." She moved back towards the control room.

"May I remind you, Captain—" Jason put heavy stress on the word, "—that you cannot issue orders to your equals?"

Erica halted three steps from the door. One deep breath ran through her chest, across her shoulders, and down her spine. "That wasn't an order," she said, her voice low and soft, "just a warning." She looked over her shoulder at him. "But when Keraun comes, it will be far more than that." She left.

Jason stood alone in the hallway for a long time. He knew that Miyasato was watching him, but she kept her distance and waited as he collected himself. Finally, he turned and started towards her, and she met him halfway. She gave him another odd look, but it was fleeting, and she helped him make the slow journey to his private quarters in silence.

When they had nearly reached the door to his room, Jason hesitated, and Miyasato stopped with him.

"Ranae Ramirez," he said.

"What?"

"My sister. Her name is Ranae. She's an architect, married and living on Sciyat, last I heard. If you can get verbal communication approved, I'd like to speak with her."

Miyasato nodded slowly. "Last name Ramirez, you said?"

"Yes."

"I'll do what I can."

"Thank you."

Miyasato gave him one final physical examination before helping him ease down on to his cot. She told him that she would check on him periodically, but for now, she left him to rest. Jason thought that he'd never get to sleep, but weariness outweighed all else, and he drifted off soon after she was gone.

CHAPTER 4: SILENCE

There was darkness, but it was far from peaceful.

Voices swarmed around her ears, and try as she might, Lissa could not make out the words. There was just an unending drone of whispers and breaths, and she tried to track the sources of the voices through the dark, but she never found them.

She listened for familiar voices, hoping to follow one out of the dark, but the sounds blurred and meshed together, and all of the whispers sounded alien to her, just an unfamiliar rush of words echoing across infinity and back. She tried to close her ears, but the voices always found a way in, filling her until she threatened to burst.

She tried calling out, but her own voice had been stolen, and she could only scream silence.

Lissa tried to run. She did not know where she was going, or if she was moving, but her breath slowly melted out of her chest. The air grew tight and warm around her, and the voices grew more frenzied, buzzing and pressing into her ears until they finally aligned into a single voice that whispered, "Welcome to the Light."

The darkness exploded into searing brightness, and Lissa gasped in agony, her lungs and vision burning and sweat streaming down her face. The breath came back into her in shaky bursts, and her eyes slowly adjusted to the light as she returned to reality.

The world fizzled into focus.

She was in a small room. She rested on either a table or a hard cot—she could not tell which—in the center of the room, and there was a door off to her right. To her left were a few machines, probably monitoring her vital signs, all out of reach. They were definitely medical technology, but she could not see their readouts all that clearly. The room smelled sterile enough to be a hospital room or a division in a ship's medical bay, but something felt off about it. She glanced around the room again, and saw a lot of gray. There was a spark of blue—a cluster of flowers that were harshly out of place on top of one of the machines—but the rest was gray. Bare gray walls, gray ceiling, gray floor. For a brief moment, she thought that it might be the signature gray of the Star Federation that she was looking at, but it was too light. Far too light. Not a gray room, but a white one.

White-hot, killing shot.

Not the Star Federation, then.

She squinted at the medical machines, and realized that they were not displaying data in the Written Unified Voice. The characters were strange but familiar to her, something that she'd seen a long time ago and forgotten, and Lissa found a sense of dread sneaking into her. Then recognition clicked, and Lissa realized that the language was Neo-Andromedan.

The breath fled from her all over again, and hot, angry tears ran down her face. She thrashed and struggled, but something was restraining her, and the most she could do was whip her head back and forth and curl and uncurl her fingers. Her breath returned to her, and with it came the raging thirst to scream and tear apart the silence of the room. One ragged half-shout escaped, but she bit back the rest and forced the screams to die.

The Seventh Sun had taken everything from her, her hope, her light, her brother Aven, and even Blade—fierce, brave, loyal Blade—and they were about to take her life, but she would not give them her voice. That much she could keep. That much was hers, and hers alone.

She still wanted to scream, but she took a deep, shuddering breath instead.

I'm going to die, she told herself, *but that's all right. I wasn't fighting for anyone, not even Aven. I wasn't protecting anyone. Not anymore. It's okay. There is nothing left to survive for.*

Lissa lifted her head and glanced around the room. It looked the way she felt: cold and empty.

Nothing left.

Numbness washed in, and Lissa welcomed it.

She did not know for how long she lay alone in the room, the hard surface of the table-cot pressing into her bones, but at some point the door opened. She dimly registered the noise.

The footsteps were a bit more entrancing, and despite her numbness, she focused on their sounds. They were brisk, heavy steps, the movement of someone agitated. The footsteps drew closer, a face appeared in Lissa's vision, and Lissa stared at the ceiling just beyond the curve of the face's cheek.

"*Sen valasha?*" the face said. "No screaming?"

Lissa blinked in slow response.

The face considered her. "They said that you were angry when they brought you down. They said you fought them all the way." The face came a little closer. "Are you going to fight now?"

Lissa blinked again.

There was a small sigh. "I need a fighter. A fighter is my only hope." The face dipped closer still, and Lissa registered warm breath against her skin. "Will you fight for me," the face whispered, "Little Light?" The lips curved into a mocking smile, and Lissa finally focused on the face.

It belonged to a woman with an unpronounced jawline, and a chin lost in extra flesh. Her skin was rosy copper, her eyes were large and round, and her nose darted down her curved face in a straight, sharp line. Her lips were thin and red, her teeth large and off-white. Her hair was light brown and wavy, pulled back into a loose bun that rested against her neck, but wisps hung down over her ears and small forehead. She had a thick neck and a gentle slope to her shoulders, and she lacked the quick, certain movements of the Sun's predatory field agents. But in spite of all that, she had the same hungry fervor of the field agents. Lissa could see it in her eyes. They were very pale, white gold almost, but without the harsh light of an Awakening in them. The absence of that light left her eyes shallow and flat.

Lissa did not know this woman, but it was as though she had haunted Lissa's nightmares for as long as she could remember.

"I'm going to fight for you," the woman said softly, still smiling. "I'm going to do everything I can to keep you alive." She brought her fingers up and slowly caressed Lissa's cheek. "I want to see you Awake." Her fingers dropped to Lissa's throat. "I want to see you fight." Her free hand brought something up, and she fastened the thing around Lissa's neck almost lovingly. "But Awake or dead," she purred, "you're going to help a lot of people."

Lissa felt herself start to shake. She wanted to scream at the woman, break loose from the bindings that held her down, claw and bite if she had to, fight her way out of the room, but most of that she would never be able to do, even if she tried. The rest she forced herself to keep in.

It's mine, she reminded herself. *This one last thing is mine.*

The woman smirked at Lissa. "So silent," she murmured. "But you won't be for long." She cocked her head and studied Lissa for a moment. "You belong to the Light now, Arrilissa." Her full name rolled off of the agent's tongue with calculated ease, and Lissa's skin crawled. "All of you. Even those screams you're holding inside."

Lissa released a hard breath.

"You can try to defy us now," the woman said, withdrawing her hands and straightening, "but we'll break you if we have to." She moved around the table-cot, circling behind Lissa's head, and stepped to the strange medical machines. She reached out to hit a few buttons, and through her fresh tears of frustration, Lissa got her first good look at the woman's hands.

Her fingers were not her fingers. They were far too long, almost twice the length that they should have been, and they looked delicate and spindly, but they moved with more speed and dexterity than the woman possessed in the rest of her entire body. There were neat lines of scar tissue along the woman's knuckles, and Lissa realized that the operation had not been a necessary one. The woman had been enhanced, modified to make up for clumsy shortcomings.

When she turned back to Lissa and saw the direction of her eyes, she dropped her hands and curled her bionic fingers up tight.

And Lissa began to laugh. It was little more than soft, delirious giggles, but it was laughter all the same.

For all their power, for all the fear they had packed into her heart, for all the nightmares they had forced her to live, the Seventh Sun was still only a group of people, and people could be hurt.

"Be quiet," the woman hissed.

"You weren't good enough for them," Lissa managed to gasp out, "were you?"

"I said be quiet."

"And you're *still* not good enough."

Suddenly, the woman was standing over Lissa again, one hand with its too-long fingers clamped over her shoulder, the other gripping her face with two pointed fingertips poised over her eyes. Lissa stopped laughing, blinked, and felt her lashes brush the tips of the bionic fingers.

"I could blind you if I wanted to." The woman's voice was a venomous whisper. "Or I could pierce your throat and watch you drown in your own blood."

A slow, vicious smile spread over Lissa's face. "Are you allowed to harm candidates?"

The woman clenched her weak jaw. "I am the overseer here," she snarled. "I have total control over your life, and your death."

"But you're still worthless to them," Lissa said. The smile died. "Not like me."

The woman said nothing. She only stood looking at Lissa for a long, silent moment. Then she abruptly straightened up, withdrew her modified hands, and fled the room.

Lissa did not laugh again. She had wanted to push the overseer into acting harshly, maybe even cutting Lissa's life short and sparing her the pain of an Awakening. Now that she had left, Lissa knew that she would live to taste an Awakening, but maybe she had forced in some room for mistakes on the overseer's part. She did not expect an opening, but if she found one, she would take it, no matter how small it may be. Any opening was certain to end in death, but there was nothing left. There was nothing to lose.

Nothing, except me.

The Sun wanted her body and her life, and probably would take both no matter what she did, but there was one escape, one tiny fleck of shade in a world that was far too bright.

But to reach it, she had to embrace the light.

CHAPTER 5: BREAK

The worst of Jason's headaches had passed by the time the return journey to Phan was complete.

Major Miyasato—given name Malia, he had learned from her file, though until she invited him to call her that, he would continue to address her as Major Miyasato—had monitored him closely over the course of the trip, and though she had cleared him to enter the field, she also had urged him to take things slow and avoid physical exertion whenever possible until his headaches had fully subsided.

"Unless someone wants to fight me, I don't think that's going to be a problem," he had assured her before leaving the ship. "Well, Captain Anderson might, but maybe I'll pick a scrap with Keraun before she can get to me."

"Commander Keraun wouldn't want to *fight* you," Miyasato had responded, "just kill you."

"You think he already hates me that much?"

"No, but he is a Hyrunian that has tainted his tongue with an impure language. Every time he speaks it, he falls a little further out of favor with the Hyrunian gods. As far as he's concerned, he has already been condemned in his next life, and it doesn't matter what he does in this one." She had given Jason a hard smile. "If I were you, Captain, I'd stay on his good side."

"You know an awful lot about Hyrunians."

"You have to, if you're going to treat them medically." She had handed Jason a pill to swallow, and a final word of advice before sending him off. "But if you do ever have to fight a Hyrunian, watch out for the feet. They like to kick."

Kicking Hyrunians were the least of Jason's concerns, however. Erica had successfully untangled the signal from the stolen shuttle, and traced it to its landing spot on Phan, though she had found what looked to be the same signature leading back out into space. Before she could sprint after it, orders from the admiralty board had come through. Ashburn had been stripped of his rank and honors, declared a Beta Class criminal, and the void of his rank was to be filled by the freshly promoted Fleet Commander Erica Anderson. With her new rank came a reassignment of territories, and a few officers were shuffled out of her command, including Jason. She had to drop him and the others on Phan before racing after Ashburn, and the detour frayed her already threadbare patience.

As they came in to port, Jason asked Miyasato to give his subordinates a few basic etiquette lessons regarding Hyrunians, then made his way to the control room to watch the final approach. He had counted it a lucky dodge that Erica was not his commanding officer now, but he still tried to avoid her whenever possible. When he stepped into the control room and saw her hovering over the soldiers, growling orders and monitoring every last detail of the final approach, Jason strongly considered stepping back out into the hall and disappearing until the touchdown was complete, but he forced himself to remain.

He had accepted that he could not tell Erica the truth, but there was still one thing he wanted to say to her before she ran after Ashburn.

Tense and agitated, Erica prowled up and down the room, watching every move the soldiers made. Jason saw nervousness roll over the soldiers with Erica's movements, but they kept their focus and no one slipped up. Finally, to relieve herself of some stress, Erica stalked over to the communication system and contacted Phan's Monitors. She started to ream them out for letting Ashburn slip under their noses, but they told her that there wasn't much they could have done about a solitary shuttle.

"Phan is a huge trading port, Commander," the head of the Monitor team told her apologetically. "We get a ton of ships coming and going every day. We catch most of the illegal ones, but shuttles are just too small for us to see."

Erica snarled something back that Jason did not quite catch, though it sounded like she had compared the skill level and usefulness of the Monitor team to a pack of blind, nose-less sewer rats trying to shit shit from mud.

The Monitors disconnected shortly thereafter.

Still fuming, Erica turned away from the communication system, and her gaze fell on Jason for the first time. Her eyes narrowed and her hands went to her hips, but she waited for him to speak.

Jason took a deep breath, then plunged in. "May I have a word, Commander?"

For a moment, she looked as though she was about to say no. Then she barked a final order at a soldier, clipped across the room, and led the way out of the control room. She did not speak or look at him until she had found an empty room, gestured Jason inside, and locked the door behind them.

Jason faced her squarely. "There's something you—"

"No," Erica cut across him. "There's nothing that I have to do other than my job. You, however, need to tell me the truth. Now." Before he could speak, she cut in again. "There's something going on with you and Ashburn, and you are jeopardizing so much by keeping silent. Need I remind you that we're soldiers, Jason? We swore to protect the galaxy, and that's what we need to do, first and foremost."

Jason looked at her for a long time. Maybe he could tell her after all, but he needed to be very careful. Slow and soft, Jason asked, "And what if we're not doing that? What if we're moving towards killing a lot of innocent people?"

Erica froze, the glare upended by confusion. Then her brown eyes sparked with triumph. "I knew you were hiding something from me." She stepped towards him. "Something happened at that hospital, and I want to know what."

Jason made an angry, cutting gesture with his hands, feeling the caution melt away. "You need to step back and think about all of this. You're so damned eager to get information, but you don't want to understand what any of it means."

"I understand that you are trying to hold me back from all of this, and that's why you've been keeping your mouth shut!"

Jason erupted. "No, I kept my mouth shut because I didn't want Keraun finding out about us. I kept my mouth shut because I didn't want the Star Federation reaching into my life and ripping it to shreds. I kept my mouth shut because *I could not go through that again!*" Jason was breathing hard, and the headache had crept back in, but he felt as though a weight had slid off his shoulders.

Erica stared at him, her mouth partly open. "Oh," she finally said, and her face hardened again. "*You* couldn't go through it again." She took a step back and folded her arms across her chest. "Look, Jason, whatever happened to you and… whoever she was, it happened, and you can't change that, but you shouldn't have tried to make up for it with me. I mean, you never even asked if I—" She broke off, and her face twisted with disgust. "No, this is the wrong time entirely to be talking about this." She turned away.

Jason followed her. "Then when is the right time?" He heard his own voice growing louder, hotter. "After you've left? When I'm under Keraun's orders? While I'm on the battlefield trying to decide if I should stay and fight or try to make a run for it? When, Erica? When can we talk about it?"

She rounded on him, eyes blazing. "Never! There will never be a time to talk about it, because there is nothing to talk about! And there was never anything for Keraun to find, either. You only thought there was because you never bothered to open your fucking eyes!"

Jason only looked at her in silence.

In that moment, he was very aware that, with a word, she could turn the Star Federation against him, and bring down repercussions far worse than anything Ashburn would deal with, because he was actually there to take the punishment. She seemed aware of that, too, and it looked like she was ready to give in to the temptation.

But she only sighed and shook her head, shaking off some of the anger. "You and I had been whatever we were for almost a full sidereal year, and we spent most of that time apart." She turned her head a little, looked at him sidelong. "I told you that we're soldiers, and that we're sworn to protect the galaxy, but there are people that I try to protect above all else. I'm sorry, but you are not one of them." She spread her hands through the space between them. "So, there you have it. Now will you please, please tell me what happened in that hospital, and why you let Ashburn go?"

Jason felt as though his heart had dropped out of his body and been lost somewhere in the empty space between stars. He could feel it beating, but it felt cold and heavy, and not at all like it was sustaining his life anymore. "I found out that..."

That Nandros are so much deadlier than we thought they were? That the ultimate leverage over the Shadow is lying helpless in a hospital bed? That I'm not as good a soldier as I pretended I was? That I wasted life, love, and breath on someone who could drop me in a heartbeat?

"Yes?"

"I found out that the Seventh Sun may not be as strong as they'd like us to think they are, and that not all Nandros are flocking to them willingly."

"But you don't know that for sure," Erica said flatly, but without heat or malice.

"No," Jason agreed, "but if one of the deadliest bounty hunters in the galaxy thinks that the Seventh Sun is too extreme, then maybe there's some hope for the rest of the Neo-Andromedans."

Erica sighed and crossed her arms again. "And Ashburn?"

Jason looked at Erica for a long moment. He couldn't tell

her. He knew that for certain now. "I didn't let him go."

She rolled a disgusted noise off her tongue. "So let's see. Against your word is a recording of you interacting with Ashburn and then presenting your back to him moments before he makes a straight rush for the arkins and then takes off in the best escape shuttle the ship had to offer. And, just in case that's not enough, we also have your weird fixation with Nandros."

"It's not a fixation," Jason said. "I just think that the Star Federation needs to act very carefully. There are so many wrong moves we could make, and I know that Keraun especially won't give a damn. If it were up to him, he would initiate a purge, and that's exactly what he's going to try to do. I bet he's already working on getting more support, but you're our human fleet commander now. If you don't sign off on a purge of Neo-Andromedans, none of the others have any reason to do it." He took a deep breath and stared into Erica's eyes, trying to remember what it was like to trust her. "I need you to promise me that you won't side with him." He reached for her hand, but she pulled away, and Jason quickly took a step back.

Wrong move entirely.

"Eight fleet commanders need to sign off on a purge before it can happen," Erica growled.

"Five in times of galactic war."

"We're not at that stage yet."

"Not officially, but if it happens…" He looked back at her, feeling desperation burning behind his eyes. He so badly wanted to tell her the truth, but he knew that he could not. "Don't do it, Erica. That is too high of a price to pay for peace."

Erica held his gaze. "I know that purges seem vicious, but this would be our chance to eradicate a threat from the galaxy." She clasped her hands behind her back, drawing herself up to her full height and looking every bit the way a fleet commander should. "We have a chance to do what the Star Federation should have done a long time ago."

Jason felt cold horror settle in his gut. "A lot of people are going to be killed. Innocent people."

"Nandros."

"Innocent. People. And you just might drive the few Neo-Andromedans who you actually would not want to shoot into the waiting arms of the Seventh Sun."

Erica gave a bark of laughter devoid of all humor. "You really believe they're out there. Nandros who would help you rather than kill you." Her eyes took on the stony hardness once again. "They were *built* to go to war and forcefully take the place of humans, and they were more than ready for that back when the Andromedans were here. With this Seventh Sun group in power, they're ready for it all over again." She stepped forward, moving to pass him, but paused when her shoulder was level with his. "This time," she said, staring him straight in the eye, "we're cutting them off before they get the chance." She stepped forward, moving towards the door.

Jason turned after her. "Erica, if you initiate that purge, you are going to make the Seventh Sun even stronger. They will become the only option for every Nandro out there. Don't force them into that corner. If you do, they will strike back."

She hesitated. "We can't do nothing, Jason. They've already struck once, and probably even more than that. We just don't know the extent of their reach. We can't sit idly by and let them grow any more than they already have."

"You don't need a purge to do that."

"But a purge will thin their numbers, spread their focus, and let them know that we're coming for them. That's the message that we need to send. We have to rise to meet them, and it's not your place to say that we should not." She took the final few steps away from him, and reached the door. She unlocked it, but did not step outside. Instead, she took one long last look at Jason. For a moment, her eyes were their usual soft brown again, but a moment was only a moment, maybe even a little less. "Whether you want to admit it or not, we need to do what's right. I hope you realize that soon. For your sake."

She left before Jason could say anything more.

CHAPTER 6: BEGINNINGS

Vinterra stood in the overseer's balcony, watching the grunt team perform the final checks on the Awakening machine. It was an ugly thing, large and hulking, all dark metal jutting out at mismatched angles and curves to form a rough shape that sat uncomfortably somewhere between a sphere and a cube. Bundles of exposed wires snaked out of the machine and trailed over the floor towards the lower power station, where part of the grunt team ran the initial calibrations. Their voices drifted up to Vinterra's ears, but her gaze had settled on the Awakening machine, picking out the dark, gaping hole that led into the interior. The darkness was mesmerizing in a way, cool and quiet and so unlike what the candidate was about to experience, which would not be pleasant. The hatch of the Awakening machine did not form a perfect seal when closed, and the candidates' screams always filtered through. Vinterra had come to know their pain all too well, and she had begun to hate the Awakenings a long time ago.

There were better Awakening machines in existence than this bulky mess, machines with smooth curves and carefully concealed wiring and circuitry, with inner chambers that held candidates more securely and contained their screams completely. Those machines were on the main base or the higher ranking outposts, guarded by larger teams as they serviced the top Awakening candidates. Here on Daanhymn, a forsaken little outpost built up from the ruins of a failed human colony, they were lucky to have this old prototype for their trials. Their machine did not have a high success rate, but the few candidates that came their way were always slated as unusable, either too unstable or too weak to make successfully Awakened Neo-Andromedans. This machine's purpose was to gather raw data from failed Awakenings and send that information to the higher-ranking bases.

So naturally, when the First Lit had contacted the Daanhymn base and promised the delivery of Candidate Arrilissa, there had been some confusion.

The reputations of the siblings Aven and Arrilissa—self-nicknamed Lissa, as the file had noted—were known throughout the Seventh Sun. Marked at an early age and then given high priority when they had deserted the organization, they were top candidates and never should have come anywhere near Daanhymn. Though Aven had always outranked his sister, Lissa would have made a powerful Awakened, perhaps even deadlier than Syreth.

Syreth had, after all, only been unleashed on the galaxy as the bounty hunter Phantom after his Awakening was complete. His targeted kills had brought in a significant portion of the Seventh Sun's funding, though his handling team had discovered that for each assigned kill, he needed at least a dozen auxiliary ones to retain a small scrap of control.

Lissa, on the other hand, had been hunting as the Shadow for a few sidereal years now. Five years, if the reports were correct. That would have dulled her to the pleasure of her first few kills while Awake, but her skills would have been unmatched. Granted, her controllability would have been shaky at best, given her rebellion against the Seventh Sun at an early age and the long years of cultivated hatred for the organization. For all of their bloodlust, allegiances mattered to the Awakened, and Lissa was anything but an ally. If she could be brought under control, she would be a very powerful asset, but Daanhymn was too understaffed and under-resourced to even attempt something like that.

There was also little to no hope of successfully Awakening her in the first place. Not on this planet.

Sending her to Daanhymn had not been a mistake, however. First Lit Rosonno had included a personal message on her file, saying that he believed that she could best serve the Seventh Sun dead. He claimed that he and the other First Lit were only interested in the data from her Awakening trials, and that there would be no repercussions if she did not survive the process. First Lit Rosonno even encouraged pushing the known limits of safe power levels during Lissa's trial. There had been no mention of Candidate Lissa's brother, or why First Lit Rosonno had struck both of their names from the list of top candidates, but that could only mean that there was something very, very wrong with both of them.

Vinterra knew that none of that had dulled Haelin's enthusiasm in the slightest. Rather, the obstacles had made the new overseer more determined, and Vinterra worried that Haelin would only be disappointed in the end.

"This is our chance to get off of this pathetic little planet," Haelin had said when Candidate Lissa had arrived on Daanhymn, firmly sedated but struggling and straining under nightmares. "If we can Awaken her, we can prove to the First Lit that we deserve better, that we should be with them on the main base." Her white gold eyes had gleamed eagerly, brighter and happier than Vinterra had ever seen them. "We could actually do something that matters!"

Vinterra had said nothing. She did not want to crush Haelin's enthusiasm, and knew that Daanhymn had been far from her first choice of station, but Vinterra had always secretly hoped that Haelin would grow to love the planet, just as she had.

Vinterra had been part of the first exploration team that had found Daanhymn and decided to test the planet as a potential location for an outpost base. The odds of any non-Neo-Andromedans stopping to scan the planet, let alone land on it, were slim to none, though the world was not without its risks. Daanhymn's flora was highly toxic to most species, and had already killed off a group of humans that had foolishly attempted to settle on the planet many years earlier. Not long after that, the toxic flowers had eliminated the native fauna and spread over the surface, choking off the indigenous flora. No one had tried to combat the mutated flowers. The world had been left to rot.

When Vinterra's team had run their initial tests, there had been very little hope for Daanhymn, but she herself had discovered that while sunlight neutralized the toxins, Neo-Andromedans were naturally immune to the deadly pollen of Daanhymn's night-blooming flowers. Vinterra's report had noted that there was little potential for a self-sustaining settlement, but if the Seventh Sun could spare the resources, the planet was an excellent choice for relatively short-term operations. The location of the outpost base had been approved shortly thereafter, and the Daanhymn facility was raised from the abandoned foundations of the dead human colony.

There wasn't much to it. Though the location was, in Vinterra's opinion, one of the safer ones, Daanhymn was too far removed from the main base to receive steady supplies. They scraped by on what they had, and stretched every delivery as far as possible. There had been bigger plans for Daanhymn as a full-fledged research station, but those had been postponed and then abandoned as more pressing matters rose up, and finally the Seventh Sun had turned it into an Awakening facility. Their outpost received the shakiest Awakening candidates, but they did what they could to gather the data and pass the information along to the larger bases.

The Daanhymn base consisted most importantly of the overseer's balcony and the Awakening chamber. Outside of those areas were the four holding rooms for potential candidates, only one of which was currently occupied, though it would likely drop back down to zero after today. Beyond the holding rooms were the small mess hall, the supply room, the ground cruiser bay, a small starship hanger housing three tiny vessels, and the sleeping quarters for the three working teams: the grunt team, which worked the Awakening trials and assisted wherever they were needed when there were no candidates present at the base; the researchers, who studied the data from the trials and communicated with the other bases, though Vinterra had nudged the team towards examining and testing the pollen from the night-blooming flowers; and the skeletal maintenance crew, which did the bare minimum to keep the building from collapsing around them, and took care of food rationing and preparation.

As the head of the research team, Vinterra had her own private quarters, though she had begun sharing them with Haelin as of a few months ago. The leader of the grunt team had his own quarters as well, and the final private room belonged to the Awakening overseer, which stood vacant now that Haelin was with Vinterra. The grunt team leader had wanted to move one of his better workers into the empty room, but Haelin had insisted on keeping it available, just in case. Vinterra had shrugged that off.

Outside of her stubborn desire to keep the private room as an escape route, Haelin was far from disloyal, and Vinterra had grown to love her and all of her stupidly brilliant ambitions. While Vinterra was content to remain on the Daanhymn outpost, studying the night-blooming flowers alongside Neo-Andromedan genetics, Haelin wanted to work on the Seventh Sun's main base. She wanted to work directly with better Awakening candidates, and with machinery that would not kill the candidates within the first few minutes of the Awakening process. She wanted to call on that hidden power in all Neo-Andromedans, and help the Seventh Sun guide them towards a better, brighter future. She wanted to bring them out of hiding, out of skulking in the shadows, and into the light.

She could do it, too. Vinterra knew that she could, but Haelin had tested poorly in the eyes of the Seventh Sun, and she had almost lost her chance. Their first night together, Vinterra had run her hand from Haelin's bare shoulder all the way to the tips of her bionic fingers, and asked how she had got them. Truthfully, Vinterra had not understood their significance, and had only meant to be playful; those fingers had brought her a great deal of pleasure moments earlier.

Instead, Haelin had slipped from blissful exhaustion into melancholy monotones, and Vinterra had learned that Haelin had wanted to be a field agent, but lacked the physical prowess needed to pass the Seventh Sun's tests, and no amount of training had been able to help her. That had destroyed Haelin's confidence, and her intelligence and mental examinations had gone even worse.

Shortly thereafter, Haelin had been given a choice: volunteer as a test subject for new bionic tech, or step into an Awakening machine and serve the Seventh Sun in death as she could not hope to in life. Haelin had considered the second option very seriously, far more seriously than she liked to admit, but her determination had won out in the end, and she had let the Seventh Sun remove her thick fingers and give her the long, tapered, bionic ones.

After the operation and the completed trial period of the bionic tech, Haelin took her tests again, and though she failed the physical examination once more, she qualified for Awakening work. But even though she'd wrangled her concentration and achieved a remarkably high score, the Seventh Sun had assigned her to the Daanhymn outpost as the new Awakening overseer. It was the highest position she could have held at any given base, but the worst location for any Awakening worker. Haelin had been depressed for most of her early time on Daanhymn, but Vinterra had drawn her out, and helped shift her mindset into a more positive light. Though it was slowly dying, Daanhymn was a beautiful planet, especially at night when the flowers bloomed, and Haelin had begrudgingly admitted that it wasn't such a terrible a place after all. But she also had come to believe that the Seventh Sun was testing her. The arrival of Candidate Lissa had only heightened that belief.

Vinterra sighed and leaned against the railings of the

K. N. SALUSTRO

overseer's balcony, crossing her arms and hugging herself tight. Even if they were successful with Candidate Lissa, Vinterra thought that it was highly unlikely that the First Lit would pluck Haelin off of Daanhymn and assign her to a better facility, which would depress Haelin all over again, perhaps beyond recovery this time. And if they did promote her, she would be happy, but Vinterra would lose her.

Vinterra did not know which to hope for.

Candidate Lissa is not even likely to survive, Vinterra reminded herself. *Best not dwell on the possibilities that depend on her living.*

She almost regretted putting the flowers in the candidate's holding room. Recent tests had confirmed that the pollen had a slight rejuvenating effect on Neo-Andromedans, and it even seemed to help the candidates fair better during Awakenings, though so few came to Daanhymn that it was impossible for Vinterra to provide accurate data. She had begun to send out samples of the pollen to other Awakening bases along with her findings, and her work had attracted the attention of the Daraax Beta base. The last she'd heard, they were going to expose the in-stasis Awakened to the pollen and see if it had any effect on their vitals. Vinterra was hopeful that it would; if the pollen had enough of an impact, there was a good chance she could get the Seventh Sun to dedicate more resources to the Daanhymn base, maybe even convert it completely into a research station. Then they could get rid of the awful machine—

And probably Haelin with it, Vinterra realized.

Her hopes were painfully conflicted these days. She slumped over the railing and tried to untangle some semblance of a future that had both Daanhymn and Haelin in it.

The grunt team had nearly finished their final preparations of the Awakening machine when the door of the overseer's balcony opened and Haelin stepped through. She came up short when she saw Vinterra, white gold eyes wide with surprise.

"I didn't expect to see you here."

"I didn't expect to be here," Vinterra returned. While she

50

was primarily part of the research team, so skeletal was the Daanhymn crew that Vinterra also served as Haelin's assistant from time to time, though she usually skipped the actual Awakenings. She did not like the screams. "How is our candidate?"

Haelin's round face twisted into a disgusted snarl. "Horrible."

Alarmed, Vinterra straightened and took a few quick steps towards Haelin. "What happened? Does she need medical treatment? We can—"

Haelin dropped the snarl and shook her head. "She's fine, physically. Mentally, too, I think." She glared at the floor. "She was not right at first. Very quiet, very… submissive, almost. Not what I had hoped for. Or expected." Haelin stepped past Vinterra and curled her long fingers around the balcony railing. "So I tried to stir her up a bit. I thought that I could rouse her to fight back against the machine and up her chances of survival."

"Did it work?"

"No." Haelin's eyes narrowed. "But she did respond to… something else."

"What?"

Haelin looked down at her hands, flexed her fingers, and said nothing.

Vinterra felt a cold twinge at the base of her spine. "Oh." She reached out and took one of Haelin's hands. Lightly, she traced a line from Haelin's wrist to the tip of one of her bionic fingers. "You're beautiful, Haelin," she murmured. "All of you."

It took a moment, but the corner of Haelin's mouth finally twitched up into a half-smile, and her eyes took on a soft glow that Vinterra had always found enticing. She took a step forward, closing the distance between them, and planted a firm kiss on Vinterra's lips. She broke away after a few seconds and rested her forehead against Vinterra's, wrapping her long fingers around the back of Vinterra's neck. She gave a content little sigh, but whispered, "We have work to do."

Vinterra nodded, and Haelin released her. The overseer moved to her computer, leaving Vinterra to stand at the balcony and watch as half of the grunt team began the final manual calibrations of the Awakening machine. The other half disappeared for a few minutes, then reappeared with the candidate, passing directly under where Vinterra stood.

The candidate was still strapped to the hard hover cot from the holding room, arms and legs secured by thick bindings. They had removed her traveler's clothes when she had first arrived, then dressed her in a loose-fitting garment that could be easily removed if necessary. Injuries to candidates were not uncommon during successful Awakening processes, and the sooner they were cleaned and treated, the better. Not that Vinterra expected to treat this candidate at all.

Vinterra had seen a few others go into the machine, having served as a temporary overseer prior to Haelin's arrival. They had all thrashed and fought against the restraints, and some had started screaming long before the machine had fully powered up. Candidate Lissa, however, lay perfectly still, her face turned straight up and eerily calm. Her hair spilled over the cot in a black wave, and her skin was golden brown against the white garment she wore. She was very thin, Vinterra noticed, lean and probably fast. From her position on the balcony, Vinterra got a good look at her face when it appeared: all clean angles and sharp features, a bit too harsh for Vinterra's taste but beautiful all the same.

As Vinterra watched, the candidate's eyes suddenly snapped open, and she looked straight at Vinterra. She kept looking at her as the grunts pushed her hovering cot towards the machine, twisting her neck to keep Vinterra in her line of sight.

Vinterra felt herself go cold, and she turned away from the candidate's piercing silver stare, only to meet Haelin's white gold one.

"Technically, you're not on the Awakening team," Haelin said, not unkindly. "You don't need to be here."

Vinterra took a deep breath, then glanced down at the

Awakening machine once more. The grunts were beginning to load the candidate into the inner chamber, and Vinterra could no longer see her eyes. "Condemned by the First Lit or not, she is an important candidate." She gave Haelin a weak smile. "I think I should be here for this one."

Haelin gave her a sidelong look, but did not press the matter. Instead, she turned to the computer and began calibrating the Awakening machine. She finished her preparations at the controls, waited for the grunt team to scurry out of harm's way, then activated the machine.

The lights of the Daanhymn facility dimmed as the machine sucked up the power. Faint blue pulses emanated from the inner chamber as the power washed through the candidate, surging towards her inner light. The machine hummed with the energy, a self-satisfied monotonous drone. Before long, though, the screams had started, and Vinterra winced as they scraped against her ears.

CHAPTER 7: CONTRAST

Aven's fever-dreams swung back and forth between fantasies and nightmares.

He dreamed of huge monsters with the Star Federation insignia tattooed across their chests swimming through space, pushing the stars aside like bright little insects stuck in water, drawing closer, ever closer to the Seventh Sun's base. The monsters circled the base, eyeing it hungrily, then charged in and tore through the structure, ripping it apart and greedily devouring the pieces.

He dreamed of metallic eyes burning with power, so bright that they seared his own vision and burned the world to black, and as the colors and the shapes around him faded, so did his life.

He dreamed that he could breathe again, that he wasn't even aware of his own lungs as he drew in gulps of sweet, clean air, sitting on a grassy hilltop on a nameless planet, running his fingers through cool dewdrops and watching the dawn crack the horizon and split open the sky.

He dreamed that he was Awake.

He dreamed that he was not.

He dreamed that Lissa had finally let him go, and he could slip into the void in peace.

He dreamed that Dr. Chhaya was shaking him awake.

But that was not a dream after all.

The real world slowly came back into focus, but when it settled, it was a little too sharp and there was far too much contrast between the light and the shadows. Aven felt alert and tired all at once, and as though he was not inside his own body but stuck somewhere just above it, out of synch with himself.

Chhaya stood next to him, one hand tight on his shoulder and still shaking Aven back into consciousness, the other slowly emptying a syringe of clear liquid into his arm. The strange contrast of Aven's vision made the doctor's skin seem even darker than its natural sepia brown, and when Aven raised his hand to look at his own flesh, he saw that his formerly bronze skin had been bleached even further to a sickly off-white.

Aven dropped his head back on to the pillow and blinked slowly up at the doctor.

Chhaya met his gaze, and his gray eyebrows slowly dipped into a frown. "I needed you awake." His voice sounded more like an echo than an original sound.

"No," Aven said, and his own voice sounded just as distant and just as small. "Never Awake. Never again."

Chhaya's frown deepened as he removed the needle from Aven's arm. He cast a lingering look at the medical machines next to the bed, then looked down at Aven grimly. "Aven," he said gently, "I'm going to try to tell you all of this again when you're more lucid, but I'm worried I'm not going to get the chance, and I need you to be prepared."

Aven blinked again.

"I don't know what's going to happen to Lissa," Chhaya said. The words echoed on top of each other, and Aven strained to hear. "If she…. Well, funding for your treatment is dependent on her. But you already know that."

Aven closed his eyes and rolled his head away. "I don't mind if I die," he heard his own voice echo out, and he knew that it was true.

"Well, there are others who do," Chhaya said, and the

echoes were hard and brittle this time.

Aven swiveled his head back around. For all the strange colors of the world and the other bizarre side effects of whatever Chhaya had given him, Aven suddenly saw with total clarity what Chhaya thought of him. "I am not a coward," he growled.

"And yet you fear to live."

"I think we've had this talk before. Many times before."

"That doesn't make it any less true. Your sister is out there risking her life for you, and you—"

"I risked more. I sacrificed more. For her. Always for her. I gave up everything. And I became this. And now, I want to stop. I want peace. But I can't get that. Not in life. So yes, Dr. Chhaya, I want to die. And don't you dare condemn me for that."

Chhaya looked as though Aven had slapped him. After a long pause, he murmured, "I suppose, after everything that's happened, you truly believe that there are things worse than death."

"So many things," Aven agreed.

Another pause.

"Aven," Chhaya finally said, "what happened to you and Lissa? What broke your family?"

"The Seventh Sun," Aven murmured.

"No, they broke your life, but I want to know what happened between you and your sister. What broke you two?" Chhaya hesitated, but when he spoke again, the gentleness had returned to his voice. "What happened?"

And Aven had to laugh because the memories finally came back, and he knew for certain that they were not dreams. The group of Antis that had targeted them after he and Lissa had fled from Terra-Six had been real. His fear and Lissa's anger had been real. Her reaction had been real, and so had Aven's decision to protect her one last time.

So he told the doctor that story. He snarled the details, but he thought that he got the basic points across. "After her first Awakening," he told Chhaya, "she blacked out. When she came to, she didn't remember anything, except the smell of heartbeats and the taste of death. It scared her, and I didn't want her living with that over her head. So I told her that I was the one who had Awakened and killed those people, and that she had watched me do it, but she had been so scared that she had passed out. She could barely look at me after that. Like she thought that I was a monster. But I was all she had, and she had to put her life in my hands again eventually."

"Did she ever find out?"

"No. And I don't want her to. I hate that she won't let me go, but I won't put her through that. She's all that I have, too." Aven rolled his head towards the doctor and met his dark gaze. "I played big brother. I did everything I could to keep her safe. I gave up food so she could eat. I gave up clothes so she wouldn't freeze. I looked for work so she wouldn't steal. I tried to protect her." He turned his head away. "But I couldn't stop her from forgetting what she was. She tried to pretend that she was human. She so badly wanted to be. And she almost threw our lives away."

"She remembers now," Chhaya said, but his voice was not untroubled.

"Now," Aven agreed, and had to laugh again. "But first, I had to take her away. First, I had to remind her. First, I had to show her what Neo-Andromedans can do."

First, I had to be the Shadow.

But the world had fallen away again, and Aven was not sure if he had spoken those last words aloud or not.

CHAPTER 8: ESCAPE

Haelin knew that she was not supposed to give the candidates any special treatment. As the overseer of an outpost base, her purpose was to gather raw data from fixed trials with the test subjects themselves providing the only variables. First Lit Rosonno had made a point of emphasizing as much in his personal notes on Candidate Arrilissa's file.

But Haelin had already directly interacted with Candidate Arrilissa, and if she'd broken that rule, she figured she might as well break the others.

Besides, she got the sense that this candidate did not want to be Awake in spite of all her seemingly calm acceptance. She would fight. After her scornful looks and mocking words, Haelin was more determined than ever to bring Arrilissa into the Light.

Out of the corner of her eye, Haelin saw Vinterra watching her over her shoulder. She was fidgeting a little as she leaned over the balcony, shifting her weight back and forth across her thick legs. She was dressed in baggy, casual clothing, much like Haelin was, but she wore her pristine blue researcher's coat today. Quiet, beautiful Vinterra, with her full figure, smooth onyx skin, tightly coiling black curls, gentle curving cheeks, full lips, and blazing silver eyes streaked with dark purple.

Haelin tried to avoid her eyes for the moment, much as she loved them. She knew that Vinterra was uneasy about this Awakening, not that she had much of a stomach for Awakenings to begin with, but this one in particular had put her on edge. Haelin had not tried to comfort her. Not this time. This time, everything circled back to Haelin herself, and she did not want Vinterra trying to talk her out of her decision.

She was going to Awaken Arrilissa no matter what it took, and then she was going to get herself off of Daanhymn with Vinterra in tow, if she would come.

If.

Haelin flexed her bionic fingers, and focused on the data readouts from the Awakening machine.

She had started Arrilissa at the lower levels, feeding her more controlled bursts of energy at a steadier stream. The Awakening machine was too unstable to give an ideal power feed, but Haelin had done what she could, adjusting wherever and whenever she needed to.

Candidate Arrilissa was doing very well at the initial stages. Her heart and brain activity were exactly where they needed to be, and her stress readings were still far below the Awakening threshold.

"She's holding strong," Haelin said into her communicator. "I want to raise the power levels and hold her steady for a few minutes. Let's see how she does, but be ready to adjust the feed lines as needed."

The leader of the grunt team acknowledged the decision, and Haelin dimly heard him relay orders to his underlings. "Grunt team ready," he barked over the communication line after a few moments. "Surge when ready."

"Surging in three... two... one..." Haelin's bionic fingers hammered out the code, and fresh power thrummed into the Awakening machine.

Candidate Arrilissa's data readings jumped, but nowhere near as high as they should have. Her stress levels were still far below the Awakening line, which was unusual by itself, but there was also far too much restraint in the other areas.

Haelin stiffened. She saw Vinterra glance at her, but she ignored the look and snatched up the datapad with the candidate's electronic file, skimming through the information.

Candidate is known to be the bounty hunter Shadow... replacing older brother as... no longer a top candidate. No repercussions if... unlikely to have experienced prior Awakenings, but no known data regarding this.

The last section went on to speculate about Arrilissa's possible activities prior to her capture. Haelin reread that part twice, but her eyes kept lingering on a single phrase.

No known data.

She bit her lip and studied the readouts again. If Arrilissa had been Awake prior to coming to Daanhymn, that could account for the anomaly, but Haelin could not say for certain if that was what was happening or not. She had barely any experience with successful Awakenings, and what she did know came from second-hand data. As far as she knew, there had not been anything like this during other trials. Not even the legendary Awakening of Candidate Syreth had been this steady.

"Something wrong?"

Haelin jumped a little, but forced herself to relax. She had not heard Vinterra come up beside her, and now the scientist was standing just over her shoulder.

Haelin passed Vinterra the datapad, wordlessly pointing to the bit about Candidate Arrilissa's Awakening history. Vinterra read the information silently, then checked the data readouts.

"Even if she has been Awake before," Vinterra said thoughtfully, "she should still be having a stronger reaction to the power feeds."

Haelin nodded in silent agreement. She flexed her bionic fingers, fired off a warning to the leader of the grunt team, and made a few adjustments to the power levels.

The readouts spiked a little higher, but still not high enough.

Vinterra drummed her fingers against the datapad, then winced as another scream shattered the air. "Other bases have found that candidates with solid eye colors have a higher tolerance to the Awakening process," she said. "They don't have an explanation for it yet, but it is a definite trend. Do you think that's happening here?" Vinterra glanced down again. "Haelin?"

Haelin had barely heard her. She had focused on the scream instead. Normally, when she oversaw an Awakening, she could ignore the screams and fill all her senses with the data, pouring over the numbers and blotting out the world around her. This Awakening had not been any different at first, but now Haelin found herself listening very closely to Candidate Arrilissa's screams.

There was something off about them. They had the sharp rings of pain that had been present in all the other candidates' screams, but there was something hard beneath the surface of Arrilissa's, something cold and calculated.

"I'm killing it," Haelin snapped over the communicator. "This one is done."

The grunt leader did not hide his surprise. "She's still alive and you haven't—"

"Shut it down," Haelin shot back, "and stand by for extraction."

The grunt leader did as he was told, and Haelin performed her part of the shut down process, bionic fingers flying over the controls. As the machine powered down, the screams died away, but the data readouts did not change.

"I don't understand," Vinterra said, moving back towards the balcony's railing.

"Neither do I," Haelin muttered. To the grunt team, she said, "Something's not right with this one. Get her out of there, but be careful."

The reply came back immediately. "Is there any danger of her being Awake?"

Haelin drew in the breath for the reply, but held the words at the back of her throat. She looked back at the data, and felt the tension wrinkle across her shoulders.

"Is she Awake?" the grunt leader asked again.

"I don't know," Haelin finally said. "Proceed with caution."

"If you don't know, we shouldn't be moving in."

"And if you don't move in, she could die from shock. You need to extract her if we're going to get any solid data from her." Haelin rubbed her forehead with the tips of her bionic fingers. They felt hard and dead against her skin. "What we have now is unclear. We need to rest her and then put her through another trial."

Silence from the grunt leader. Then Haelin heard him order his team to arm themselves before they moved back in to the Awakening chamber.

Haelin bit her lip again and entered the required sequence to activate the sedatives in the candidate's collar. She did it more out of reflex than anything else.

She had not given Arrilissa the right kind of collar, opting instead for the weaker class given to allegiant Awakened rather than uncontrollable ones. When she had selected the collar, Haelin had only thought about keeping Arrilissa alive to the best of her ability. The right kind of collar would have killed the candidate when activated. The wrong kind, the kind Haelin had given her, would only pump tranquilizers into her bloodstream. If Arrilissa really had Awakened, there was a chance that the sedatives would not be strong enough to subdue her; uncontrollable Awakened could only be brought down through death. Haelin regretted not taking that risk more seriously. All surviving candidates were weakened by the Awakening process, but there had been a few instances of particularly hostile candidates lashing out with deadly force, striking down collared agents before they could be brought down. Arrilissa had hated the Seventh Sun before going into the machine, and she had tasted kills before.

Haelin could only hope that she was wrong about the data, or that the sensors within the machine had been faulty, or that anything else had gone wrong, anything but Arrilissa slipping into the Light. By the time Haelin stepped to Vinterra's side at the railing of the balcony, the tension in her shoulders had spread through her chest, and her bionic fingers were curling and uncurling almost of their own free will.

The grunt team moved in after a few minutes. They all had enerpulse pistols drawn, and the leader had them work slowly as they manually opened the Awakening machine and accessed the inner chamber. Four of the grunts slipped inside, including the team leader, and an impossibly long silence played out.

Finally, the voice of the grunt leader drifted over the communicator. "All clear. She's unconscious."

Haelin exchanged a sharp glance with Vinterra.

"She can't be," Haelin replied to the grunt leader.

Vinterra moved back to the data readouts and frowned hard at them. She looked at Haelin and shook her head.

"There's no way," Haelin told the grunt leader. "We're still getting readings that say she's conscious."

"Well, something's definitely wrong," the grunt leader said, "but it's with the machine, not your candidate. The sensors must have blown out or something."

"You should have checked them beforehand."

"We did," the grunt leader said. "We can't do anything during the actual process, though. You know that."

In the background, Haelin heard one of the underlings say that they were releasing the candidate's bindings.

"I'll take a look at them while we're in here, but if it's not the sensors, then it's probably the—"

"SHE'S AWAKE!"

The scream ripped over the communication line, and at that same moment, Haelin heard Vinterra give a startled cry as a warning beeped out from the main computer, and the data readouts jumped into Awakened levels.

Haelin heard enerpulse shots, and she saw the flashes of light inside the Awakening machine, but over that, she heard the sounds of the grunt team dying. There were shrieks of pain cut off by silence, and the enerpulse shots dwindled down to nothing. The grunt leader came stumbling out of the machine.

"Fall back!" he was shouting. "Evacuate! Get to the—!"

Then the Awakened Arrilissa came flying out of the

machine. She slammed into the grunt leader's back, driving him to the ground, and Haelin watched her rip the enerpulse pistol out of his hand. She fired off three shots, killing three members of the retreating grunt team, before pressing the barrel of the enerpulse pistol to the back of the grunt leader's head, and pulling the trigger.

Numb, Haelin watched the Awakened straighten up. Her hair hung loose and wild, and her breath pulsed through her body. She stood over the dead grunt leader with her back to the Awakening machine, looking at nothing in particular now that the few surviving members of the grunt team had disappeared. Then her gaze snapped to the overseer's balcony, and her silver eyes found Haelin. The Awakened raised her hand, and Haelin flinched back so violently that she cleared half the distance from the railing of the balcony to the exit door.

She forced herself to go back and trigger the evacuation alarm, then wrapped her bionic fingers around Vinterra's wrist and pulled her towards the exit. Haelin glanced down into the Awakening chamber as she and Vinterra skirted the edge of the balcony, keeping their heads low, but Arrilissa had already fled, and more likely than not, she'd gotten out before the room had fully locked down.

She was loose, and she was hungry for blood.

There was no point in trading speed for caution; if the Awakened found them, they were dead. Haelin sprinted through the halls, pulling Vinterra after her, the pounding of her own wild heartbeat closing her ears to all sound, and it wasn't until Vinterra wrenched her wrist free and ground to a halt in the middle of the hallway that Haelin realized that the scientist had been shouting over the evacuation alarms, trying to get her attention.

"Her collar," Vinterra was saying. "We have to trigger her collar!"

"I already did," Haelin panted, reaching for Vinterra's hand again.

Vinterra pulled away. "You... She should be down by

now." Horror bloomed in Vinterra's eyes. "Which collar did you give her?"

"The wrong one."

"Haelin!"

"I couldn't give her one of the kill ones! Not if I wanted her to survive."

"She wasn't *supposed* to survive!"

"I know, okay? I know that I was supposed to let her die, but I didn't want to. I wanted her to live."

"Well congratulations, she is alive, and you have probably just killed us all!"

"I KNOW!" Haelin took a shaking breath. "This is entirely my fault, and I will take the blame, but I need to be alive to do that, and so do you if you want to see me do it. But we *have* to get to the hanger. Now!"

Vinterra looked angry, far angrier than Haelin had ever seen her, but she did come. She ran with Haelin through the narrow halls of the facility, their footfalls drowning in the shrieks of the alarms. She passed the mess hall and the teams' sleeping quarters with Haelin, and neither of them stopped to even consider taking any of their belongings when they sprinted past their private room. There wasn't much of value in there as it was, except maybe the necklace of dried flowers Vinterra had woven for Haelin, but neither of them thought to take it.

With Daanhymn's resources stretched as thin as they were, the ground cruiser bay had never received a vehicle, and the evacuating agents had no choice but to take the three starships and retreat off-planet until the escaped Awakened either collapsed from exhaustion, or "starved" from a lack of kills. The ships were all kept stocked for such emergencies, but Haelin had always assumed that discovery would be a bigger threat than an escaped Awakened.

When they reached the starship hanger, Vinterra worked with Haelin to sort the three teams into the ships and avoid over-crowding, though with half of the grunt team lying lifeless in the Awakening chamber and another two missing and probably already dead, there was no real danger of that. Vinterra pulled Haelin on to the research team's ship, and sat her down in the copilot seat. Vinterra was the one to pilot the tiny starship out of the hanger with the other two ships close behind, and send them leaping away from Daanhymn's blue-speckled surface. And, when they had cleared the atmosphere and settled into orbit, trying to monitor the escaped Awakened through infrared scans and waiting for the Seventh Sun to reply to the evacuation report, Vinterra was the one to reach out and steady Haelin's shaking hands.

Haelin was grateful for the touch, and so relieved that she and Vinterra had made it off the planet. But she could not bring herself to tell Vinterra that just before they had left the overseer's balcony, the Awakened Arrilissa had looked straight at Haelin with her clear, burning eyes, raised her hand, and flexed her fingers.

Haelin looked down at her own hands. One set of bionic fingers was wrapped tightly around Vinterra's hand. The other set rested on her knee, long, tapered, and still.

CHAPTER 9: DOUBTS

When word of what had happened on Daanhymn reached him, Rosonno wanted to kill the overseer himself. The report had come from one of First Lit Tyrath's agents with the note, *Thought you should know,* as though the loss of a base and the deaths of several agents were on par with his starship suffering a scuffed hull. He could not fathom why Tyrath would be so calm about this, and he fumed over the report again as he waited for her to respond to his demand for communication.

The one consolation was the knowledge that the escaped Lissa would not survive long on Daanhymn if she had not already dropped dead from Awakening starvation, as had happened with some of the earliest trials. Without enough kills to slake their bloodlust, freshly Awakened candidates were prone to driving themselves so far past the point of physical exhaustion that they dropped dead. The more lucid ones sometimes turned whatever weapons they could find against themselves as a means of escaping the Light. There was a chance that Lissa would have fallen into that latter category, but that knowledge was not secure enough to ease Rosonno's restless heart.

On top of that, reports from the fleeing Daanhymn operatives had indicated that a Star Federation shuttle had arrived on the planet shortly after Lissa's escape from the Awakening chamber and the evacuation of the base. The shuttle was thought to be a scout, and the large ship following hot on the shuttle's trail suggested as much, but Rosonno was leery of it all. The Seventh Sun had gone dark on the inner workings of the Star Federation after the Ametria incident. Rosonno had a nasty itch at the back of his brain and he could feel something unraveling, but if that was his mind or the security of the Seventh Sun or something else entirely, he could not say. The only thing he knew for certain was that he was having a lot of trouble accepting the idea that Lissa had perished on Daanhymn.

Ever since the failed attempt to capture her on Yuna, Rosonno had known that Lissa was too far beyond control. Gone was the small, soft girl named Arrilissa, born and raised on the main base, the one he had studied closely and finally determined was too psychologically fragile to survive an Awakening. Her brother had shown much promise, but Arrilissa had been too soft-spoken and gentle.

Rosonno wondered if he had somehow been mistaken about that, and he tried to recall if there had ever been a time when Arrilissa had stood back and watched the world with the same predatory shades he had seen in Lissa—he could not even think of them as the same person—on Yuna. He did not think so. He would have noticed.

When he had made the decision to strike Lissa's name from the list of primary candidates, he had felt a deep sense of loss. With the state of Aven's health, that was two potentially great Awakened thrown away. Rosonno had hoped that Aven would rival Syreth in ferocity and stability, and then he had shifted that hope to Lissa when he had learned that she had become the bounty hunter Shadow, but now that hope was gone. It had died long before Lissa had been taken to Daanhymn, leaving Rosonno tired and empty, but when the evacuation report had come in, panicked rage had begun to seep in and fill the void.

She has to be dead by now, Rosonno tried to convince himself once again. *If she didn't starve, then the Star Feds will pick her up, and they have no reason to keep her alive.*

And yet, he could not quite believe that. Lissa had escaped the main base as a child, escaped death by Syreth's hand the night she had scarred him, escaped Rosonno himself on Yuna, and escaped the Ametrian surface, taking down a base with her. He could not shake the feeling that she had somehow escaped Daanhymn, too.

If only that self-righteous overseer had done the simple duty the Seventh Sun had assigned to her, but no, that had proved too mundane for her. And now, rather than being punished to the degree that her actions demanded, she was being reassigned to the location of her choice.

Rosonno felt sick with rage. He had demanded communication with First Lit Tyrath as soon as he had learned of the treatment of the overseer, and now he waited at the private communication terminal of his personal starship, his gut performing angry backflips as time stretched around him.

Finally, the terminal came alive as the other First Lit checked in, and a hologram projection of her appeared before Rosonno, showcasing in full scale her long, pale face, piercing red-and-gold eyes, narrow shoulders, and slim body. She was dressed in loose, light clothing layered on top of her thin frame; whites slashed with green, brighter colors than what Seventh Sun agents typically wore, though as Rosonno recalled, Tyrath had never been fond of dark colors. She was quite a bit taller than Rosonno, and even via hologram, she looked down her straight, narrow nose at him as though being thrown into an exploding star would be preferable to his company.

The feeling was mutual.

It had not always been this way, but after the desertion of a group of uncollared Awakening candidates—including Aven and Arrilissa—Rosonno had begun to doubt Tyrath's capabilities of overseeing Awakening operations, and had gone so far as to suggest she step down from her position as a First Lit and bring up one of her secondary officers. Tyrath had fired back with the point that had Rosonno paid closer attention to the behaviors of the candidates in question while he had been evaluating them, the warning signs would have been marked long before they had become Tyrath's responsibility. When the time had come to vote on the issue, the First Lit had been split, and Arrevessa—oldest and solemnest of the First Lit—had cast the deciding vote in favor of Tyrath.

Though she had won, Tyrath had never forgiven Rosonno for sparking the battle in the first place. For Rosonno's part, he had never forgiven Tyrath for letting those candidates escape, and now he was ready to rip in to her decisions regarding Haelin.

But first, procedure.

"The seventh star burns brightest," Rosonno and Tyrath intoned in unison. For all their friction, they were still First Lit, and they held Seventh Sun customs in the highest regard. "May our Light touch the darkest corners of the galaxy, and may we shine forever."

"So," Tyrath said as soon as the greeting was complete, "you have a problem with the way I'm supervising the Awakening efforts."

"I have a problem," Rosonno returned, "with you rewarding an overseer who blatantly defied orders, jeopardized an entire base, and cost us the lives of several agents."

"Haelin is a dedicated and talented individual," Tyrath said easily. "We saw fit to reward that."

Rosonno kept his voice slow and deliberate, but he could feel the warmth of his anger deep within his gut. "Haelin deliberately ignored protocol and acted out of her own self-interest. Because of her, we lost an important candidate, and just turned control of an entire facility over to the Star Federation!"

"Correct me if I'm wrong," Tyrath said, "but didn't you mark that candidate as unusable, First Lit Rosonno?"

"Yes, First Lit Tyrath, and in the wake of recent events, I'm sure you can see why I did."

"I see that the overseer in question Awakened the

candidate on a low-ranking outpost with outdated machinery and no hope of success."

"And people died!" Rosonno spat.

"Yes, they did, but what this overseer did was next to impossible. Imagine what she will do if she goes to a high-ranking base and is given access to fully functioning machinery."

"I imagine she'll doom the rest of the bases," Rosonno said acidly. "We've already lost two."

"Yes," Tyrath said, and her eyes narrowed sharply. "But that had more to do with Arrilissa, didn't it?" She folded her arms across her chest, long limbs nearly losing themselves in the fabric. "As I recall, you were the one who insisted that we track her and her brother down. You demanded it."

"I made a mistake," Rosonno said, the words snagging in his throat like barbs.

Tyrath's thick eyebrows arched in shock, then a wicked grin cut across her face. "I never thought I'd hear you say those words."

"Much like I never thought I'd hear that you were promoting an overseer who let an Awakened loose."

The smile slid off of Tyrath's face. "It may interest you to know that First Lit Niradessa was the one who suggested it."

It was Rosonno's turn to be surprised. "And why did she think this was a good idea?"

"She said that it would be good for morale now that we're moving towards the first strike. Show that we're willing to reward those who put faith and determination into the Awakenings. Obviously, we're going to keep your notes on Arrilissa a secret, and Nira's going to spin the entire incident like it was some great act of heroism. She's already getting ready to correct the survivors, and we're lucky that only the overseer and the lead researcher were present to see what actually happened firsthand." Tyrath reached up and pushed her dark hair behind her ear, offering a clear view of the quick slant of her cheek, the line of her jaw, and the black collar around her white throat. "Regarding Haelin, something interesting did come up. We found out that she has romantically partnered with the research lead from Daanhymn. A woman named Vinterra, I believe." Thoughtfully, Tyrath ran the ball of her thumb over her bottom lip. Rosonno looked away. "She's quite brilliant from what I understand. Discovered the stabilizing effect the mutated flower pollen from Daanhymn has on the Awakened. It's not much use for throwaways, but she sent us a few batches a while ago, and we've found it to be quite effective on those in stasis."

"Fascinating," Rosonno said, "but what does this have to do with the overseer?"

Tyrath dropped her hand, and Rosonno could look her in the eye again. "Vinterra and Haelin are both capable agents, but I do agree with you in one regard: they cost us quite dearly. From what Niradessa and I have gathered, what happened on Daanhymn was because of Haelin, and she'll bear the brunt of the cost.

"Vinterra will not know about the choice we will give to Haelin. If allowed to live, Vinterra will be given a new assignment at our stasis facility on Daraax Beta. I expect she would accept. She'd like it here. Plenty of candidates to study without the nasty part of the Awakenings themselves to worry her.

"As for Haelin, it is in her best interest to fully accept the version of the truth Niradessa has crafted. If she cooperates, Haelin can choose to go to the main base and work with top Awakening research teams and occasionally oversee Awakenings at the closest facilities, but only if she names a suitable replacement for the candidate that she lost. And Nira will make it very clear that the fewer left who know about what really happened on Daanhymn, the better it would be for the Seventh Sun."

"But the only two left who know firsthand are Haelin and Vinterra," Rosonno said.

"Exactly."

Rosonno considered this for a moment. "That does sound like one of Niradessa's ideas."

"Through and through," Tyrath agreed. "I'm hoping Haelin decides to be selfless for once in her life. I could use Vinterra's research for the in-stasis Awakened, and maybe even fresh candidates." She breathed out heavily. "We're stuck at the sixty-eight percent survival rate."

"That's enough for what we have planned."

"Barely, and based on recent tests and the way we're losing our grip on Syreth, we're going to have to keep the bulk of the Awakened in stasis until exactly the right moment." She gave Rosonno a hard look. "If you hadn't kept Syreth running around the galaxy, we might have been able to pull him back in reserve, then let him loose with the final wave."

"That was never the plan for him."

"Neither was him deteriorating this rapidly. Ever since the Ametria operation, he's been slipping further and further beyond control."

Rosonno winced. He had felt the shift in Syreth, and remembered how danger had crackled through the air that night on Yuna. They'd kept him under control with the false promise of a hunt for Lissa, but when that went sour, he'd nearly killed Rosonno. It had taken three hard doses of sedatives to bring him down, and even then, his hunger for blood had radiated off of him. The run-in on Phan had yielded similar results, and his handling team was reporting more aggression towards them, barehanded fights with the massive brown arkin, and longer response times to the collar. Out of desperation, they had taken him to Daarax Beta with the intent of putting him to rest until they could find a truly satisfying task for him, or a way to repair some of the psychological damage. Rosonno braced himself and looked back at Tyrath. "How bad is he?"

"Ros, we couldn't even put him back into stasis. He kept fighting his way out of it, and we had to send him back into the field. First Lit Sekorvo's people have been trying to keep him calm by feeding him auxiliary kills, but those are having almost no effect." Scorn flared in her eyes. "I don't know why you thought you could use him as your own personal bounty hunter."

Rosonno's face twisted with disgust. "It's not as if I broke him."

"Didn't you?" Tyrath fixed him with a piercing stare. "Awake or not, he has a memory, and from what I understand, you've denied him revenge twice. All for the sake of bringing in a candidate that you've marked as unusable." She took a slow, steady breath, and considered him. "The other First Lit might take that as a sign that you're losing your touch. Maybe you're putting personal pride ahead of the Seventh Sun?"

"And maybe you're putting petty grudges ahead of proper judgment."

Tyrath smiled. "At least you still have your bite." She became serious again. "You have handled Arrilissa poorly, though."

"There was a reason," Rosonno said slowly, deliberately, "why I wanted her brought in alive. I thought that we may as well try to get some useful information from her, but your precious Haelin ruined that." He felt the rage boil up in his gut again. "I still think we should take a harsher course of action against her."

"Like you did with Yuna?" Tyrath rocked back on her heels, still looking down at him. "You're lucky the Star Feds don't care about that planet. If they did, they'd call up one of their purges."

Rosonno spread his hands. "And then we'd welcome back our lost brothers and sisters with open arms."

Tyrath snorted. "The survivors, at least. However few there would be." She sighed again. "In the meantime, Haelin will help us keep morale up among the collared. She'll become a hero, the very image of dedication and determination, and whatever she chooses, our agents will aspire to be like her. Or at least the version of her that Niradessa puts together."

"And the Daanhymn base? It'll be crawling with Star Feds soon."

"First Lit Arrevessa says let them come. Much like the Ametria base, the Daanhymn outpost is minor enough that the loss of it will not ultimately matter to us. To our people, we play the exposure of the Daanhymn base as intentional. Then, when we trigger the failsafe, they can see how many Star Feds we've caught in the trap. Beyond that, we proceed as planned. Nothing has changed."

Rosonno took a deep breath and held it in his lungs, waiting until it burned before letting it out in a whisper. "I'm not so confident about that. I can't shake the feeling that Lissa somehow survived."

Tyrath considered him for a long moment. "Evaluation of Awakening candidates is your field. If she did survive, and if she somehow made it off of Daanhymn, what do you think she'd do?"

Rosonno turned the idea over in his mind. "If she's alone, she might run and never look back. She's gotten a taste of what happens when we find her, and if we leave her be..." He frowned. "She might stay hidden this time. Maybe." He swallowed, and felt the comforting grip of the collar around his throat. "If she's even alive."

"And *if* she's alive, and *if* she doesn't stay away, we know where Aven is."

"Yes, we do." But Rosonno's voice was far off, and he thought that it might have been a mistake to play that advantage as early as they had.

CHAPTER 10: TRACES

Aven's tracker had pointed to the Paradise Void, and Lance had set himself on the trajectory without hesitation. He had brushed off Dr. Chhaya's offer to take a closer look at his enerpulse wound and had rushed out of the hospital. Chhaya had escorted him back to the alley access door and sent him off with careful directions, a small bottle of fresh water, and a wish of luck.

To Lance's relief, the arkins had been waiting for him with no Star Federation soldiers in sight, though there had been a half-eaten feathered thing lying just inside the shuttle's airlock, and Orion had looked fairly pleased with himself. Blade had only looked depressed.

Lance had launched the shuttle as fast as he could, doing his best to scramble the shuttle's signal. He had made it off Phan and plunged back into space without Anderson appearing to gun him down, and then he had begun the long trek to the Paradise Void. It was a three-sidereal-day trip. By the time they had reached the edge of the system, Lance had been just as restless as the arkins, and sweating as he ground down to his last stim. He had decided to save it for the Paradise Void, and as the shuttle rocketed past the first few stars of the system, Lance hit himself with the final dose.

I'll either be sober or dead when this is all over, he thought as the stim burned through his veins, but it did its job and Lance felt more alert almost immediately. His enerpulse wound was healing cleanly as far as he could tell, and he had more mobility in his arm and shoulder, but he forced himself to go slow. At least until he found Lissa.

If he found Lissa.

Lance had tried to repair Aven's navi-sphere, but the technology was beyond him. He'd gotten it to flicker to life at one point, but its hologram displays had been snarled and staticky, and Lance had given up and accepted that he was just going to have to work off of what he'd seen at the hospital.

Aven's tracker had not settled on a planet. Either Aven had broken off the system before it had traced out the path to its completion, or the traced signal had dissolved. Neither possibility guaranteed that Lissa was anywhere near the Paradise Void.

Lance did not give the doubts any ground in his mind. He was here now, and he had to work with that. He brought up a map of the system and scanned the names of the planets. "Where would you hide?" he muttered, flicking from name to name. "Where would you build?"

Many of the planets in the Paradise Void were beautiful, idyllic worlds as long as they were viewed from a safe distance. Ruwei and Rulei emitted deadly radon across their sparkling surfaces. Uutera was a breathtaking display of rising and falling rock formations, carved and weathered into liquid shapes by the eons, but an asteroid had ripped the atmosphere from the planet's surface, and now the formations rose against a black sky. Daanhymn boasted beautiful, mutated flowers that bloomed at night and secreted a deadly toxin, and even the planet's indigenous flora and fauna had not evolved fast enough to survive the new species. Jathorix was a blissful world, pure and clean as mountain air from ancient Earth, but it hosted an intelligent species still in its pre-Contact stages, and interactions from off-world travelers were likely to be treated as demonic happenings more than anything else.

Still, a planet like Jathorix was the most likely place to find Lissa. It was habitable, and galactic law prevented most starships from traveling anywhere near its orbital path. Jathorix was a good place to hide, provided the indigenous population had been dealt with.

"But they're disrupters, not conquerors." Lance frowned at the star map, squinting at the little blip that was Jathorix.

The Seventh Sun would have nothing to gain by building on Jathorix. If anything, a move like that would have brought them too much attention. The Star Federation would have known if a pre-Contact planet had been encroached upon. No, the Sun preferred to lurk in the least-expected places, proving that they could exist where no one else could. They wanted to topple the Star Federation, but their sights were set on the post-Contact races, that much Lance knew for certain. They would not waste their time or their resources on Jathorix.

But they would waste them on Ametria.

The Seventh Sun had ducked under the radar at Ametria, had built a small space station just outside the hostile planet's atmosphere, and they had hidden from the Star Federation for years.

Least-expected places. Where no one else can live.

Lance looked at the star map for a long time, and then felt realization and cold certainty slam into his gut.

Once again, they were living where other species could not.

No, they were living where *humans* could not.

They were on Daanhymn.

Lance sent the shuttle streaking towards the planet, but as he drew closer, he felt his certainty wavering. He did not know what he had expected to find, but the space around Daanhymn was void of activity, save for the rogue meteoroid that deflected off the shuttle's shields as the craft came down from light speed. Daanhymn filled the thick window at the nose of the shuttle, and Lance eyed it anxiously. He approached the planet at a slow, steady coast, but nothing rose up to greet him, no fighter starships or even a pulse beam fired from the ground. The planet drifted along its orbit, as silent as it had ever been since the failure of the True Eden colony.

As the shuttle drew closer, Lance initiated a scan of the planet. Scans had gotten him into trouble on Ametria, and he rubbed his jaw, remembering how Lissa had punched him for that decision. He had not been prepared for her fist, and he had let the attack pass, knowing that retaliation would get him nowhere, but Lissa wasn't here this time, and if he triggered a trap that brought the shuttle down, at least he'd know for certain that he was on the right planet. He did not have much hope for getting Lissa out of the Sun's base as it was.

"May as well go down in a blaze. Literally."

Orion grunted somewhere behind him, and then Blade's head appeared next to Lance's shoulder. Her injured wing hung limp at her side, but she had roused herself and was staring at the speckled blue planet with fierce intensity.

"Easy," Lance murmured, reaching out to gently touch her head. "Don't get your hopes up just yet."

But the scan returned full data on the planet, and Lance found a building down on the surface that should not have existed, along with three small starships that were coasting just outside of the atmosphere on the far side of the planet. There was a long, tense hesitation as Lance sized up the starships— and he assumed they did the same for him—before they suddenly turned and shot out into space, disappearing out of range.

Lance doubted that a solitary shuttle was enough to send three starships running, even if his scans had revealed that they were decidedly unarmed. A solitary shuttle with a Star Federation insignia tattooed on the hull was another matter entirely, however.

That confirmed that Lance was in the right place. The reassurance was far from comforting, but he had come this far and with the ships gone, there were no other threats to him outside of the toxic flowers. He had the feeling that he needed to move fast and press that advantage while he had it, though it dawned on him that if Lissa had been aboard one of those three ships, she was out of reach now. The ships had darted away too quickly for him to follow, and the current power levels of the shuttle would not let him keep up a light-speed chase for long. The best he could do was land on Daanhymn, search the base, and figure things out from there if he came up empty.

He brought up an image of the Seventh Sun's base. It was clearly a cannibalized structure, built up from the salvaged ruins of the decaying human colony in the middle of a dying forest. The structure was purely a utilitarian box, no embellishments in sight, save for the small starship hanger jutting off the side.

Daanhymn's night-blooming flowers had started their slow journey up the sides of the building, having already conquered the surrounding trees and ground. All the petals were closed up tight, shielding their stamens from the bright sunlight and holding their toxins in.

"At least we have a few hours before nightfall," Lance murmured, bringing the shuttle into the atmosphere and setting it on a direct course for the base. "But I don't think we're going to find anything."

He knew that the base was empty long before he landed. The behavior of the three ships had suggested recent abandonment, and as he drew closer and saw the gaping starship hanger, his suspicions were confirmed. The hanger stood wide open and empty, and looked to be just large enough for three small starships. Whatever the Seventh Sun had been doing here, they were done and gone now.

Lance steered the shuttle into the empty hanger, landed, and powered down without any alarms sounding or traps activating. When he stepped out of the shuttle into the thin air with a breathing mask securely covering his face and the arkins close behind, nothing greeted him.

Nothing, except the total silence of a dying paradise.

Lance had heard stories of the failed True Eden colony. It was a mixed source of shame and outrage for most of the human race, though now that some time had passed, it was mostly a reminder of what happens when off-worlders become too alien on their host planet.

Glancing out of the open hanger, Lance saw a sweeping sea of blue flower bulbs.

Once, Daanhymn had been predominantly green, with wide meadows and healthy forests. Its surface had danced with a huge array of animals, and its skies had swarmed with flying life. Not everything on the planet had been lovely and docile, but the True Eden colonists had been able to settle and survive.

Files from the Star Federation database had noted that the colonists had lived on Daanhymn for nearly a full sidereal year before the night-blooming disaster. The True Eden colonists had believed that they had found paradise, a world untainted by extraterrestrial contact, a world sweeter and purer than Earth had ever been even before the First Contact. But their paradise had not been complete, and the colonists had brought in seeds from Earth, hoping to create a plant that would grow in Daanhymn soil and produce edible fruit.

Instead, one fateful cross pollination with an indigenous Daanhymn plant had produced the mutated night-blooming flowers that had spread like wildfire, and killed off all of the colonists and most of the planet's fauna before the end of the next sidereal year. The Paradise Void had fallen under the jurisdiction of a non-human fleet commander at the time, and the colonists' distress call had not been heeded. At least, not in time to actually help anyone.

When aid had finally arrived, it was far too late, and the planet was condemned, though the corpses had not yet fully decayed. Agonized faces and stiff, bulging veins stained blue by the toxins had dominated the visual records, and a shiver ran up Lance's spine. Daanhymn was one of those planets with a record that stuck out in his memory, having come to his passing attention once or twice when it had fallen under his jurisdiction as a fleet commander. Though he had been morbidly fascinated by the planet's history, he had never expected to stand on its surface, and he pressed the breathing mask deeper against his skin as his eyes swept over the landscape. The flowers had begun to creep up the trees and root out the rest of the flora. Before long, Daanhymn would be completely dead, a rotted core drifting around and around a pleasant little star.

Lance stood looking at the sleeping blue flowers for a long time, entranced by the seemingly endless sprawl of them, so innocently peaceful in the daytime now that the sunlight had burned the toxins out of the atmosphere.

A grunt from one of the arkins roused him, and he turned away from the flowers to see Blade standing near a closed door, staring intensely over her shoulder at Lance. Orion was near her, sniffing the ground, yellow eyes bright and wide. Lance had not been able to get a breathing mask on either of them, and while they were not showing any signs of poisoning and appeared perfectly healthy, Lance couldn't bring himself to remove the mask around his own head.

He moved towards the arkins with his breath loud in his ears. Even over that exaggerated sound, he could hear how eerily out-of-place his footsteps sounded in the starship hanger, but when he opened the door and slipped inside the abandoned base, he felt even more like an intruder.

It was a strange feeling, walking through a Neo-Andromedan facility built up from a human structure. There were elements that did not quite go together: adjacent walls made from different materials, rooms somehow positioned in places that humans never would have put them, hallways that were just a bit too narrow to be comfortable, with turns cut on diagonals on the inside walls.

The power was on in the building, with lights and ventilation holding just fine, but everything felt too still and too quiet. Lance kept close to the arkins as they padded through the hallways, letting them guide him. There weren't too many branching paths, but Blade had picked out a trail almost immediately, and was following it at an eager clip.

She led Lance and Orion past what looked like crewmen quarters, a mess hall, and four very formidable doors that

Lance could not open no matter what he tried. They were sealed tight, and their control panels bore a language that Lance had seen maybe once before, and that was when a superior officer had been assuring his training group that it was a defunct language already eradicated from the galaxy.

He gave up on the doors before long, and followed Blade past a room with complicated electrical equipment in it, to a door that had been blasted by wild enerpulse shots and then bent out of place by blows from a heavy, blunt object. Lance had no idea what to make of that, but he squeezed through the damaged door into a wide, open room that looked like it had once been some sort of announcement or gathering hall. Whatever it had been, it now held only a large, clunky machine and four bodies lying facedown on the floor.

Lance tensed when he saw the sprawling figures, but even from a distance, he could see that there was no life left in them. Three were on the far side of the room and the fourth rested near the machine. A shiver ran over Lance's skin, but he forced himself to take a step forward, and then another.

Blade and Orion whined as Lance moved away from the door, but he waved to them, and they quieted down. Blade kept her head near the opening, and Lance was very aware of her hard, amber stare as he moved towards the nearest body.

When he reached the dead man, he crouched down and studied the enerpulse wound burned into the back of the skull. The hair and flesh had been seared away, the bone blackened and scorched beneath. Lance's stomach roiled, but he forced himself to keep looking, to take in the metallic color of the dead man's blank, staring eyes and the tight black collar around his throat, just visible over the neckline of his shirt.

Lance remembered collars just like the dead man's from the attack at Ametria.

Whatever had happened here, the Seventh Sun had lost some agents, and been driven off the planet, probably for good. They must have taken Lissa with them. Lance was sure he would not find her here.

As he stood, his eyes lingered for a moment on the three

bodies on the far side of the room, then on the machine. It was a strange thing to Lance, and he moved towards it slowly, curious about its purpose.

The machine was a mess of circuits and exposed wires, of jutting angles and awkward curves. As he drew closer, he saw that its surface was pockmarked by the scorch marks of enerpulse shots. They looked disturbingly fresh. Then he saw that many of the exposed wires had been torn from their sockets, and the circuits had been hit by their own wave of enerpulses.

Whoever had destroyed the machine had done it viciously, and done it well.

Uneasy, Lance glanced around the room. He saw Blade's eyes in the opening of the destroyed door, and he saw a flash of Orion's yellow gaze. He saw a long row of windows showcasing more rooms with complicated machinery, and above them, he saw a balcony. Beyond the railings, he saw what looked like a computer and several data reading machines. If the Seventh Sun's agents had evacuated as quickly as it looked like they had, Lance thought that they might have left something of value up there. He turned to take one last look at the dead machine, and saw a hatchway on its side, wide and gaping.

Lance peered around the edge of the opening, into the dark chamber within the machine. The shape of some sort of harness slowly emerged from the gloom, and Lance saw more damaged machinery, dangling wires, and circuitry ripped from its structures. Then something moved.

Lance stumbled back, and the something came surging out of the dark, slamming into his chest and driving him off his feet. He came down hard and the air went out of his lungs. His vision swam with dizzy tears as fresh pain raged through his side, but through it all he saw black hair, golden brown skin, and hard, metallic, silver-white eyes.

"Lissa!" Lance said, but the breathing mask muffled his voice. The barrel of an enerpulse pistol swung towards Lance's head, and he reached up and ripped the mask from his face.

"Lissa, it's me!"

The butt of the pistol slammed into Lance's temple, and his vision went dark. He felt the barrel of the enerpulse pistol bite into the skin of his forehead.

"Lissa!" he gasped out again, squeezing his eyes shut and bracing himself for death.

The enerpulse shot never came.

Lance cracked open his eyes, and as his vision returned, he saw Lissa staring down at him. Her eyes were still too bright, and she had her hand tight on the enerpulse pistol, but she looked confused, and there was something flickering behind her stare. Her hand that held the enerpulse pistol was shaking, but Lance saw her let up on the trigger. Her irises darkened slightly, and her mouth formed, "Ashburn," though no sound came out.

Then a high-pitched cry pierced the air, and Lissa's gaze snapped up. She stared towards the broken door, and Lance saw recognition and disbelief bloom across her face. Her breathing became deeper, more ragged, the tension went out of her arms as the pistol dropped away, and she half-slid, half-fell off of Lance.

"It's okay," Lance said, trying to keep his voice from shaking. He slowly pushed himself up, wincing. "It's all right, Lissa." Lance saw a single tear spill on to Lissa's cheek, and he reached out to lightly touch her shoulder. "We're here now. We're going to get you out of here."

She shuddered, but did not pull away from him, and Lance rested his hand more firmly against her shoulder.

"We're here," he said again.

Lissa swallowed hard and nodded, but she did not take her eyes off of Blade.

Lance slowly tugged the enerpulse pistol out of Lissa's hand, whispering reassurances. She offered no resistance, and after gently tossing the weapon away, Lance clambered to his feet. He turned to Lissa, but caught sight of the breathing mask. He knew that he was doing all right without it, but fear won out in the end. After jamming the mask back over his face, he reached down and helped Lissa up. He regretted not bringing an extra mask for her, but there was time to get her out of the base before the flowers bloomed, and she was surprisingly unaffected for spending what must have been at least a few days on Daanhymn.

Lance revised that assessment almost immediately. She reeled drunkenly as she staggered to her feet, and Lance caught her against his uninjured side before she crashed back to the ground.

"Easy, now," he said softly. He pulled her arm over his head and wrapped his good arm around her waist. "We'll take it slow."

Supporting her weight as best he could and skirting wide around the dead Seventh Sun agent, Lance helped Lissa cross the room. He could feel her shaking, and when he looked her up and down, he saw that she was barefoot with nothing but a thin medical garment thrown over her in place of clothing. She must have been freezing, but the shivers felt more from trauma than from chill.

"Almost there," he encouraged her. "Just a little further."

When they reached the door, Lissa was still unsteady, but her breathing had leveled a little, she was supporting more of her own weight, and she was able to slide through the opening. Blade received her eagerly, and the arkin pressed her head into Lissa's gut, knocking her to the floor.

Lance pushed the arkin away as he came through the opening, but she surged right back to Lissa as soon as he was through. She dropped to the floor and lay with her head in Lissa's lap, whining softly and nuzzling up against her. Lance moved to push the arkin away again, but stopped when he saw that Lissa was smiling. There was a lot of pain behind it, but it was a smile all the same.

Lance straightened up and glanced around. He knew the way back to the shuttle, but a small staircase off to the side held his attention.

That must go up to the balcony.

He dropped to a knee in front of Lissa, and she raised her

eyes to meet his. They were fully back to their natural silver color. They were still hard and metallic, but they were familiar now, and Lance felt relief wash through him.

"I'm going to go check upstairs, okay? I'll be right back."

Lissa nodded, the smile dropping off of her face to be replaced by numb exhaustion, but she seemed better now that Blade was with her.

Lance told Orion to stay with them, then moved up the staircase.

He found himself on the balcony that overlooked the open room with the machine. He paused at the railing, wondering what it would have looked like from this position to see Lissa leap out of that machine and pin him to the floor. He shuddered a little at the thought, and pushed away from the railing.

He saw that the computer and data machines were still on, though they all displayed text in the language he had seen earlier, and he had no hope of reading it. If he could have relayed the text back to the Star Federation's Intelligence Unit, they could've deciphered it, but he could not risk that kind of contact. Not yet.

He looked around for any kind of drawers or compartments that might have contained something that he could have used, weapons or maybe even clothing for Lissa, but all he found was a single datapad, left on the floor where someone had dropped it. Lance picked it up and gave it a quick study. It was undamaged, but whatever data it held was a mystery to him. Nothing here was in the Written Unified Voice. He took it anyway, hoping that maybe Lissa could translate at least part of it once she felt up to the task.

With the datapad in hand, Lance left the balcony and rejoined Lissa and the arkins.

Lissa had managed to regain her feet, but she was leaning heavily against the wall, and she looked exhausted.

Lance gave her a few moments to collect herself, not quite believing that he'd actually found her, even if she had tried to kill him, but the attempted murder had not been entirely unexpected. He was not about to let his guard down now. As he watched Lissa, however, he felt a spike of alarm. She did not seem to be improving, just growing more tired with each passing minute. He had to get her back to the shuttle and let her rest. He stepped to her and pushed himself under her arm again, taking her weight against his uninjured side. "We have to go," he said gently, voice warped a little by the breathing mask. "Are you ready?"

She nodded.

They pushed off from the wall, and began the slow trek back to the starship hanger. They stopped once at the crewman quarters, and Lance snatched up a fresh change of clothes and a pair of boots for Lissa, though everything looked far too big for her. They would remedy that later.

They were halfway to the starship hanger when Lissa suddenly spoke.

"Wait," she breathed out.

"You all right?"

"My belt," she said.

"What?"

"I need it. My belt."

"Really?"

She gave a sharp nod.

"All right." Lance looked around, spied a sealed door that looked vaguely promising and nowhere near as indomitable as the four he'd seen earlier, and led her to it. "Let's try here." He looked at the door's control panel for a long moment. The buttons clearly had not been designed to make sense to a human. "I don't suppose you can read that?"

Lissa lifted her head. She frowned at the control panel, reached out, and hit a button. The door hissed open, revealing a small storage room. The shelves were packed with miscellaneous supplies, but Lissa pointed almost immediately. Lance helped her move to the shelf she had indicated, and she reached out to take her belt.

He saw why she had wanted it. The thick leather surface was covered with pouches and clips, and he could only guess what supplies were in there. Most of them were probably even more useful than what he had on the shuttle.

Lissa pulled the belt off the shelf. It did not look heavy, but it plummeted towards the floor. Lissa grit her teeth and held on, jerking the belt to a halt. Anger burned in her eyes.

Lance understood the frustration at physical limitations, though he doubted that an enerpulse wound was fully comparable to whatever the Seventh Sun had done to her. When she had a firm grip on the belt, Lissa shuffled around and they moved out of the storage room, but Lance saw how much she was straining just to keep her fingers closed around the thick leather.

"Do you want me to take it?" he offered.

There was another flash of anger, but she let the belt swing towards him.

He was right. It wasn't very heavy at all. Whatever the Seventh Sun had done to her had drained more of her strength than Lance had realized. He whistled to Orion, and slung the belt around the arkin's neck. Orion gave a disapproving grunt as it rubbed against his fur, but made no move to rip the belt off, and he carried it the rest of the way to the starship hanger while Lance kept one arm around the bundle of clothing, and the other supporting Lissa.

The sun had begun its descending sweep towards the horizon by the time they stepped out of the facility and into the hanger. Lance took one look at the growing shadow of the hanger bay, and pulled Lissa along a little faster. She wasn't prepared for that and she stumbled a little. Lance steadied her, and forced himself to go slower. They made it to the shuttle with plenty of time to spare, though the flowers in the shade were beginning to take on an otherworldly glow as they stretched towards the darkness. Inside the shuttle, Lance lowered one of the wall cots and put Lissa on it, then took a quick inventory check. He was more than relieved to see that they had enough food and water to last them at least one more trip, wherever they went. He loaded up the arkins, sealed the shuttle, and moved to the controls.

"Ashburn?"

He turned to see Lissa staring at him. She was finally breathing levelly, but she looked like she was using the last of her strength just to keep her eyes open. Blade was curled up on the floor next to her, injured wing spread out, and Orion sat near the cockpit. Lance had to pick his way around the arkins, but he reached the cot and dropped to a knee next to Lissa's head.

She lay on her side, looking at him. He saw her take in the signs of his own exhaustion, the plain traveler's clothes that he wore, and the way he held his arm away from his injured side. "You left them," she finally said. "The Star Feds."

Lance winced and nodded, the words stinging more than the enerpulse wound. He had to admit, it was easy to forget that he was no longer a fleet commander or even just a soldier when he was flying a Star Federation shuttle. He still felt the ties that bound him to his rank.

"You gave up everything."

He shrugged. "I would've given up more if I hadn't left."

Lissa frowned at him, but after a few moments, her eyes slipped closed.

"We'll talk about this later," Lance said, standing. "Rest now." He turned away, but Lissa's hand suddenly closed around his. Startled, he looked down at her.

Her eyes were open once more, and she looked up at him with bright intensity. "Welcome to the hunt," she said. Then she released his hand, rolled over, and finally let herself drift off to sleep.

And Lance, unsure of what else he could do, found a blanket among the shuttle's supplies and threw it over Lissa. Then he slipped into the seat at the controls, powered up the little craft, and piloted them out of the hanger and away from the Seventh Sun's base, away from the toxic night-blooming flowers, away from Daanhymn, away from whatever horrors Lissa had been forced to face. He scrambled the signal and let the shuttle coast as it soaked up energy from the nearby star that was Daanhymn's sun, trying not to think about the trials that still awaited him, but Lissa's words had perturbed him.

He wasn't in the hunt. He'd chased after and found Lissa, sure, but his goal had been—and still was—information. Something the Star Federation could use. Not wild chases through space and stalking targets across planets. He'd let Lissa rest, maybe even let her think that she had control for a little while, but eventually she'd see that there was only one real way to take down the Seventh Sun. She did not have the power or the resources to damage the Seventh Sun without Star Federation support, and he doubted that she could allow herself to slip back into hiding and let the Sun continue on after everything that had happened. And even if she could, Lance was there to nudge her back towards the Star Federation, slowly, quietly, but steadily.

No, he wasn't in the hunt now. Neither of them were. Not unless they were the prey.

CHAPTER 11: ARRIVAL

Upon disembarking back on Phan, Jason checked in with the squad of soldiers that was stationed at the hospital where all the trouble had begun. They reported no suspicious activity, and Jason felt a small twinge of relief, but he knew that information would not stop Keraun.

He knew the Hyrunian fleet commander by reputation only, but that extended to his "get the fucking job done" attitude and the tendency of the admiralty board to give assignments to Keraun that they wanted completed at all costs, never mind the danger to civilians. What little Jason knew about the Hyrunian species suggested that those might have been the only kind of assignments Keraun would have taken. He was the Star Federation's first Hyrunian fleet commander, appointed in hopes of strengthening diplomatic relations with the leaders of the species. No real progress had been made on that front, as far as Jason knew. Outside of their dominated space, Hyrunians were exceedingly rare, and those that ventured beyond those territories had no desire to return. Or at least, Keraun had never shown any desire to return, and Hyrunian territory remained far beyond Star Federation jurisdiction. Meanwhile, Keraun had filled his agenda with harsh action in Star Federation-controlled space rather than serving as a diplomat.

Keraun was the galactic media's favorite officer to love to hate, which took some heat off of the other questionable actions the Star Federation occasionally made, though those had started to fade as the admirals had begun to push more towards peacekeeping. With the reshuffling of territories in the wake of recent events and Keraun gaining authority over the large, jutting arm of the galaxy known as the Andromeda Reach, Jason knew that the admirals were swinging back towards fear, and drastic actions were not far behind. With Erica gone, Jason could feel any hope he had of stalling the initiation of a purge slipping away. Keraun was coming, and the formal declaration of war could not be far behind.

When Jason received word that Keraun's ship was on its final approach, he prepped his soldiers for the reception, and had them wait with him at the ground port for the arrival of the fleet commander.

True to his rank, Keraun had brought a small fleet with him, though his flagship was too large to dock at any of Phan's ground ports. He took a shuttle down instead, and Jason met him at the port with his squad.

Jason's soldiers stood at strict attention. They all wore the formal gray Star Federation uniforms, and Jason had inspected each of them himself before moving to meet the arriving fleet commander. His soldiers were immaculate, not a wrinkle in any uniform, even those on the non-human figures. Those who had the heads to support caps wore them light and low on their brows, the flat tops running straighter than a horizon.

Overall, they cut an impressive line, and Jason could feel the glances of the civilian crews at the ground port. They kept a respectful distance from the soldiers, but the space between them crackled with a mix of admiration and tension. Not everyone across the galaxy loved the Star Federation, and Jason felt particularly hard glances landing on the captain's badge secured over his heart. He wore the fancier, decorative badge today, and had polished the metal surface until the red bars gleamed and the gold edging almost pulsed with life in the weak light of Phan's sun. His dress uniform was as crisp and clean as his soldiers', and his cap was embellished with a thick braid of gold across the visor, but he felt oddly deflated.

There was still a hole where his heart had been, and he was acutely aware of Erica's absence. She had only stayed long enough to deposit the soldiers that were not under her command. Then she had nodded a curt goodbye to Jason, taken her ship and her underlings, and gone back out after Ashburn.

As she should have, Jason told himself, but throwing off the sting of that departure was proving difficult. He shook himself and settled back in to his formal stance. Erica was gone, and he had to focus.

If nothing else, Keraun should at least be satisfied with the reception.

He dared not hope for more.

Jason had a bad itch on his shoulder, and he could feel sweat running down his back despite the cool air, but he held himself at the ready long before Keraun's shuttle broke through the atmosphere, and he kept holding the stance as the shuttle landed, docked, powered down, and broke open to let the fleet commander emerge. Jason snapped into the formal Star Federation salute, and his soldiers mirrored him.

Sunlight glinted harshly off the Hyrunian as he emerged. It shone on his curling horns and metal chains threaded through them. It flickered on the hard yellow-green scales of his body, but snagged on the dark mark burned into the top of his reptilian head and around the back of his long neck, a Hyrunian symbol that Jason had never known the true meaning of, though he understood that the closest translation was "outcast".

Keraun did not wear a Star Federation uniform. Instead, there was a short, loose vest over his shoulders, and his fleet commander's insignia was blazed in blue and gold against the gray fabric, but outside of that, he wore nothing related to the Star Federation. There were heavy metal cuffs around the thin wrists of his stubby arms, dark against his light scales, but they were nearly the same color as his black iron claws. There was another set of metal cuffs around his ankles, looser than the fetters at his wrists, and they shifted with each step the Hyrunian took, chafing against the scales of his feet. Jason could see areas on his large, three-toed feet that had been stripped raw by the metal, though the Hyrunian either ignored the pain or felt none. There were no decorative elements on his tail or around his hip joints. The bareness probably left him with a better sense of balance and freedom to run. And made it easier for him to rear back on to his tail and lash out with his feet, Jason suspected.

They like to kick, Miyasato had said.

Jason did not doubt that she was right.

Keraun moved with a swaying stride, his long, thick tail thrust out behind him to counterbalance the swing of his neck. He held his arms curled against his chest, but Jason saw his claws flexing with each step, as though ready to tear into anything that dared come close enough to threaten his heart. His back arched with the forward swing of his feet, but never flattened out to the sleek, deadly dart of a Hyrunian running form.

Keraun's yellow eyes flicked around the ground port as he drew closer to Jason, pulling in the details, and Jason felt the tension in the port shift and focus on the fleet commander. A few of the crews pointedly turned away and disappeared among the docked starships and shuttles. Others dropped their gazes, and made themselves as busy as possible. The rest stared openly at the Hyrunian, but looked ready to scatter like fat rabbits before a wild, starving arkin let loose on an Earth reservation.

Jason stood his ground.

"You are Captain Stone?" the fleet commander said as he closed the last few steps, voice clicking on the hard syllables. It sounded more like an accusation than a greeting, and Jason caught glimpses of hard, sharp teeth as the Hyrunian spoke.

"I am, sir," Jason said, still holding the salute. "Welcome to Phan."

Keraun came to rest in front of Jason, looking distinctly

unimpressed. He dropped his tail and pulled his spine back and up, bringing himself eye level with Jason. The lines of his horns joining with his skull cut a permanent glare into his brow. He peered at Jason's group of soldiers, registering their neat, clean appearance and sharp attention. His own small squad was equally polished, though they were not in their dress uniforms. Keraun was the only Hyrunian present, but Jason noticed that there were far fewer humans among the fleet commander's ranks, and those that were present bore heavy combat scars. But human or not, they all looked mildly bored.

"At ease," Keraun finally scraped out, and Jason and the other soldiers dropped their salutes. "Fleet Commander Anderson is where?"

"Off-planet," Jason said with careful neutrality. "She traced the signal from the shuttle Ashburn stole, and is following the trail."

"Good," Keraun said. His head jerked and bobbed as he threw quick glances around the port. More crews dropped their gazes and turned away. "As I'm sure you know," Keraun clicked out, "Ashburn has been ejected from the Star Federation."

"As he should have been," Jason returned.

"Ejection is not enough for traitors, particularly at this level." Keraun's eyes glittered harshly. He took a step to the side, curling his toes. "I urged the admiralty board to take stronger action, but they are slow to hear, and slower to listen."

"I'm sure they will act as circumstances demand."

"One can only hope," Keraun growled. "Ashburn should be an Alpha criminal, not a Beta."

"I suppose the admiralty board would prefer for him to be brought in alive," Jason suggested. "It would be better for the investigation."

Keraun made an unpleasant face, curling his mouth into a snarl and slitting his yellow eyes. "We know what he has done. We do not need someone like him alive. He and others like him would open every world in the galaxy to Nandros and all the other impurities without a second thought."

Jason opened his mouth, but closed it again without speaking.

Major Miyasato's voice drifted back to him: *I'd stay on his good side, if I were you.*

"I care not to discuss this at a ground port," Keraun clicked on. "We have things to do." He glanced at Jason's soldiers. "You all remain here with my shuttle. My squad will accompany us."

He took a long step around Jason and loped into the central aisle between the rows of docked starships. Keraun's scarred squadron surged after him, and Jason almost had to jog to keep up with them. As he fell in beside Keraun again, the crowds of the ground port parted like water before them, but Jason almost had to fight through the nervous fear that remained in the wake of the scattering masses. The soldiers surged into the connecting city, and as they cut their way through the crowds, Jason realized that they were heading for the hospital.

He had no idea what Erica had told Keraun since their final conversation, if anything. He would have to be very careful when shaping his words, and did his best to appear calm as he jogged next to Keraun.

Keraun did not bring up the hospital. Instead, he spoke of the Ametria incident, and Ashburn's defecting to Nandros. "We will give him and whomever he is working with no place to hide," the Hyrunian said, turning his permanent glare on Jason. "We will find and expose them, all of them, and deal with this new Nandro threat harshly."

"Of course," Jason managed to get out.

"A tragedy, what happened at Ametria." There was no trace of sadness or remorse in the fleet commander's voice. "Perhaps a bigger tragedy still that those who died under Ashburn's command have not been put to rest as of yet."

Jason frowned. "No one has performed the memorial services?"

"Services fall to the commanding officer present at the time of death. With Ashburn gone, that's you."

The breath in Jason's lungs turned to stone and he almost tripped. He had forgotten about that policy in the wake of recent events, and guilt pricked at him, but more than anything, he felt a small surge of panic. If the Star Federation was waiting for correct protocol to be followed, then they were ready to go public with the incident. Jason was about to become the face of the Star Federation's first contact with a Nandro threat since the end of the Andromedan War. He could think of nothing that he would have liked to experience less.

"Your service speech will come at an important time, Captain," Keraun clicked on. "The admirals may be dragging their feet on Ashburn, but they are ready to engage in war. We need to show the galaxy that we will stand against this threat." He suddenly lurched forward and threw a sputtering hiss at a man who did not step out of the way quickly enough.

The man jumped back, stumbled into a child behind him, knocking the young one to the ground. The child clearly wasn't his, wasn't even of the same species, but the man snatched the child up and dove out of the way. Keraun stormed into the space they had filled. Jason glanced at them over Keraun's curving back, trying to at least show some empathy, but the man and the now-crying child would not meet his eye, and they disappeared before long.

"We need to make it very clear how dangerous the Nandros are," Keraun continued. "I trust you to do as much in your speech."

"The point of memorials," Jason gritted out, "is to honor the dead."

"The dead are not important. They can do nothing for the living," Keraun spat. "What is important is that we remind everyone what we are dealing with, and how dangerous it is to allow the Nandros to live. We need to wipe those things from the galaxy, every last one of them." Keraun's putrid yellow eyes glittered once again. "And this is where we start."

Jason looked up and saw that they had reached the hospital. Two soldiers lounged on the front steps, lazily watching the Phanite crowds as they halfheartedly guarded the main entrance, but the moment their eyes fell on Keraun, they snapped to tight attention. Jason heard Keraun mutter something in Hyrunian before he stalked past the saluting soldiers and darted into the hospital.

The reception staff tried to block Keraun's access, but his fleet commander rank allowed him to push past them, and Jason had no choice but to follow. He saw a nurse give him a long, careful look before slipping away. Jason thought that he recognized her as one of Chhaya's team members, and only hoped that she could warn the doctor.

Frantically, Jason tried to work out the details of what Keraun actually knew. Erica had reported back to the Hyrunian shortly before Ashburn's escape, of that much he was certain, but she had not known about the sick Neo-Andromedan called Aven. All she'd known was that the bounty hunter Shadow had received medical treatment at this hospital. Jason had kept Aven and Dr. Chhaya's warnings about the Nandros' Awakenings a secret.

Hide him, doctor, Jason prayed. *Hide him and hide away any reason for a purge.*

Keraun moved even faster through the hospital than he had the streets. He did not break out into a run, but his loping trot had Jason and the scarred squad running after him. Keraun had demanded Dr. Chhaya's location from the staff, and had been given the information without much resistance. He charged through the halls, slowed only by a decontamination checkpoint, and Jason felt dread spreading through his gut. If he remembered correctly, they were heading straight for Aven's room.

Hide him, doctor, hide him.

CHAPTER 12: DEATH

When the nurse came running, Aven knew that something was about to change.

Chhaya had come to check up on him, and Aven was having a rare bout of semi-lucidity, though everything still felt dull and fuzzy. The doctor had been saying something about weaning Aven off of some sort of drug or other, presumably to make him more comfortable as his life slipped away, but the nurse came skidding in, murmured something to Chhaya, and made the doctor look like he had just glimpsed a little piece of Aven's nightmares.

"Stay with him," Chhaya said, and turned to go.

"What happened?" Aven demanded, forcing the words through his raw throat.

"Nothing," Chhaya snapped, and did not look back.

Aven looked at the nurse the moment the doctor was gone. She was one of the nice ones, one of the trusted ones, round in face and figure with lots of easy smiles when things went well and lots more nervous tics when things went wrong. Aven watched her slide her weight back and forth from foot to foot, chew her bottom lip, and curl a loose wisp of hair around her finger while her other hand played with a fraying thread on her sleeve.

He asked her the same question.

Jolting as if from a daydream, she flashed a nervous smile at Aven and patted her auburn hair flatter than it already was. "Problem with another patient," she said a little too quickly.

Chhaya had a strong stomach. Illnesses gone wrong had never drawn that reaction out of him before. Aven had been in the hospital long enough to know that firsthand.

"Who's here?" he asked.

"No one," the nurse said, and turned her back to him.

"Lissa?" Aven tried.

The nurse shifted her weight.

"People with collars?"

The nurse shifted back.

"Star Feds?"

"It's no one," she snapped.

Aven struggled his way into a sitting position. If the Star Feds were finally here, he wanted to talk to them. He had information for them.

I shouldn't have thrown away the navi-sphere, he lamented, but he could give them at least a rough guess on where they should look. *Out beyond the Reach*, he thought, keeping the words fixed at the front of his mind. *Where there are no stars.*

The nurse heard him rustling and turned back to him. "Oh, no," she said, and jumped to his side. "You need to rest." She pushed him back down, and Aven pushed back against her hand and his own weakness.

"I want," he panted, "to talk to them."

"Aven, no," the nurse said, and pushed harder.

"I have to," he said, forcing the words out. They burned in his throat, but the need to be heard burned hotter. "I need to!"

"Aven, calm down."

"No!" he cried, and his voice was louder. He began to struggle again, and with what little strength he had, managed to whip one of his arms out from under the blanket. It hit the nurse's shoulder with a limp *thud*, and she grabbed his wrist and fought to hold him down.

"Stop!"

"NO!" The shout ripped through Aven's throat, and he thrashed harder.

"You don't understand," the nurse said, wrestling Aven flat but trying so hard not to hurt him, just as she always had. He could feel it in her grip, and if he had even half of the strength that had rippled through him when he had been a hunter, he would have broken free of her with ease. "If he finds you," the nurse grunted, "he'll kill you!"

"Don't care!" Aven snarled. "Let me go!"

There was a sudden flash of movement in the hallway, but the nurse's body shifted into Aven's line of sight.

"It's Keraun!" the nurse shouted. "Fleet Commander Keraun!"

Aven fell still.

The nurse stood over him, panting lightly. "He won't listen. If he finds you, he will—"

The door hissed open.

The nurse twisted around to look, giving Aven a clear view of the Hyrunian as he stalked inside. Glittering yellow eyes fixed hungrily on Aven, and the reptilian mouth pulled back into a nasty snarl that just did not want to register as a smile.

"Leave," Keraun breathed, not breaking his gaze away from Aven.

The nurse released Aven's arms, and turned to face the Hyrunian squarely. She drew herself up. "I will not." Her hands were shaking at her sides.

Keera, Aven remembered. *Her name is Keera.*

The fleet commander blinked lazily at her, and the unpleasant smile did not disappear. Aven knew that Keraun would kill her too, given the flimsiest of excuses.

"It's okay," Aven said. His throat felt raw, and the words were whispers of what he'd wanted them to be. "Go."

Keera glanced down at him, eyes wide with fear, but sadness crept in and, finally, she left. Cold silence settled over the room in the wake of her absence.

After a few solid minutes of enduring the Hyrunian's scrutiny, Aven gathered the tattered remains of his stamina and struggled upright. He was shaking by the time he had lifted his shoulders off the mattress, but he forced himself to push his legs over the side of the bed, and sit facing the fleet commander. He let his gaze fall into his lap for a moment as he gathered his breath, and he saw his own skin, sickly pale and washed even paler in the light. He shivered as a chill ran over his bare legs, but that could not shake the wild, desperate need to tell the Star Federation where to look.

Aven knew that what was left of his life extended the short distance between himself and the Hyrunian, and he felt the cold, sharp edge of certainty against his throat.

"Beyond the Reach," he breathed.

The Hyrunian blinked.

"It's where you need to look," Aven panted. He forced himself to stand, reeling on his feet and nearly collapsing to the floor, but he caught himself on the edge of the bed and looked desperately at the Star Fed. "Beyond the Reach."

The fleet commander said nothing for so long that Aven was afraid he had not actually spoken any words aloud. But then: "Where?"

"Past the edge. Where there are no stars."

"Where?" the Hyrunian said again, slower and harsher. He wanted an exact location.

"I…" Aven tried to remember, but fog closed over his mind, blotting out his memory. *Should not have broken the navisphere.* "I don't know."

The Hyrunian stood looking at him for a long time. Just looking at him, considering him, studying him. Then he seemed to come to a decision, and in the instant it took Aven to blink, he coiled his tail behind him, and reared back.

The world somersaulted around Aven in the next instant, and all the breath had been crushed out of his lungs. But all of that lasted for only a heartbeat. He had been dying for so long that his true moment of death, when it came with a dark and startling swiftness, did not feel real.

CHAPTER 13: BETA

In the end, it did not matter if Dr. Chhaya had intended to hide Aven or not. The doctor met the soldiers in the hallway, and had tried to block Keraun's path, but they were close enough to know which room he was shielding, and Keraun stepped around Chhaya and dashed to Aven's room.

Chhaya turned to follow the Hyrunian, but Keraun's lieutenant—a light-skinned human of medium height and build with a layer of dark scruff against his pale jaw and a raw, jagged scar running from one ear down the side of his neck—brandished his enerpulse pistol a little too liberally before running after the fleet commander, and Chhaya remained where he was.

Jason went after Keraun. "Commander," Jason called out as the Hyrunian slipped inside the decontamination chamber, "that man is in no condition to—"

"Do not," Keraun snarled, twisting his long neck around and focusing his permanent glare on Jason, "test my patience, Captain."

Jason held Keraun's stare, but the door slipped closed between them, and Keraun's soldiers pointedly blocked the control panel.

"Move," Jason growled, but they shook their heads.

"Commander's orders," the lieutenant quipped smugly.

Over his shoulder, Jason watched Keraun confront the nurse and the dying man, and Jason could only hold his breath, watching and waiting.

When the nurse emerged from Aven's room, she pushed past the lieutenant without a word, and refused to meet Jason's eye. She walked down the hall, and her path brought her past Dr. Chhaya, who only looked at the soldiers with disgust before turning away.

"Hey," the scarred lieutenant called out, but neither Chhaya nor the nurse turned back. "Hey!" he called again, and raised his enerpusle pistol.

Jason grabbed the soldier's wrist and shoved the barrel of the weapon towards the floor. "Stand down!" he snarled.

The lieutenant looked as though something slimy had touched him. He jerked out of Jason's grasp and gave him an angry stare, but did not raise his weapon again.

There was a heavy, meaty *thud* from inside Aven's room, and Jason looked up in time to see Keraun bring his legs down and spring back on to his feet. Aven had disappeared from sight.

"All of you, wait here," Jason snapped, and did not bother reprimanding the lieutenant for that glance. He did not have time. Instead, he charged after the doctor. Jason found him around the corner, one hand braced against the wall, the other on his knee. The nurse had disappeared, but the doctor looked as though he was about to be sick.

Chhaya glanced at Jason as he drew near, and anger sparked in his dark brown eyes. "Of all the officers you could have brought," he said, each word heavy, "it had to be the Hyrunian."

"I didn't bring him," Jason said quietly. "He came here on his own. I couldn't stop him."

"No, you couldn't," Chhaya said, and gave Jason a look that made him flinch. "And now Aven is paying the price."

Jason groped for the words, but all he could get out was, "I'm sorry."

"You're sorry?" Chhaya shook his head, straightened, and faced Jason squarely. "Captain, you're not the one who has to tell someone that the brother she trusted you to save is now dead, and not because of the disease that has been gnawing away at him for years, but because a Star Federation officer came in one day, and decided that his life was not important."

"There wasn't anything I could do."

"Oh really?" Chhaya crossed his arms. "As far as you all are concerned, his only crime was that he was a Neo-Andromedan."

"We know he was a bounty hunter," Jason said softly.

"But he was not part of the organization that the Star Federation is trying to destroy. He was also very sick, and not able to defend himself. You all promise to 'Stand and Protect' but so far, you've done neither."

"I'm doing what I can."

"That is not enough."

Jason looked at the doctor in silence.

Chhaya held his stare, almost as if daring him to say more, but after a while, his eyes flicked over Jason's shoulder. He sighed heavily, and uncrossed his arms. "I have to go now. Goodbye, Captain Stone."

Jason heard the soldiers coming then, and Keraun's scarred lieutenant fired off a brisk order to have Dr. Chhaya detained for questioning.

"You were ordered to stay," Jason said to the lieutenant, watching the doctor allow himself to be led off by the soldiers.

"Commander Keraun told us to go," the lieutenant shot back, adding a slimy smile. "He also says he has fresh orders for you." Then he turned on his heel and followed the doctor.

As he made his way back to Aven's room, Jason's chest felt tight, and there was something cold and unpleasant running its fingertips along his spine, but he held himself tall. He knew what he was about to find, and he could not let Keraun think that it would have any impact on him. Not if he wanted to keep trying to help.

Keraun was waiting for him outside of Aven's room. His

expression was as neutral as the permanent glare allowed, but at a quick glance, Jason saw the stains on his feet. His yellow-green scales had turned brown under the color, but there were blood-red, three-toed footprints on the floor next to him.

"The Nandro's heart gave out," Keraun said as Jason drew close. "He died before I could get any information out of him."

Jason swallowed past the hard lump in his throat, and said nothing.

"A waste of time," Keraun growled. "So, I expect you not to spend any more time here than is absolutely necessary. Get off this planet, and broadcast your memorial speech back to the space station while you're en route to assist with the salvage efforts."

Jason thought that he must have heard that wrong. "Salvage efforts, Commander?"

"I want that crashed starship recovered. Analyzing the hacked systems should help us build up a defense against further attacks. We'll need that for future strikes."

It took Jason a moment to understand which ship the Hyrunian was talking about, but the realization hit him with cold force. "Commander, that ship is on Ametria."

"I see no problem with that," Keraun retorted. "As long as the salvagers work quickly, we should recover the systems that we need with minimal casualties. Now," he stepped past Jason and started down the hall, following the footsteps of his scarred squadron and Dr. Chhaya. "I have another interrogation to conduct. You're dismissed, Captain."

As the Hyrunian walked away, Jason had a clear view of the dark mark burned into his skull and down the back of his neck. *Outcast,* Jason remembered. He had once heard that "nothing" was another possible translation of the symbol, but he could not remember who had told him that.

CHAPTER 14: BURNT

Lissa's sleep was deep and black. There was no room for dreams, only the sweet nothingness of pure exhaustion. She did not know for how long she slept, but when she swam back up into the waking world, she felt better. Fuzzy, drained, and a little broken, but better.

She opened her eyes to see a lot of gray.

And all at once, the nightmares rushed back in.

She saw the face of the woman who had come to her before the Awakening, round and fleshy and eerily hopeful, with her white gold eyes that hung on the brink of Awakened light. Then her face bleached into brightness and Lissa saw only her heartbeat. She felt the raw power coursing through her in blue waves, synching with her own pulse and reaching deeper, ever deeper to touch the hidden spark and explode it into a raging inferno. She relived the ache of having to lie still while the smell of heartbeats filled her lungs, waiting for the sources of the pulses to release her from the biting harness. She remembered the way their deaths had tasted, sweet and clean but just not satisfying, and she had wanted more, more, always more, and there had been voices in her ears again but this time, they were joined by another one that murmured, "Fight for me, Little Light."

Lissa cried out and began to thrash. Something tangled around her, closing off the movement of her legs and arms, but she managed to twist free before the hand gripped her shoulder. She swung her fist around wildly, but another hand caught her wrist and someone was shouting her name and there was a growl and a whine and then the nightmare lifted, and she was back on board the Star Federation shuttle, a blanket tangled around her legs, Blade watching her from the edge of the cot, and Ashburn standing over her. His fingers were wrapped tight around her wrist.

"It's okay," he was saying, bringing her fist down slowly, away from his head. He sank into a crouch, bringing his face level with hers. "It's over. You're safe now. I promise it's over."

The breath scraped through Lissa's chest, and she felt her eyes burning, but she didn't think there was anything left in her that would let her cry. She had survived the Awakening, and she had survived the Seventh Sun, but she felt dead inside. Just cold, empty, and entirely devoid of life.

Ashburn did not say anything for a long time. But he didn't move away, either. He just stayed crouching next to the cot, his hand over hers, letting her catch her breath.

Blade was less patient. She inched closer to the cot and put her head on Lissa's leg, still tangled in the blanket. She gave a heavy sigh and stared up at Lissa, amber eyes wide.

Lissa sat up and moved her hand out of Ashburn's, dropping her palm on to Blade's head. He let her go, and made no moved to touch her again.

After a few minutes of silence, Ashburn spoke. "There's some food if you want it. Clothes too, if you want to change."

Lissa glanced down at the thin garment she wore, loose and baggy and drowning her in a wash of white. She swallowed the hard lump that came into her throat, and felt something tighten around her neck. She reached up, and felt the panic sweep back in when she felt the thin collar. She ran her fingers over the surface, feeling the studs of the seven little stars, but there was no clasp, no seam, no weak point. She scratched at it, growing frantic, and there were voices in her ears again, but Ashburn grabbed both her hands and pulled them away from her throat.

"We'll get it off," he promised. He held her hands firmly this time. "Lissa, whatever they did to you, it's over."

She shook her head. She might have been out of the base and away from the Sun for the moment, but they had marked her, and that brand extended beyond the collar around her throat. It ran deep inside, right through her heart, and she knew that no matter how hard she tried, she would never be truly rid of it.

"Do you want to talk about it?"

Lissa squeezed her eyes shut, trying to force the lingering whispers out of her ears.

Ashburn's grip tightened a little more, but not painfully. "I know it doesn't feel like it, but they can't hurt you anymore." His voice was soft and gentle. "They're gone. It's just you and me and the arkins."

Through the whispers, Lissa felt the weight of a lie behind the words, and she fixed her eyes on Ashburn again. She saw in his face that someone was coming after them, closing in on their trail, fast and hard.

Welcome to the fight for me Little Light, the voices whispered.

Ashburn's face changed, and he gave her a tight, forced smile. "Are you hungry?"

"I was," she heard herself mutter.

Ashburn did not release her hands. He only dropped the smile and waited for her to speak.

Blade whined and edged closer, and Lissa moved a hand back to her head, but she left the other one in Ashburn's.

They should be dead, she realized. *Both of them.*

Yet here they were, both of them, survivors of the Seventh Sun. Like her and not like her all at once. Their wounds were on the surface. Hers went to her core.

Welcome to the fight for me Little Light, the voices whispered.

And here she was, too. Alive, and back in the cool, dark world outside of an Awakening. Still alive, with her hand on

Blade's head, running her fingertips over the arkin's soft, thick fur.

It took a long time, but the words did come, and they helped drown out the whispers.

"I can still taste the kills," she heard herself say. She could not look Ashburn in the eye, but he stayed with her, and held on to her hand. His touch was warm and Blade's fur was smooth against her fingers. Those sensations helped ground her in reality. "I can feel their heartbeats, and the silence that soaked their deaths. I can hear the voices nibbling on my ears, tapping on my brain, begging me to come back into the light, to lose control all over again."

Her breath hardened again, tightening through her chest.

"I was lost in the light," she pressed on, "blinded by it, but I could still hunt. I could trace these people and touch their fear, just reach out and twist it through my fingers. I knew I was doing it, hunting and killing them, but the hunger was so strong that I couldn't stop. I just followed it from heartbeat to heartbeat and I felt myself falling a little further into the light with each kill."

Her fingers traced the line of Blade's skull, but she couldn't feel the arkin's fur beneath her fingertips anymore. She was numb all over.

"There was just the light and the hunger and the heartbeats, and every time they pulsed, they ripped me a little further out of myself until I couldn't take it any more, and then they were just gone. All of them, gone." She squeezed her eyes shut. "That almost killed me. I could feel the hunger tearing me apart, but there was nothing left to kill. There were just the dark dead spots of the lives I already took, and the machine." Her eyes cracked open again, and found Ashburn's. "The machine. I remember the machine."

Blue power coursing through her, synching with the rhythm of her body. She shuddered at the memory.

"Lissa," Ashburn said gently. "I know that this was hard for you, but…" He held her gaze for a moment, and looked as though he regretted speaking. He plunged ahead anyway. "This isn't the first time you've killed."

She swallowed, and felt the collar close around her neck again. "This was different." She looked away from him, and her gaze snagged on Blade's amber eyes. She squirmed under their stares, suddenly wishing they would not watch her so closely.

Welcome to the fight for me Little Light, the voices whispered.

"Hunting is cold and calculated," she said, desperate to make Ashburn understand but suddenly angry that she had to. He would never taste an Awakening, and he would never know what it was like to have the world burn through his eyes. He would never understand. The words poured out of her anyway. "Hunting is distance. It's done for a purpose, and no one that I've ever hunted has been clean and pure. They were people that you would have killed yourself, if you'd ever tracked them down." She looked at him then, and felt the intensity strain behind her gaze. His skin was suddenly too hot against hers, and she pulled her hand away. "You would have killed them, and called it justice, and never lost any sleep."

Ashburn's eyes narrowed and he opened his mouth to say something, but closed it without a word a moment later.

"An Awakening," Lissa growled, feeling the anger grow, "is not like that. An Awakening is searing heat and hunger, but none of it is yours. It's fueled by death and burns white-hot until it boils you away, leaving only a husk that keeps hunting and killing and trying to slake the emptiness but it's infinite." Lissa pressed her hands over her eyes, trying to take refuge in the dark, but the world still felt too bright. "If you stay too long in the light, you can't break free. And if you go to it willingly, you don't want to."

Welcome to the fight for me Little Light, the voices whispered.

"Willingly?" Ashburn said, and she heard the jagged beginnings of distrust and fear in his voice.

Lissa dropped her hands. She tried to take a deep breath to steady herself, and felt the collar tighten its grip again. "I thought that I was going to die. I thought that there was no point in fighting them anymore, and that maybe, if I embraced the Awakening, I could keep some control. I thought that I could focus it, and tame it, and use it to get myself out." The round, hopeful face of the woman who had visited her before the Awakening filled her vision. "But I couldn't. I lost it all to chaos. Instead of trying to get out, I only wanted to go further in, to hunt them through the light and kill them, just because I could." She met Ashburn's gaze again. "Just because I wanted to."

He shifted uneasily, but something flickered behind his eyes, and he stood. He squared his shoulders as he looked down at her, and there was hard certainty when he spoke. "When I found you, you were still Awake, but you weren't totally out of control. You didn't pull the trigger when you had me on the floor with a pistol pressed to my head."

The memory of the moment flooded back in. Her inside the Awakening machine, trying to gut the thing in hopes of slaking some of her hunger, but halting when the sudden warm, heavy smell of a fresh heartbeat drifted around her, caressing her and pulling her towards the source. There was the bright flash of life filling her vision, the solid and satisfying crash of her body into his, the sweet taste of holding his life in her hands, and the savory feel of having the power to shred it as she pleased. Her hunger for the life. The gnawing, burning hunger, and the bitter confusion when the life did not go out when she pulled the trigger of the enerpulse pistol.

"But I did." She looked up at him, her voice sticking in her throat and her skin suddenly feeling too tight over her bones. "I wanted to kill you. I pulled the trigger. But the capsule was dead."

Ashburn opened his mouth, stood still for a long moment, then closed his lips without a word. He turned to leave, paused, and turned back. "I got lucky, then. I admit that. But you did recognize me."

Lissa said nothing.

"You said my name. My last name." Ashburn sighed. "I don't know if you had recognized me as an enemy or as a friend, but you did see me, and that has to count for something." He looked down at her for a long moment. "And I'm sure you know ways to kill that don't involve firearms."

Lissa dropped her gaze.

"Look," he said, sinking to a knee once again and positioning himself back in her line of sight. "Whatever they did to you, you held on. Somehow, you held on, and no matter how small that part of you was, the part that you kept, it was still you. That has to count for something, and it's not something that you should ever forget."

Welcome to the fight for me Little Light, the voices whispered.

Ashburn rose after a moment, and took a step back. "There's a change of clothes for you in there," he gestured to a storage compartment, "and there's food in the next unit over. It's shuttle food, so it's not the finest thing you'll ever eat, but it'll get the job done." He held her gaze for a steady moment before moving back to the shuttle's cockpit, and slipping into the seat at the controls. He sat sideways, watching her over his shoulder through the open, narrow door. "When you're ready, we can figure out our next move against the Seventh Sun."

"And what if I don't want to?" Lissa said, her voice low. "What if I just want to disappear? What if I just want to vanish into a little corner of the galaxy, and hide from them forever?"

Ashburn shrugged. "Then I couldn't stop you. I couldn't make you come with me to try and take down the Seventh Sun. I probably couldn't even stop you from killing me and taking this shuttle for yourself, or leaving me for dead on some forsaken planet, or even just ejecting me out of the airlock without killing me first." He cocked his head and considered her. "But I don't think you really want to do any of that. I think you've had enough of hiding, enough of running. And I think that the little part of you that you held on to during your Awakening, that little piece that you refused to surrender, is the part of you that wants to fight back."

Lissa forced another gulp of air past the collar.

"We can't undo what they've done," Ashburn said. "We can't take back what they did to you or anyone else. But we can stop them from ever doing it again." He turned to the controls of the shuttle, offering his back and his greatest blind spot to her. "When you're ready, we can begin."

Lissa sat looking at Ashburn's turned back. She saw the rise and fall of his shoulders as he worked the controls, but she also saw the tension. He was afraid of her, but he had decided to trust her. She thought that was a very stupid decision.

Welcome to the fight for me Little Light, the voices whispered.

Ashburn's gray arkin Orion lay sprawled on the floor near the cockpit, and he lifted his head and watched Lissa when she finally stood up from the cot. She swayed a little, very aware of the arkin's yellow stare even through the dizzy, airy feeling wrapped around her head, but the cold touch of the shuttle floor on her bare feet helped ground her. Her steps were unsteady, but she made it to the storage compartments, and Blade moved with her, matching her stride and never letting Lissa more than a pace beyond her reach.

Lissa dressed in the clothes Ashburn had found for her. They were oversized and baggy, prone to snagging on anything that so much as considered jutting out a tiny bit, and they had come from the Seventh Sun's base, from a life that may or may not still be pulsing somewhere out in space, but they were not the thin garment she had been forced to wear. They were a solid bundle of neutral browns and blues, not the bright white of her Awakening. The boots that came with the clothes were a little too big for her feet, and they were heavy, clunky things, but boots could be replaced.

Welcome to the fight for me Little Light, the voices whispered, but they were softer now.

Lissa found the food and water Ashburn had promised in the next storage compartment. It was pasty, plastic-tasting stuff, but Lissa chewed it gratefully, finally feeling the hunger abate. She chased it down with a full ration of water, and took another container with her when she went to join Ashburn in the cockpit. She sipped at the water, and felt the collar around her throat with each swallow, but she fought past the thing's grip. She would get it off somehow.

When she stepped into the cockpit, Ashburn glanced at

her clothes, then up at her. He considered her for a moment, then reached beneath his seat, grabbed something, and held it up. It was her belt. He handed it to her without a word, and took the container of water so that she was free to handle the belt.

Lissa held the thing in her hands, staring down at it and drinking in the details. The belt had always been hers, even before she had taken up the mantle of the Shadow. The leather was worn and weathered, soft against her fingers, but not thin enough to risk falling apart. It bore the burden of her tools and supplies with solid grace. She slipped it around her waist, feeling the familiar comfort of the thing against her hips, and fastened it. She secured the secondary strap of the empty enerpulse pistol holster around her upper thigh, and rested her hands on the edges of the belt. She'd fill the holster with a weapon later, but for the moment, she only focused on the weight of the belt, and the security of it.

"So," Ashburn said, handing the water back to her. "Where to? Back to Phan?" He asked it casually, but Lissa heard a small catch in his voice. It was all she could do to keep herself calm, but she knew what he was up to.

There was a very good chance that the Star Federation was still on Phan, and Ashburn knew it as well as she did. His clothes were different, and he did not have the rank badge sewn over his heart, but he was still a Star Fed. Killing him would be the easiest and safest course of action, but if she did and the Star Federation caught up with her, there would be no chance of outmaneuvering them. Better to keep him alive, and keep a close watch over him, and be very, very careful around him.

"No." She took another sip of water, but her throat still felt dry, and the words snagged on their way out. "There's nothing to do there that I haven't already done."

"You're sure?"

Lissa nodded, looking Ashburn in the eye this time, but careful to keep her gaze as non-challenging as possible.

He still held her stare a fraction longer than necessary. "All right." He rolled his shoulders as through shrugging off a weight, but Lissa saw him wince and push his left elbow out, away from his wound. "Where do we start?"

How sweet. He's letting me think I'm in control.

Ashburn was counting on her to fail. He was giving her room to play, but fully expected her to have nowhere to turn, nowhere to run, except the Star Federation. He wanted her to turn to them on her own.

She would take advantage of that.

Lissa glanced around the tiny shuttle. It wasn't a bad vessel, just small and cramped and not quite fast enough to suit their needs. But it was also stolen, and the Star Federation was bound to be tracking it. The sooner they were rid of it, the better, but they could not just drop the thing on a random planet. They needed their own ship. And for a ship, they needed money.

There was still a bit left in the reserve funds for Aven's treatment. As much as she trusted Dr. Chhaya, she had not given him access to that hidden, locked account, and she had always wanted to leave a little in storage, as much for Aven's emergencies as her own. She could withdraw the money remotely, and though that would give the Star Feds a line to trace, there wasn't much they could do once the account had been drained. Minted money was one thing, but virtual credits that were stripped of tracers by black market sellers were another matter entirely. If the dealer did not try to press her desperation, the reserve funds would put her close to the price of a decent starship.

They would also guarantee Aven's death, but that had been guaranteed for a long time.

There's nothing left for him, she reminded herself. *Nothing left to do for him. Let him go.*

If Aven was still alive whenever—if ever—she returned to Phan, she would say goodbye. If he wasn't, then he wasn't and there was nothing to be done about it. Lissa had never given Dr. Chhaya a way to contact her if the worst should happen; communication lines were too easy to trace. She had always waited for either confirmation with her own eyes or a steadily draining bank account to prove to her that Aven was still alive. And besides, Lissa had said goodbye to her brother dozens of times over during the early stages of his sickness, just in case an organ failed or the treatment went sour or she failed to return from a hunt. Eventually, the words had lost their meaning, and she had stopped saying goodbye.

Aven had not cared. He understood what a tether was. He might actually be happy to see it cut.

Nothing left, except Blade and me.

Even with Aven's reserve funds, Lissa knew that she would probably have to hunt again. There just wouldn't be enough if she wanted to buy from an untraceable dealer, and that by itself severely limited her options. She could think of one or two dealers who might take the shuttle against the remaining value of a starship, but they would gladly feed information back to the Star Federation in hopes of avoiding a nasty confrontation. Then that untraceable ship would suddenly blaze a trail as bright as daylight.

Asburn was another problem entirely. She needed a dealer that would not be intimidated by his Star Federation ties, even if he had deserted. If she could keep Ashburn outside of negotiations, she could remind him that while he had gotten her off of Daanhymn, he was not in control. He'd be beyond wrestling his way back into power at that point.

Lissa considered the shuttle again. It was in pristine condition, and the controls were top-of-the-line. Only the best for Star Federation vessels. Someone was bound to want the thing for parts. Someone who would love to see Star Fed tech, and would never surrender it willingly, even with the Star Federation bearing down on them.

And then Lissa realized that she knew someone who would love to get her hands on the shuttle, never mind if it was stolen or not.

Lissa almost discarded the idea as soon as it had occurred to her. Too much had happened for Min to ever want to see her again, let alone make a deal with her for a starship. And yet, with Aven dying and maybe even already dead, it might not hurt to try. After all, Lissa did have Star Fed tech to offer.

"Mezora," she said to Ashburn. "We start on Mezora."

CHAPTER 15: TURN

Erica wasted as little time as possible on Daanhymn. Ashburn's trail led to that forsaken little planet, but it doubled back into space and headed across the Paradise Void. Erica wanted to follow it immediately, but the shuttle had landed on the surface and that could not be ignored. To Erica's surprise, scans around the touchdown point revealed a building that should have collapsed alongside the True Eden colony. Imaging showed that the building had been maintained far after the colony had failed, and there were elements that suggested someone had added to the structure. Erica was leery of this discovery, but she dispatched a small salvage team under the command of Lieutenant Bachar to Daanhymn's surface. Erica left them with plenty of supplies, but signaled for reinforcements from the Star Federation space station.

"Work fast," she told Bachar, "and be careful. Flowers aren't the only thing you may have to worry about."

After receiving confirmation that the salvage team had safely landed and set up a secure base camp, Erica pointed her ship away from Daanhymn and tore after Ashburn.

She was getting close. She could feel it. The signal from the stolen shuttle was growing stronger with each light-year that drifted off in the wake of her sprinting starship, and she knew that Ashburn would have to dock somewhere soon.

He has to be getting desperate, Erica thought as her ship tore across the galaxy. *At this pace, he'll blow most of his power and supplies before he puts in to port. And with his Star Federation accounts frozen, he won't be able to restock.*

Without access to money, it was unlikely that Ashburn would be able to make it off of whatever planet he ended up grounding himself on. He risked starving out in space if he did not put in to port soon, and Erica would catch him either way. It was just a matter of patience, but Erica was swiftly running out of that.

To fill the empty time and distract herself, she contacted her captains for status reports, and learned that the galaxy was relatively quiet, all things considered. There were the usual troubles with illegal endeavors, but there had been no Nandro activity since the encounter at Ametria, and Erica's captains were handling their own agendas without much trouble.

Sporadic replies to her messages to the other fleet commanders revealed that they were all having similar luck in their own territories, though Yukarian-dominated space was churning with more activity than usual, and the Hyrunians had gone chillingly silent.

We think they're waiting to see how we handle recent events, one fleet commander's message read. *We don't know how, but they know what happened at Ametria. Watch yourself, Commander Anderson. They're probably watching you.*

Erica's mind twinged when she read that.

She had expected tension to come with her promotion, considering she had taken over as the human fleet commander and there were plenty of expectations that she now had to meet, but when the admirals had transferred jurisdiction over the Andromeda Reach to Keraun, she had thought that they were only temporarily lifting the weight of that unstable territory off her shoulders as she settled into her new role; she had assumed she would get the Reach back after catching Ashburn. Now, she wondered if they had put her aside so they could use Keraun as a demonstration to the Hyrunians. If he caught even a trace of something related to Nandros, he would rip through the territory until he found what he was looking for, or killed everyone and everything connected to the Nandros. That would probably impress the Hyrunians, and terrify the rest of the galaxy into obedience.

Not for the first time, Erica found her thoughts turning to whatever it was that Jason had not told her. She knew that there was something, and that it had to do with that damned hospital and the doctor. They were Keraun's problem now that Phan was under his jurisdiction, not hers, but she wished she had been able to get the secret out of Jason before she had left. Erica knew that she could have threatened him with the promise of turning him over to Keraun or the admirals, and letting them review the security footage and question him, but she had not been able to bring herself to do it.

Part of her wanted to, but there just wasn't enough evidence. The scene from the footage certainly played out like Ashburn had gotten the jump on Jason, snatching a tranquilizer while the captain's back had been turned. And Erica had to admit, it was still a bit difficult to fully think of Ashburn as a traitor. Most soldiers would have been perfectly comfortable turning their backs to an officer like Ashburn, no matter what charges had been levied against him. Erica was not one of them, but she could understand that sense of security and trust.

But look where that got us, she reminded herself.

Something was off about everything, and Erica knew that she needed to bring down Ashburn in order to fit it all back together, but she hated the feeling of charging after him half-blind.

You should have told me, Jason.

She sighed quietly, thinking back to her final exchange with the captain. Jason was a good man, and she regretted that things had ended the way they had. She knew she had left him with a lot of pain, but there were more important things to worry about than shallow love affairs gone sour. Things like shady Nandro organizations and rogue fleet commanders and all the other reasons to initiate a purge, but Erica kept thinking back to Jason's quiet urging to avoid that route. She knew that there was something that was not fitting into place, and in spite of everything she had said to Jason, she feared that he was right, that there was something going on that she did not understand, that a purge would destroy all chances of bringing that unfathomable thing into the light.

Then the transmission from Lieutenant Bachar came through. The lieutenant shakily informed Erica that the building they had found on Daanhymn had indeed been a Nandro base, but it had exploded while most of the salvage team was inside, killing them. The small remainder of Bachar's team had not been able to determine if the salvagers had tripped something during their search, or if the explosives had been detonated remotely. They were not confident that they would ever know. There was nothing left of the building but rubble, bits of destroyed machinery, and a large number of dead Star Federation soldiers.

Once the initial shock had subsided, Erica felt the rage bloom in her gut. She forced herself to take a deep, steadying breath. "Did you get *anything* out of that base before it blew?"

"Very little," Bachar said, her voice thick with distress, "and what we do have is in the Nandro language."

"Relay what you have to the Intelligence Unit on the space station. Maybe they can puzzle it out. Have you found any survivors from the explosion?"

"Not yet, ma'am, but we had to halt the search when the sun went down."

A heavy weight settled in Erica's gut. "If the sun's down on Daanhymn, then there are no survivors," she told Bachar. "Double check the airlocks of your basecamp, and rest part of your team until morning. The rest of your team needs to get back in there and focus on the machines. Take everything you can, and preserve it until the reinforcements arrive."

"Commander, we need to wait until dawn. The flowers have released their toxins."

"You don't have respirator packs and breathing masks?"

123

Bachar hesitated.

"Then you're going back in," Erica said firmly. "Find what you can, and do it quickly. We cannot waste time."

"Yes, ma'am." Her voice was shaky, but Erica knew that the Nandro danger was already past.

If the Nandros had blown up their own base, they were not coming back. As long as Bachar and her team were careful, they would survive the toxic flowers. Lieutenant Bachar was a capable soldier, shaken by the explosion and the loss of her subordinates, certainly, but Erica was confident that she would lead a successful salvage expedition once she calmed down and returned to the task at hand. The sooner that happened, the better.

Erica cut the transmission, and ordered a soldier to bring up a star map with the stolen shuttle's signal projected on it. The trail cut across the map in a thin red line, and Erica's own ship was creeping up on the source of the signal, but not fast enough for her taste. As she stared at the trail, her brain chewed over the facts of Ashburn's desertion, and the trouble he had caused. That only brought unanswerable questions racing to the front of her mind.

Could Ashburn really have betrayed humanity, and defected to Nandros? Had he meant to lead her and her soldiers into a trap on Daanhymn? If so, had he known that the base would blow?

Was that even worth asking at this point?

Whatever Ashburn was up to, his betrayal was taking lives, and Erica's hands clenched into fists at her sides, turning her knuckles bone-white.

I will find you, Ashburn, she thought. *Traitor.*

CHAPTER 16: SACRIFICE

After Arrilissa's disastrous escape and the sudden appearance of the Star Federation, the Seventh Sun moved the survivors to another outpost base, this one almost as austere as the Daanhymn facility, but without the pretty blue flowers to fill the nights.

Haelin was miserable on the new world. She avoided people as best she could, even Vinterra, and snuck off to sit alone in the bright, unending light of the planet's binary suns, feeling the weight of her decisions crush down on her. But the First Lit reached out to her before long, and her time on the new base was cut short.

Haelin expected a harsh message promising harsher punishment, but to her mortified shock, she was given total power over her fate. All the First Lit wanted was a name, and they gave Haelin the power to choose. So she chose.

Saying goodbye to Vinterra did not go well. There were angry tears and demands for the truth, but Haelin could not tell her. She wasn't sure what Vinterra was hoping to hear or not to hear, but whatever it was, Haelin could only say, "I'm sorry. This is how it has to be."

And Vinterra crumpled before her eyes.

Haelin wanted to kiss away Vinterra's tears, to take her in

her arms and make up for the absence she had forced Vinterra to feel, but Haelin could only stand there and breathe out silence.

She so badly wanted to tell Vinterra the truth. She wanted to tell her that the First Lit had demanded a replacement for Arrilissa, but they would not accept just anyone. Someone had to pay for the crime of disobeying orders, and the First Lit wanted the one responsible. They had demanded that Haelin give them a name for a new Awakening candidate, and Haelin had known exactly what the First Lit had wanted to hear.

To her, there had been no choice. There had been only the one name she could never speak, and the one she had blurted out immediately. She had felt cold and empty afterwards, and now, standing before Vinterra and watching her heart break, she felt cold all over again, but oddly calm.

Haelin forced herself to say goodbye, even though a million other words buzzed behind her lips.

And Vinterra, beautiful, sweet Vinterra, turned away to hide her tears, but finally screamed, "Just go!"

So Haelin went, thinking, *It will be easier if you hate me.*

But even if that was better for Vinterra, Haelin's resolve cracked at the last minute, and she rushed back to Vinterra's quarters, ready to spill the truth, but Vinterra was gone and Haelin had no time to look for her. Instead, she scrounged up one of Vinterra's datapads, entered a hasty message, and then took her leave, hoping feverishly that Vinterra would find it.

The world blurred around her as she walked from Vinterra's room to the starship that would take her to her fate. As she boarded the ship and took her seat, escorts scattered throughout the vessel, Haelin's mind kept flitting back to all of the things she had forgotten to pack, but she would not need them where she was going, and most of those things were back on Daanhymn anyway.

Haelin's fingers twitched whenever she thought of that planet. She had hated it, but with it far, far behind her and receding beyond the horizon, she was starting to miss it. Daanhymn was where she had met Vinterra and carved out some semblance of a life, and where she had been as close to being happy as she could remember. Daanhymn was where Vinterra had touched her hands and not flinched away from the feel of her too-long fingers. Daanhymn was where Vinterra had lain next to her in the dark, whispering into the night until they both drifted off to sleep. Daanhymn was where Vinterra had woven a necklace of flowers bursting with color and given it to Haelin after a bad afternoon of wrestling with depression. Daanhymn was where those moments had lived, and Daanhymn was where those moments had died forever, but Haelin held the memories close.

She held on to the memories all the way to the Awakening facility, all the way through the preparation process, all the way through the final moments between the dim, cool, normal world and the searing brightness of an Awakening.

Haelin had promised in her final, hasty message that she would think of Vinterra until the very end, and she kept that promise.

CHAPTER 17: SCARS

After the lifeless silence of Daanhymn and the long trek between distant star systems, Mezora was a welcome sight. Lance was eager to land on the planet and get out of the cramped shuttle. Space had been limited before he had picked up Lissa, and with the mistrust between him and her combined with the restlessness of the arkins, there was little room for relief. Lance had tried to diffuse the tension between himself and Lissa at first, but as the sidereal days slipped past and they shot towards Mezora, it had become all too clear to him that Lissa would not open up to him at all, let alone give him any information about the Seventh Sun. He was beginning to doubt that she even had the knowledge he'd expected her to possess.

When he had left the Star Federation, Lance had thought that Lissa would know how to root out the Neo-Andromedan organization's hidden agents. Now, he had the distinct impression that all she had to offer were a few names and some traumatic memories, not the least of which was her Awakening on Daanhymn. She did not sleep much on the trip to Mezora, but when she did, nightmares plagued her.

Lance had not tried to shake her from her dreams after she had confessed that she had tried to kill him on Daanhymn. He worried that she would try to do it again if he broke into her nightmares and gave her a physical target. That fear and paranoia mixing with shaky, sweaty withdrawal from the stims meant that Lance had not slept much during the journey, either.

He had filled the sleepless days by pouring over information from a Star Federation database entry on Mezora pulled up from the shuttle's main computer. Exhaustion and the gently gnawing need for stims had kept him from absorbing everything he read, but some details had managed to stick to his brain.

Not entirely unlike Earth, with large continents and larger oceans of water, Mezora was a wealthy, prosperous planet. Its flora grew red instead of green and humans needed respirator packs to walk the surface, but it was not otherwise a hostile environment to off-worlders, provided they were willing to embrace Mezoran social customs and took the time to review and understand the Mezoran justice system before entering the atmosphere.

Thrilled as Lance was at the prospect of getting out of the shuttle, reading about how the Mezorans handled crime and justice made him nervous. Mezora was a fully independent planet and had declared itself outside of Star Federation jurisdiction a long time ago, and the planet's warped views on what was and was not illegal were often in conflict with Star Federation laws, most notoriously their approval and enforcement of registered kills if there was enough evidence to justify the action. While in recent years, a healthy population of humans and other off-world races had immigrated to the planet and successfully integrated themselves into Mezoran life, the ideologies of the world remained beyond the grasp of much of the rest of the galaxy, including the Star Federation as a whole. There had been very few efforts towards diplomacy between the galactic military and the independent planet. The database entry described Mezoran-Star Federation relations as cool at best, and warned soldiers to expect snubbing or even hostile treatment from the Mezoran planetary council and the police force known as the Justice Keepers. The database entry's final words advised Star Federation soldiers to avoid Mezora altogether whenever possible, noting the location of several alternative port planets should an emergency arise.

I'm not part of the Star Federation anymore, even if the shuttle is tattooed with the insignia, Lance had reminded himself grimly when he had read that. *What do I have to worry about?*

His eyes had snagged on the brief section on approved registered killings within the justice system, but there hadn't been enough information to ease the sudden anxiety roiling in his gut.

Still, when Mezora finally came within striking distance, the recycled air inside the shuttle was thick with relief.

The planet bloomed across the cockpit window, all vibrant shades of blue, turquoise, white, sandy-brown, and fiery red under the light of its orange sun. Cities glittered across the night side of the planet, dotting the inky black with golden warmth. Ships came and went from the trading ports, and Lance hid the shuttle from security scans by engaging the shuttle's cloak and dipping close to a large freighter for extra protection.

Lissa struck up a rare conversation prior to entering the atmosphere, running through the best way to breach the sky and make certain they could get to where they needed to go. Lissa claimed to understand the Mezoran justice system far better than Lance did, even after studying the database entry. She said that while explaining why they were arriving in a stolen shuttle might have prompted the Mezorans to let them in just to spite the Star Federation, the procedure would burn time, and if the Mezorans turned them away, there was a very good chance that Anderson would catch up to them before they could disappear.

Lance did not argue the point. He did not like the idea of broadcasting their arrival as it was, warped alien perceptions of justice aside. He and Lissa agreed that they should risk a stealth entry. It was a tense ride into the atmosphere as Lance strained to match the flight path of the freighter, but once they were beyond the checkpoint, the shuttle broke away and streaked towards the largest Mezoran city, coming in just as the bloated sun began to slip over the horizon.

Lance had seen some striking settlements during his travels with the Star Federation, from buildings that had stretched above the clouds into the skies and been nearly abandoned at the ground level save for maintenance workers; to underwater civilizations that had viewed air as unclean and evil, and shunned anyone who required it to live; to cities that had been built in the sky and relied on hover-tech to keep them from falling to their doom. He was accustomed to either heavy dependence on technology or stagnant refusal to advance, though in the latter instance, he had seen plenty of cases where there had been no need to fix what was not broken, and everything had made perfect sense once he had gained a grip on the core concept of the cultures.

The Mezoran city, however, stuck out as one of the strangest he had ever seen.

Scorning hover-tech and force fields, the city was built on three solid black platforms, rising out of each other in increasing height and subdivided by what Lance thought was an indicator of wealth, though as the shuttle drew closer, he could not say for certain if that were true or not. From what Lance could see, the platforms that served as the city's foundations did not use any technology, and were simply massive, solid disks sitting on top of each other with the city sprawling over their surfaces.

The outermost district rested on the lowest platform, running in a neat ring around the middle level, and though the buildings were graceful and tapered and looked to be made from the same materials as the rest of the city, they lacked the showmanship of the higher levels. The buildings of the lower district all looked to be in good condition, however, and far more residential than the middle and upper districts. Traffic was minimal in the corresponding airspace, with only a few ships and fewer sky cruisers streaking through the air, though most of these glided quickly over the outer ring, heading for the higher areas.

The middle district towered above the first ring, the platform rising in a wall of domineering black above the roofs of the lower district's tallest buildings, and the massive disk that served as the perch for the upper district rose even higher than the mid-level buildings. The city had an odd silhouette that Lance found displeasing, but the individual buildings themselves were striking.

The middle and upper districts had the bizarre, unnerving structures that Mezora was famous for: buildings with wild twists worked into their designs, others bent into smooth arcs, still others sweeping across an excessive amount of airspace, and all reaching with odd grace towards the sky. Mezoran architecture was legendary, perhaps overshadowed only by the construction materials harvested from the planet's twin moons that made such buildings structurally possible, and at this time of day, with the sun slanting low in the sky and staining the buildings and their glittering windows soft shades of gold, pink, purple and deep blue, the city was reluctantly beautiful, particularly the slender, reaching upper district.

Studying the city, Lance felt that nauseous mix of excitement and wariness again. Even though they had managed to successfully run a stealth breach of the sky, the shuttle was bound to attract attention, and Lance was not certain what kind of attention he should hope for. And Lissa still had not told him who they were meeting on Mezora, just that they would be willing to trade for the shuttle. Lance had serious doubts about the certainty of that, given that the shuttle was marked as stolen and the Star Federation was coming for it.

At that moment, Lissa slipped silently into the space beside him, and Lance flinched at her sudden appearance. He was slowly becoming accustomed to her presence and learning how to hone in on her quiet movements behind him, but it was unnerving how easily she could still sneak up on him, especially in such close quarters.

Lissa gave his tense expression a slow, thorough scan. "Don't worry," she said, turning to stare out at the Mezoran cityscape, her jaw tight and her gaze hard. She had insisted on this planet despite Lance's gentle nudges towards somewhere more Star Federation-friendly, but now that they had arrived, she looked as though she would rather be stranded on Ametria all over again. "A stolen shuttle will catch enough of the business owner's interest to open a communication line."

"And you're sure this dealership will want to cut a deal with us?"

"No."

Lance looked at her sharply. "You said that this was our best chance of getting rid of the shuttle and cutting the trail cold."

"It is. If this dealer won't take it, I don't know anyone else who will."

Lance groaned. "You sounded more confident when you first suggested this planet."

"I had to," she said, never once tearing her eyes away from the approaching city. "You never would have agreed to come otherwise."

"No," Lance said. "I would've just suggested that we dump the thing and try to buy a starship without it."

"It wouldn't have been enough."

Lance had nothing to say to that. Lissa had already offered the reserve funds from Aven's treatment, and that was all she had. There was a decent amount of credits tucked away in Lance's retirement account, all of his savings from a salary that he had barely ever touched, but one of the first things the Star Federation would have done after his desertion was completely freeze his accounts. If he even so much as thought about accessing his funds, he would have an entire fleet bearing down on him.

He did not like this feeling of helplessness slowly creeping over him. He had known that deserting the Star Federation was likely to result in this exact situation, though he had expected being caught or being dead to be the more likely consequence. Desertion had felt like the right thing—the only thing—to do at the time. He was still harboring the dangerous hope that Anderson would find them, but that hope was fading into nothing, and all illusions of control were slipping further and further out of Lance's grip.

I never should have left the Star Federation.

But it was far too late for that.

As the shuttle glided closer to the private port, the communication system came alive, and Lissa accepted the transmission.

The voice that cracked over the communicator was stern and cold, but not impolite, and it pointedly addressed them as the Star Federation shuttle. It informed them that they were trespassing, and that if they did not turn around immediately, they would be forcibly removed from the surrounding airspace.

Lissa ignored the warning. "We're here to meet with Chief Executive Officer Fang Min of the Fang Galactic Cruiser Dealership. We have business with her."

"Do have an appointment?" the voice asked, still not quite impolite but far from friendly.

Lance saw Lissa take a breath and brace herself. "Please tell Executive Fang that Arrilissa would like to speak with her."

There was a delicate pause.

Then there was a muffled exchange.

Then there was a tense silence.

Then there was a burst of words in a language that Lance had never heard before, fired off in a new voice, a man's voice.

Lissa winced as the strange words filled the shuttle, then gave a halting reply in what sounded like the same language.

There was another pause.

"Please land your craft on the upper pad," the man said in Galunvo. "You will be met by a representative." The voice cut out, and silence filled the cockpit.

"What language was that?" Lance asked, not bothering to hide his shock.

"Terra-Six Chinese."

"And you can speak it?"

"Not fluently." Lissa refused to meet his eye. "Let me handle this, all right?"

"I'm not staying on the shuttle."

"Fine, but just stay as quiet as possible."

"Are you serious?"

Lissa finally looked at him. "Let me handle this."

Lance threw up his hands. He had no idea what to expect, but he was less than thrilled to leave everything to Lissa. She had barely recovered from her ordeal on Daanhymn, and though she had been evasive on the journey to Mezora, this was another level of ambiguity. It did not help that he was feeling more and more like an unwanted lackey than a partner. That was a dangerous state. Lance had no idea how stable Lissa actually was, and if she did not need him, he did not doubt that she would cut him loose. Or just cut him. He had done his best to hide the weapons that had been onboard the shuttle while Lissa had slept, but he had not been able to identify every item tucked into her belt, and he was fairly certain that he had misjudged the lethality of at least five seemingly harmless things. Lance knew that he needed to stay on her good side, but being kept ignorant was frustrating him.

Seething internally, Lance piloted the shuttle to the private landing pad. It was small, built more for sky cruisers than spacecrafts, but it was large enough for their needs and swept out in an elegant curve that mirrored the side of the attached building. As Lance manipulated the shuttle into position for the touch down, he caught a glimpse of a smooth hologram sign projected over a large doorway. There were a few unfamiliar characters on the sign, but below them were the words "Fang Galactic Cruiser Dealership" in the Written Unified Voice. In smaller text beneath that: "Breathe easier with us."

Lance eyed Lissa, but she offered him nothing in return.

When the shuttle touched down, Lissa rose without a word. She stepped over the sprawling arkins, and they lifted their heads to watch her as she moved to the airlock.

"We need respirator packs," Lance reminded her.

Lissa shook her head and told him to wait.

Lance gave a hard sigh, but settled back into his seat. He

did not have to wait long. Through the cockpit window, he saw a force field shimmer out from the building, reach over the landing pad, and descend around the shuttle, closing off the Mezoran atmosphere. Pale gas pumped into the sealed bubble, mixing with the un-breathable air and dissipating almost as quickly as it entered. After a few minutes, the shuttle's communicator cracked to life again.

"You may breathe easier," a cool, pleasant voice informed them, "knowing that Earth-like conditions have been restored. Welcome to the Fang Galactic Cruiser Dealership."

If that was true, Lance thought that that was a wild waste of money.

Lance threw another look over his shoulder at Lissa, but she had already opened the airlock and slipped outside without a breathing mask. Lance drew an involuntary sharp breath, but forced himself to release it and breathe normally. The air held a faint artificial tang, but breathing it brought on no ill effects as far as he could tell, and the arkins seemed unaffected as well. They rose with him when he stood, and they stepped out of the shuttle close behind him.

The force field pulsed around the landing pad, holding out the Mezoran air and the winds that ripped across this level of the planet's atmosphere. The field made the twisting buildings around the landing pad ripple and dance, and a light glaze of dizziness settled over Lance's brain. He had seen plenty of force fields as a Star Federation soldier, and that experience kept the shivers at bay, but the thing still felt unstable to him, or maybe just acutely unnecessary. Respirators were not that much of an inconvenience.

Turning away from the field, Lance saw the large, transparent door of the building hiss open, and a man stepped out. He was dressed in an immaculate suit, charcoal gray and not unlike what Lance would have expected from Earthborn humans, but it had a distinct Mezoran flare. The suit jacket was trimmed in deep red, and there were two red lines running down the seams of the pants. The trimming matched the color of the sash that hung from the man's left shoulder, ran across his breast and wrapped under his right arm.

The man was young, Lance realized, maybe twenty-three at most, but he walked with a brisk, easy confidence. He was shorter than Lance, but held himself straight, and his figure was all hard, strong lines. In contrast, his face was round and smooth, with a gently curving chin and lightly sloping brow. His cheekbones were low, his nose was small and flat, and his dark eyes had sharp, upturned corners. His skin was smooth, pale ochre with bronze undertones, and his hair was a neatly combed wave of black.

He smiled as he approached, but Lance thought that he saw uneasiness behind the expression.

"Welcome," the man said brightly, and Lance recognized his voice as the one that had spoken in Terra-Six Chinese over the communications system. He extended his hand to Lissa, and she took it for a light, quick shake. "It's wonderful to see you again. I hope your journey here was pleasant?"

"Pleasant enough," Lissa said, and to Lance's shock, her smile looked warm and genuine, though there was a bit of wariness in her eyes, too. She turned to Lance. "This is Mr. Fang Deshi."

"Director of Operations," Fang added.

"Oh, I'm sorry," Lissa said. "I didn't realize. Congratulations."

"Thank you," Fang said, nodding to Lissa.

"Director Fang," Lissa continued, "this is Mr. Lance Ashburn."

"Mr. Ashburn." Fang extended his hand and gave Lance the same light, quick handshake he had given Lissa.

Lance returned the gesture with an easy smile and greeting, but he felt an unpleasant twinge at the back of his mind. He did not know how safe it was to have his name given out freely.

Then again, he had just stepped out of a stolen Star Federation shuttle. Discretion was far beyond his reach at this point.

Fang eyed the shuttle over Lance's shoulder. His eyes

lingered on the empty cockpit and open airlock. His gaze caught on the arkins, and he lightly gestured to them. "Is this your whole party?" he asked.

"Yes," Lissa said.

Lance distinctly saw relief wash over Fang's face, but he quickly hid it behind a pleasant, neutral mask.

"Chief Executive Fang will meet with you in her office," he said to Lissa. "Please come with me."

He led them through the large door of the building, but before they entered the dealership, Lance and Lissa entered a secure chamber and went through a thorough weapons screening. Lance was given a clean pass, but Lissa was forced to surrender her belt.

"It will be returned to you unharmed," Fang assured her.

She handed it over reluctantly.

Fang placed the belt in a storage locker and entered the security code, sealing it out of reach. Then he led them through another large door.

They stepped into a huge, open space. It was brightly lit by the overhead lights, but sunlight slanted in through the long bank of windows that faced towards the setting sun. Evening crept up against the opposite windows, but Lance's attention was fully captivated by the displays in the showroom.

There were small-scale hologram projections scattered throughout the room, showcasing a dozen different models of starships. They ranged from small, fast cruisers to medium-sized freighters, although their basic framework was very similar as a signature of the manufacturer. The holograms rotated slowly, showing off the designs from every possible angle before splitting open and offering a peek at the interiors of the ships.

In the middle of the room were the only physically present vessels: three sky cruisers resting on slowly turning podiums and illuminated by an even stronger light source. Two of the cruisers were luxury designs, with spacious cabins and room to sprawl. The third was a wicked-looking model, all severe curves and fierce points, a cruiser built specifically for slicing through the winds of the upper atmosphere and shrieking across the sky. Its hull gleamed in the light, perfectly clean and harshly beautiful.

"You have fine taste, Mr. Ashburn," Fang said suddenly.

Lance tore his eyes away from the sky cruiser. "It's a beautiful craft." *And a nightmare for the local police, I bet,* he added silently.

"One of our newest," Fang said. "Quite popular among our human buyers, but the Mezorans prefer something with a bit more legroom." His gaze slipped over Lance's shoulder.

Lance looked around again, this time past the displays of the starships and the sky cruisers. There were not many other people in the showroom. A pair of employees stood talking quietly by the windows, throwing half-curious glances at Lance, Lissa and the arkins as they crossed the room. That was trouble, but Lance forced himself to stay cool and disinterested, and noticed that Lissa did the same. Glancing away from the employees, Lance saw a human salesperson speaking with the lone customer, a native Mezoran that Lance could not believe he had not seen earlier.

The Mezoran was huge and lanky. It held itself on the balls of its feet, its legs bent double and tucked neatly against its chest. It had two sets of arms, the longer pair of which reached down to the floor, helping the Mezoran maintain its balance. The shorter pair was tucked in close to the torso, carefully positioned to minimize movement and avoid contact with everything except the Mezoran itself. In that tight, curled position, the Mezoran was roughly the double the height of the human salesperson, and she was not short.

Lance could not even imagine a Mezoran trying to get into anything but the storage space on a shipping freighter, though the showroom's high ceiling suddenly made infinitely more sense.

The Mezoran had scaly skin mottled with red and brown that faded to cream on its belly. Everything about the Mezoran looked stretched out, from its head to the four digits on each of its limbs. Two horns swept back from the sides of the creature's skull, but when Lance looked again, he realized that those were not horns but ears. Lance did not get a good look at the creature's face as a breathing mask was firmly secured to the head, but he did notice that the Mezoran wore a deep red sash trimmed with yellow across its chest, not dissimilar to the one Fang wore, and that was the Mezoran's only garment.

Lance tore his attention away from the Mezoran when he heard Lissa say something to Fang in a low voice. He did not catch what she said, but he did see Fang shake his head and whisper something back, and Lissa looked immensely relieved.

After that brief exchange, Fang led them to the far side of the showroom. They stepped through a much smaller door than the ones that led out to the landing pad, walked down a hallway past a few closed rooms, and came to a halt in front of a door with what Lance assumed were Terra-Six Chinese characters blazed at eye level. Just beneath the characters were the words, "Fang Min, CEO," in the Written Unified Voice.

"Wait here, please," Fang Deshi said. He knocked sharply, paused for a polite moment, then opened the door and slipped inside.

Lance heard low, muffled voices. He strained to hear, but they did not seem to be speaking in Galunvo. He glanced at Lissa. She was frowning and listening close, though Lance had the feeling that she did not understand much more of the conversation than he did. Lance could hear the tone, though, and it was not happy.

Lissa took an abrupt step back from the door. She stood with her feet apart and her hands clasped behind her back, drew in a deep breath, and braced herself.

The door snapped open, and a woman stood in the threshold.

Fang Min was older than her brother, probably by four or five years, Lance suspected. She held herself with the same straight, easy confidence, and her skin was the same bronzed-ochre color as that of her brother. Her hair was shiny black, cut into long, straight layers, and her eyes were very dark. Her chin was a little sharper than her brother's, her eyes a little rounder and her cheekbones more pronounced, but the siblings had the same nose and the same gently sloping brows. Fang Min wore a gray pantsuit cut differently than the one her brother wore, but like his, hers bore the Mezoran trimmings and the deep red sash hanging from her left shoulder across her chest.

"You have some nerve," the Fang sister growled, "showing up here."

Over her shoulder, Lance saw Fang Deshi standing with his arms tightly crossed and his back tense.

"I didn't know where else to go," Lissa murmured.

"How about far out of our lives? That's where you and Aven should have stayed." She threw an angry look at Lance, ready to say more, but stopped when she registered his identity. She glanced past him, at the arkins and the empty hallway behind them. "Where is Aven?"

"Not with them," the Fang brother put in.

"That's another detail you should have mentioned," Fang Min shot over her shoulder.

Lissa looked past the sister. "You didn't tell her we were here?"

The brother raised his eyebrows. "I think she would have shot you out of the sky if I did."

The chief executive shook her head and gave Lissa a heavy look. "You need to leave," she said tiredly. "Right now."

"I need to buy a ship first."

"Well, you're not going to get it here. Director Fang will show you back out, since he so thoughtfully showed you in."

"Min…" the brother began.

"Don't you dare," the sister said hotly. "You have the gall to let her in here, after what her brother did?"

"Aven is dying," Lissa blurted.

The siblings looked at her sharply.

"You'll have to forgive me," the sister said after a tense pause, "but I can't quite bring myself to mourn."

"I don't expect you to," Lissa said, very quietly. "All I want from you is a ship."

Fang Min sighed and looked away for a moment. "To do what with? Run around the galaxy collecting bounties now that Aven can't do it on his own?"

"I've already done that."

There was a small silence.

"Aven is gone," Lissa continued. "There's nothing I can do for him, and there probably never was. It took me a while to see that, but it's better this way. For both of us."

Lance looked between the two women, entirely unsure what to make of this interaction. As if sensing his scrutiny, Fang Min suddenly snapped her gaze to him.

"And what about him?" she asked.

Lissa glanced at him. "Tell her," she invited.

Lance looked at the Fang sister. She looked back at him with guarded intensity.

"I'm Lance Ashburn," he told her. "A former fleet commander of the Star Federation." The words left a sour taste in his mouth.

Fang Min's eyes flicked over his traveler's clothes. He had changed into a fresh set prior to entering the Mezoran atmosphere, but he was still a bit disheveled and looked nothing like a Star Federation officer. "Former?"

"I was stripped of my rank for assisting Lissa."

Fang Min cocked an eyebrow at Lissa. "How did a minor bounty hunter get a Star Fed in that much trouble?"

"Actually," Lance said, "when I met her, she was operating as the Shadow."

Fang Min drew in a sharp breath, and Lance saw her brother drop his arms in disbelief. They both looked at Lissa with a wild mix of fear and respect, but it looked to Lance like it was mostly fear.

"The Shadow is Aven?" Fang Deshi asked, but immediately shook his head. "The Shadow is *you*?"

Lissa nodded, almost impatiently, it seemed to Lance.

"I still don't know what you want this ship for," Fang Min said, and Lance noticed that she had inched back a little.

"It's for me," Lissa said.

"But what are you going to do with it? More importantly, why do you need to buy from us?"

"Because you're the only ones I trust not to sell my secrets."

"You throw trust around far too lightly."

Lissa shook her head. "I don't do it lightly."

Fang Min considered Lance for a long, searching moment before turning back to Lissa. "So, if we deal with you, we'll have the Star Feds on our backs."

"Yes."

"Just them?"

"Probably."

The chief executive gave Lissa a hard look. "Elaborate."

"Their activity might attract another group, but I don't think they'll come after you, no."

"Why not?"

"Because I'm going after them."

"That sounds more than just vaguely stupid."

"I'm done running, Min. I'm done."

Fang Min sighed heavily. "What's this second group called?"

"The Seventh Sun."

The siblings stiffened.

"That's that group we've been hearing about," Fang Deshi said, stepping closer to the doorway. "The one threatening the Star Federation."

"How do you know about that?" Lance asked.

"It's not on the public media waves yet," Fang Deshi said, "but we have our sources." At Lance's glance, he added, "Don't worry, officer. They're suppliers for starship parts." He smiled. "Mostly."

"Talk of them is burning through the Andromeda Reach," Fang Min said. "Rumor has it they're the ones responsible for Yuna."

"What happened on Yuna?" Lissa asked sharply.

"Last we heard," the Fang brother said, "they put something in the oasis that dried it up. Just evaporated all the water and condemned the planet."

Lissa looked at Lance for confirmation, but he only shook his head. He had not heard anything about that prior to leaving the Star Federation. But then, he had been completely focused on Phan until Lissa had dragged him to Ametria, and then he had been unconscious.

"We're too far to deal with Yuni traders," Fang Min put in, "so we don't know if that's true or not, but whatever they did over there, it was bad. Galactic news hasn't covered it yet, but we're expecting something to surface soon." She studied Lissa for a moment. "Weren't you and Aven running from the Seventh Sun when we met you?"

Lissa reached up and touched the collar around her throat. "They caught up."

Fang Min stared at the collar, seeing it for the first time, and her posture tightened. "And they could come here if we deal with you." She looked at Lissa and shook her head, almost sadly. "I don't know if we can risk that."

"You already did once."

"Yeah, but that was Jian's idea."

Lance saw Lissa's jaw clench at the name, but the chief executive took no notice.

"You're really going after these people?" Fang Min asked.

"It's that or wait for them to find me again."

The Fang sister sighed again, and a small silence played out. She wrestled with a decision, but her gaze was softening the longer she looked at Lissa. "And this is all for you," she finally said. "Not Aven."

Lissa nodded.

"All right." Fang Min moved out of the threshold. "Come inside."

Fang Min's executive office was done out with subtle lavishness. At first glance, nothing seemed ostentatious or showy, but it dawned on Lance that the deep, red-brown wood of the walls and simple but perfectly carved desk had probably been imported from off-world. They had the richness of Earth or Terra colony trees, not the pale rigidity of the Mezoran forests Lance had seen in the database entry he'd studied earlier. The carpet was a rolling wash of thick, light beige, and even through his boots, Lance felt the shift in the flooring; it was almost difficult to walk on the carpet, but standing still was exponentially more comfortable. Fang Min's desk was set forward from the bank of windows that made up the back wall; a sheet of glass that faced perpendicular to the path of the sun and offered a stunning view of the arc of the nightfall. The awakening glow of the middle and lower city lights peppered the blue evening and, beyond that, Lance saw the indigo smear of a distant ocean. There were two austere but not uncomfortable hover chairs in front of the desk, and the only other decorative elements in the room were two paintings hung against opposite dark wood walls. The paintings were carefully illuminated by concealed light sources, and looked to have been imported from off-world as well. They showed landscapes that never would have been seen on Mezora, inked out with flowing, delicate brushstrokes and gentle washes of color.

Lance felt acutely out of place in the office, and he itched for the familiar plainness of structure and strength emphasized over form and beauty.

Fang Min beckoned for Lance and Lissa to sit in the hover chairs. She took her own seat behind her desk, and her brother stood just over her shoulder.

"So," the chief executive said, with what must have been far more easiness than she usually showed in her business meetings, "I'm selling you a ship. What are you looking for?"

"Something small," Lissa said. "Easy for two people to manage. It should be fast, but we'll need to take it over long distances. Something hard to trace would be best, but I'll take a faster, farther runner before an invisible walker."

"So basically, you want the best ship that I have."

"If you have it."

"And you're planning to pay for this how?"

"We've got Star Fed tech we can trade against its value," Lissa said coolly. "Top-of-the-line shuttle, fast and with advanced signal scramblers."

"A shuttle?" Fang Min did not try to hide her amused contempt. "Lissa, I said I'd sell you a ship because it's you. I'm even cutting through all the customary bullshit because it's you. But you walk in here, after everything that happened, and want to trade a *shuttle* for a *starship?*"

"I have some money," Lissa returned. "I can pay off the balance."

Fang Min shook her head. "I don't think you can."

Her brother said something to her in Terra-Six Chinese that caused Fang Min to give him a sharp look, though after a quick but heated exchange, she paused for a long moment, considering. Then she gave a curt nod and reply, and Fang Deshi excused himself, walking rapidly out of the room. Fang Min watched him go with a hard frown on her face, but she waited for the door to close behind him before speaking again.

"There may be something else you can do for us. Save your money, you'll want it for supplies and restocking." Fang reached for the edge of her desk, brushed a subtly positioned control, and activated four hologram projectors built into the corners of her desk. A starship appeared over the wooden surface, rotating like the holograms in the showroom, and Lance heard Lissa's breath catch. "This is what I can offer you in exchange for the Star Federation shuttle and your services."

Services? Lance glanced sharply at Lissa, but she was looking intently at the starship. He could almost feel the hunger radiating off of her, and he found himself studying her eyes, but they were still their natural silver color.

Lance turned his own gaze back to the starship hologram. It was a sleek, beautiful model, all streamlined edges and austere frames, but with powerful rear thrusters burning with energy. Lance had to admit that he liked the look of it, but he didn't like the thought of blindly agreeing to perform in exchange for it. Before he could open his mouth, Lissa and Fang Min had risen from their seats, clasped hands in a light but long handshake, and both were smiling.

"We'll need to keep the shuttle here," Fang said as she

came around her desk. She began to walk with Lissa towards the door, and Lance jumped after them. "The sooner we can begin stripping it, the quicker we can kill the trail." She thought for a moment. "The Star Feds won't like it, but if we can get the Justice Keepers on our side, this should all go smoothly. It's going to take a lot of work, but the sooner we begin, the better."

Lissa nodded her assent, and Fang Min said something about walking with them back to the showroom, but Lance finally found his voice as they stepped out of the office and into the hallway.

"We're taking the shuttle with us."

Lissa froze.

Fang's smile flickered, but only for an instant. "Don't worry, Mr. Ashburn. We will provide you with a sky cruiser."

"Sky cruisers won't take us off-planet," Lance said.

"You won't be going off-planet for this task, Mr. Ashburn. In fact, you won't even be leaving this city." Fang turned back to Lissa. "Deshi will meet you on your way out. He will have the details, as well as the access codes for your cruiser."

"We're not letting go of the shuttle without getting a starship first," Lance snapped.

"Yes," Lissa said, giving him a cold, dangerous look, "we are."

Lance glared at her, but she stared him down.

Fang Min shifted stiffly next to them. "Well," she said, after a long silence. "If you change your mind about the starship, let Director Fang know on your way out. I have another meeting to prepare for, so I'm afraid I must leave you here." She stepped back inside the office. "Goodbye, Ms. Arrilissa. Mr. Ashburn." The door snapped shut.

Lissa looked at the closed door with open pain. Then she turned a hard glare on Lance. "I told you to let me handle this," she snarled as she pushed past him.

Lance followed her, rage building up. "Handle it, sure, not give away our only bargaining tool."

Lissa said nothing, only stalked through the halls.

Lance went after her, not at all ready to let her go. "We were supposed to trade it," he hissed.

"We did," Lissa shot over her shoulder.

"Trade it for something *tangible!* Not a vague promise and some shady assignment."

They had reached the showroom, and Lissa made a small, sharp gesture behind her back. The Mezoran customer was still there, haggling softly with the salesperson. Lance was rapidly losing all sense of discretion, but he caught up with Lissa and forced himself to drop his voice low.

"What services did you promise?" he growled. "What the hell did you just get us into?"

Lissa pulled up short and faced him squarely, attracting a glance from the Mezoran, but only a fleeting one. "Not us," she hissed. "Me. I said I would handle this, and I'm going to. You don't have to be involved in any way. In fact," she took a step back and spread her hands wide, "you could wait here. Relax for a bit. Test fly a cruiser. I don't care. This is my deal, with my contacts, with my whole future on the line, and I'm seeing it through." She turned and set off again at a fast walk.

Lance caught up with her as she stepped into the chamber that led out to the landing pad. Through the transparent door, he saw Fang Deshi standing with his back to them, holding Lissa's belt and a small datapad at his sides.

Before Lissa could step outside, Lance grabbed her by the shoulder, and stepped in front of her. "This is my future, too," he told her quietly. "And my shuttle, and my growing regrets, and you *cannot* keep me in the dark and expect me to just blindly follow you. I can't do that. I can't, and I won't."

She held his gaze for a silent heartbeat. "You need to prove to me that I can trust you."

Lance made a disgusted noise, and disbelief roughed his voice. "I'm the one who threw everything away. I deserted the Star Federation, destroyed my life, charged after the Seventh Sun, and got you off of Daanhymn. I came for you."

"And what did you think would happen after you found me?" she demanded fiercely. "What did you expect? That we'd go kill all of the Seventh Sun heads and ensure the safety of humans everywhere? That we'd miraculously destroy the Sun and you'd be crowned a hero? Or did you just want to clear a path for the Star Federation, and let them wipe the galaxy clean of every Neo-Andromedan they can find?"

Lance felt the heat rise to his face. He couldn't deny that those thoughts had occurred to him, but there had been more to it. "I wanted," Lance growled, "to give the Neo-Andromedans a chance. I wanted to take down the organization that is threatening not only them, but the rest of the galaxy, too. I *left* the Star Federation. I have no control over what the soldiers do, but I promise you that everything I'm doing is meant to give innocent Neo-Andromedans a fighting chance."

"I don't believe you."

"Why not?"

"Because when I look at you, I see the way you smiled on Ametria. I see the way you looked when you realized you could take out that base. I see you firing the pulse cannon. And then I see you almost hysterical with triumph when the base explodes." She looked at him for a long, silent moment. "You're not a fleet commander anymore, but you're still a Star Fed, and I can't trust a Star Fed. Especially not a human one."

"That's not fair," Lance managed to stutter out. "We needed to get off of that planet."

"But you didn't need to smile."

Lance opened his mouth, but only breathed out silence. Then he dropped his eyes, and Lissa brushed past him. He let her go, and watched as she stepped out on to the landing pad, met with Fang Deshi, and accepted her belt and the datapad from him. They exchanged a few words, and Fang threw an expectant glance at Lance through the transparent door. Lissa did not look at him.

Suddenly feeling very tired, Lance stepped through the door, and joined Lissa and Fang.

"Are you ready to leave, Mr. Ashburn?" Fang asked.

"Yes," Lance said after a small pause. "Lead the way,

Director Fang."

Lissa gave him a glance heavy with mistrust, but said nothing and walked beside him in Fang's wake.

CHAPTER 18: TARGETS

Lissa studied the information on the datapad and made a point of ignoring Ashburn's probing glances. Thanks to the structure of the sky cruiser and their seating arrangements, it was not easy for him to twist over his seat and look back at her, let alone safe given the flight paths of other the cruisers cutting across the sky, but he was determined, and he managed it at least four times before giving up.

Min and Deshi had generously provided them with the cruiser, a craft fresh from the manufacturer and not yet licensed. It was not one of the Fang dealership's signature models. That would have been too easy to trace should something go wrong, but it was a fast and sturdy little vehicle, if not a bit cramped; Ashburn had insisted on coming, and they had to make due. Lissa had barely been able to squeeze into the space behind the pilot's seat. Ashburn had not fit back there, and so had been relegated to the task of flying the cruiser. Blade and Orion had been left with the Fangs.

Lissa felt that weird blend of vulnerability and easiness without the arkin at her side, but she did not worry for Blade. She knew Min and Deshi would take good care of the arkins, and given the condition of Blade's wing, she was glad that the arkin would be spending the next few hours sprawled on a plush carpet and not out on the hunt.

Ashburn was less than thrilled by this arrangement. "First the shuttle, now the arkins," he growled as he piloted the cruiser into the air. "Why didn't we just leave our clothes with them, too, and go chasing after this guy totally naked?"

"You can if you want to," Lissa returned, not looking up from the datapad. "But I don't recommend it."

There was a delicate pause.

"Have you… actually tried that before?"

"Don't be stupid," Lissa said. In that moment, she was very conscious of the weight of the fresh, white-hot enerpulse pistol secured in her holster and the exposure of the back of Ashburn's head.

"I still don't like this whole situation," Ashburn said after a few moments.

"You're opinion has been noted," Lissa returned flatly, "but is still irrelevant. Head west."

They fell into silence after that, and Lissa had filled the time by studying up on the target.

He was a rival starship dealer, and the Fangs must have been on the verge of putting out the official bounty on his head if they hadn't already filed with the Justice Keepers for a registered kill, though given how long he had been troubling them and the amount of data they had gathered, Lissa got the sense that the Fangs had been reluctant to actually go through with it. They'd certainly had enough time to do their research, noting his place of work, his home, his most-frequented restaurants, the back alleys he took to avoid notice before slipping in to illegal gambling rings, even where he purchased his Mezoran sashes. The file noted that he generally left his workplace each evening just after sunset, and Mezoran days were uniform enough to put no noticeable variances in that timeframe, but if he worked late, he stayed until the small hours of the morning. This was, according to the file, happening more frequently. It was all technical information like that in the file, plenty enough to go on, but Lissa wanted more, though not about the target. The Fangs she knew would never have entered the hunting game without provocation.

Lissa used the datapad to do a quick information search, and learned from a Mezoran economic report that the target's dealership had begun to undercut the market, drawing a sizable chunk of business from the human part of the Mezoran population. This was generally frowned upon on Mezora, but the human buyers had been quick to embrace the change and not much had been done about it. A separate report noted that off-world trade with the Fang's Galactic Cruiser Dealership had begun to decline while the rival's had remained stable.

Lissa browsed through a few news reports relating to the Mezoran starship industry, and found that the timeline for an increase in renegade activity targeting freighters bound for Mezora matched quite neatly with the rise of the rival dealership. Most of the plundered cargo had been spare parts, according to the news reports, but a few more recent ones had been carrying actual vessels. Several dealerships around the planet were feeling these attacks, but the Fangs in particular were suffering heavy losses. The freighters and their lost cargo had almost all been exclusively from the same manufacturers that the Fangs used. Conveniently, the rival dealership used other suppliers entirely, and did not seem to be affected by these raids.

The target wasn't even subtle about all this. Lissa found three separate occasions where he had openly trashed the Fangs, saying they could stand to lose a little of their fat and have a little more courtesy, considering they were "outsiders looking at the world with their eyes half-closed," as the target had noted in a particularly nasty interview. When the interviewer had pointed out with an uneasy smile that the target himself was not Mezoran, he had grinned wolfishly and said that he "at least had the decency of being born on this world."

Lissa swallowed hard after watching that interview, and the collar around her throat gripped tight, but there was cold rage in her stomach and she could ignore the Seventh Sun's brand this time.

This kind of behavior was exactly the thing that would have pushed the Fangs over the edge, and make them consider assassination over fighting back fairly.

We're all we have left, and nothing is ever going to threaten that again.

Lissa shook her head, and the remembered words drifted away as suddenly as they had come, taking some of the cold rage with them. She reminded herself that it was better not to place any personal investment in the bounty.

And yet, after watching another interview where the target talked about the Fangs again, she couldn't help but think that this man's face would not haunt her. She would not carry his death.

Ashburn broke into her thoughts. "Is there anything you can tell me about the Fangs? Anything at all?"

She studied the back of his head, outlined by the faint glow from the cruiser's control panel. The lights of the city's middle level burned around him, and Lissa glimpsed another sky cruiser passing over them at a comfortable distance. Ashburn was holding a steady course to the coordinates she had fed him, as far as she could tell.

"They're selling us a starship." She focused on the datapad again. "That's all you need to know."

Ashburn would not be deterred so easily. "They hate Aven for whatever reason, but they were willing to deal with you. I'd love to know why, at least so I know what they expect from *me*, but all you want to do is drag me through the dark blindfolded and trip me every time I open my mouth to ask, 'Which way?'" He banked the cruiser around a slower craft in front of them, and then settled back on course. "You don't trust me. Fine. I get it. But is there *anything* you can tell me that will help me help you?"

Lissa said nothing. He didn't need to know.

"They speak a Terran dialect of Chinese," Ashburn tried again, "so I'm assuming they're not Earthborn. Logically, then, you and Aven either met them on Mezora, or the Terra-Six colony. Whichever it was, that's a strange place for two Neo-

Andromedans to end up." He turned his head a little, but kept his eyes forward. "Considering they're both heavily populated by humans."

Silence.

Ashburn let it play out, waiting for her to break.

"What do you think knowing will do for you?" Lissa finally said. "Will it really help you to know that they were farmers on Terra-Six? That their family owned a spice farm and they were comfortable and happy?"

"So what happened?" Ashburn's voice was irritatingly calm and soothing. "What pushed them off Terra-Six and into the Mezoran starship business?"

"We did." Lissa frowned. "Aven did."

"And now," Ashburn said, picking his words carefully, "you trust them to deal with you honestly?"

"No," Lissa said. "The moment I think anything is out of line, I shoot to kill. But whatever happens, I'm leaving Mezora by dawn."

"All right," Ashburn said. "So long as I know where we stand."

"And do you feel better knowing?"

"A little, actually." He rustled in his seat. "This feels familiar now."

"Chasing bounties and the prospect of taking the access codes for a starship from a couple of corpses?"

"I meant being dead if I step the wrong way," Ashburn said.

"And that's comforting?"

"It's familiar."

Lissa's mouth twitched into a smile, though she was glad Ashburn could not see it.

For the remainder of the journey, Lissa studied the physical aspects of the target. He was a human, and the file had a decent image of his face, revealing his slack jaw, square face, milk-pale skin, wavy dark hair, and wide, round, blue eyes. From a few video feeds that she pulled up from news posts, Lissa saw that he had the residual swagger of someone who had once been very fit and athletic, but he had been softened by comfortable living and his figure had rounded out. He had a habit of tucking his right hand into the fold of his Mezoran sash whenever he was standing, and the fingers of the same hand always tapped some surface whenever he was sitting.

His name was Christopher Flynn, and he would not be difficult to find.

They began with a flyby of his office. One quick look was all they needed. The target's dealership was bright and lively, but the windows of his office were dark and empty. He had left for the evening.

Lissa sent Ashburn tracing after the route the target liked to take to his gambling rings. According to the bounty file, it had been a while since his last visit, and he liked to go at least once a Mezoran month. Based on his patterns, there was a good chance he was feeling the itch tonight.

Ashburn flew low and slow, gliding quietly between the buildings. Anyone looking out into the alley would have seen the cruiser, but most of the windows they passed were quiet. Bright, but quiet.

They followed the target's route, time slipping further and further away as Mezora's twin moons danced across the sky, one striped with jet black and pale blue, the other stark bone white. Both were littered with dark, irregular craters from excavation sites, and twinkling lights from the colonies dotted their dark sides. They were hypnotic to watch, but Lissa forced herself to scan the streets as best she could over Ashburn's shoulder, and then, just before the entrance to the target's preferred gambling ring, the moonlight caught on a lone figure.

Ashburn touched the controls, sending the cruiser jumping forward, but he brought it to an abrupt standstill a comfortable distance away. It was an awkward angle, and the figure was distorted by a long coat and the hard shape of a respirator pack, but Lissa recognized the sway of the walk and the thrust of the shoulders and the slick wave of hair. It was him, and in twenty more steps, he would be inside the building and out of their reach.

Lissa leaned forward and threaded her arms over Ashburn's shoulders, enerpulse pistol in hand. "Open the cockpit," she said.

"What?"

"Do it."

"You can't make that shot. No way."

"*Open the cockpit.*"

"That is too far of a target. No one could hit—"

"Stop forgetting," Lissa snarled, "that I am not human. Now *open it.*"

Ashburn swallowed his protests, took in a long, deep breath alongside Lissa, and hit the controls. The windshield of the cruiser hissed upwards, letting the Mezoran night air spill in. Lissa's arms rested on Ashburn's shoulders, and she felt him tense.

"Steady," Lissa breathed in his ear.

The cruiser hovered in the air, humming quietly. A light breeze washed into the cockpit. Lissa held what was left of her breath and adjusted her grip on the pistol. Ashburn held himself still. The target took another step forward.

One quick shot.

CHAPTER 19: NUMB

Lance was numb. He did not know if the lack of feeling was from exhaustion, stims withdrawal, some side effect of a breath of Mezoran air, or a form of self-preservation in the face of extreme stress. He was dimly aware that he was seated on a plush couch in a circular, rose-colored room outlined in glass, Lissa next to him and the arkins—both alive and well—curled up behind the couch. There was something cold in Lance's hand, and he heard the sounds of a Mezoran newscast while images washed before his eyes, but the words were muted and the report was nothing more than vague shapes shifting back and forth.

Slowly, Lance turned his head and looked at Lissa. He registered parts of her rather than her entirety, seeing the sharp, stiff hunch of her shoulders first, then the hard grip on the enerpulse pistol that she had refused to surrender, then the lines of fatigue around her eyes, then the sharp line of her jaw, and finally the glint of the light in her eyes.

Hard, metallic, silver eyes.

Stop forgetting that I am not human.

Even though he had not forgotten, Lance still couldn't believe that she had made that shot. Enerpulse weapons had far ranges, but natural hand shakes and jitters prevented sniping without stabilizers, and those were best fitted to rifles. Lissa did not use rifles. Only pistols.

The only things that Lance could feel as he sat in the rosy room were the memory of the weight of Lissa's arms against his shoulders and her warm breath on his ear, and the momentary blinding heat of the enerpulse shot as it seared out of the weapon and across the night.

It was hard for him to believe that Lissa had barely been able to stand not long ago, and that she had thrashed through nightmares and feared to lose control. And yet, he was beginning to understand how she could keep bounty assassinations separate from her Awakening kills. Choice versus force. He understood both, and that scared him a little.

You didn't need to smile.

Lance looked away from Lissa and focused on the thing in his hand. Gradually, he realized that he was holding a glass of lilac liquid, cubes of semi-melted ice floating on the surface. He took a sip, held the sweet, fruity drink on his tongue, and swallowed. He felt a little better.

Lance threw a slow look around the room. It was something of a holding room, a place where customers could relax while they waited for the final calibrations of their new starships to be completed. The furniture and carpet were all delicate shades of pink—a luxurious color to Mezorans, according to Fang Deshi—but they were shot through with dark wooden accents, which looked to be built from the same imported wood that adorned Fang Min's executive office. The walls were a solid ring of glass, interrupted only by the doors of the lift that allowed access to the room from the sky cruiser bay. The glass walls offered a view of the stars and the passing clouds of the Mezoran upper atmosphere, though the roof of the sky cruiser hanger edged the bottom of the frame. Luxurious couches identical to the one Lance and Lissa sat on were arranged in a ring around a central pillar, and Mezoran news broadcasts illuminated the pillar's solid surface.

Fang Min sat on Lissa's other side, watching the broadcast intently. Her brother was perched on the arm of the couch, working with a datapad but often glancing up to watch and listen. Both Fangs were still in their business suits, but they had removed the Mezoran sashes from their shoulders now that there was no risk of offending their customers.

Their dealership had closed for the night, and no one was likely to disturb them while they were on the Fangs' private starship dock in the upper Mezoran atmosphere. It had been built to hold the dealership's smaller starships—the ones that were permitted to dock within the atmosphere—and was only accessible by sky cruiser.

Lance and Lissa had been instructed to head to the starship dock after successfully completing their bounty assignment, and had arrived to find the Fangs waiting for them with the arkins.

There had been some idle chatter for the first few minutes, which Lance had not been able to engage in, and at some point, Fang Deshi had handed him the drink and invited him to sit while they waited for the report to come in.

They sat in silence for the most part, the arkins dozing on the carpet and the Fang siblings occasionally exchanging a few words in Terra-Six Chinese. The stars spun slowly in the sky as the night ticked away, and the winds of the upper atmosphere howled around the starship dock, but it was quiet and pleasantly warm in the holding room.

It was a little more than an hour before dawn when the news report finally came in. Wealthy and notorious starship dealer Christopher Flynn had been found on the Mezoran streets earlier that night, shot in the back by an enerpulse weapon. Aid had come for him, but Flynn had been struck fatally and was dead long before anyone had found him. A kill register had been filed on Flynn prior to his death, and though Justice Keepers were debating the legality of the method of this killing, all agreed that it had been an approved kill, one that had been sanctioned shortly before the estimated time of death.

The report ended.

Fang Min waved her hand, and the projectors switched

off. She sat back against the couch, the tension melting out of her body. She gave a heavy sigh of relief before saying, "There should be more in the morning, but I doubt you'll want to stay for that."

"No," Lissa agreed. "It's time we left."

Lance rose with her as she stood up from the couch, and Fang Min faced them squarely.

"I don't know," she said to Lissa, "if I'm afraid or impressed. Probably both."

Lissa adjusted her grip on her enerpulse pistol. "You get used to the feeling."

"I'm sure."

There was a small pause.

"Deshi said that you gave us everything we need regarding the shuttle, yes?"

Her brother put in a quick confirmation.

Fang Min nodded. "And we have the cruiser back, which we'll need to destroy, but at least we'll have the parts." She considered Lissa for a moment. "If you've lived up to your hunting name, the Star Feds should have a hard time tracing this back to us, but if they do show up, we'll take care of them. With the Justice Keepers on our side, we should be able to keep information about you two out of the Star Federation's hands."

"Thank you," Lissa said, but kept a tight grip on her pistol.

Min shifted uneasily. "It's this other group that has me worried. This Seventh Sun. If they come..." She sighed. "I don't know what we'll do."

"They won't come."

"How do you know?"

"Because they're not the hunters anymore." Lissa holstered her pistol. "No more running, Min. No more hiding."

Fang Min nodded slowly. "In that case, it may be best to say goodbye for good this time."

Lance saw Lissa's spine straighten with tension, but she only said, "Of course."

The goodbyes were far more pleasant than the greetings had been. The handshakes were a little firmer and longer, and the Fang siblings smiled warmly throughout the exchanges. They brought Lance and Lissa to their new starship, leading them below the level of the cruiser bay and down to the starship access level. The lift doors slid open to reveal what looked like the mouths of seven tunnels, all well-lit and lined with hard, durable material that guarded the interior against the howling Mezoran winds. Fang Min led the way down one of the tunnels, Fang Deshi following with Lance, Lissa and the arkins close behind. Along the way, the Fangs gave them a few last-minute tips on some of the ship's better features, but Fang Min told them to consult the main computer should they have any questions. When they reached the sealed end of the tunnel, Fang Min gave them the access codes, and then opened the seal to reveal the closed airlock of a gleaming starship. The part of the hull that was visible inside the seal of the starship dock was deep blue-gray shot through with black and silver, and when Lance touched it, the metal felt smooth and cold beneath his fingertips. He dropped his hand to the panel that shielded the exterior airlock controls, and entered the first access code Fang Min had provided. The airlock hissed open without hesitation.

"Our ships are calibrated to human needs by default," Fang Min said as Lance ushered the arkins inside, "so you shouldn't have any trouble. There's enough food and water to last you a ways, but you may want to restock elsewhere if you have other tastes or needs."

Lance thanked the Fangs and moved into the ship. Lissa stepped inside after him.

"Wait, Lissa," Fang Min said, and hesitated.

Lance felt the renewed tension ripple off of Lissa, and he remembered what she had told him earlier about her and Aven disrupting the Fang's lives years ago. He saw Lissa brace herself, and when she turned back with a forced neutral expression, her hand was hovering over her holstered pistol. Fang Deshi eyed his sister warily, as though he, too, expected the worst.

Fang Min ignored the tension, steadily holding Lissa's gaze. "Take care of yourself," she said, and her voice was warm and sincere.

It took a moment for Lissa to register what Fang Min had said, but when she did, she relaxed, smiled, and bowed her head. The Fang siblings returned the gesture, and they stepped back as the tunnel closed itself once again. Lissa moved out of the airlock, sealed it, and turned away. She glanced around the ship with muted satisfaction before sighing quietly and looking at Lance.

"Time to go."

Lance leaned heavily against the wall. "Should I even bother asking where?"

"Do you care?"

"Yes, but I know that it doesn't matter."

"Good. You're learning."

"Or giving up." Lance pushed off from the wall. "One of those two." He moved down the hall, not caring that Lissa still had a white-hot enerpulse pistol on her hip and that he had presented a prime target to her, but he made it to one of the private sleeping quarters alive and unharmed, and he locked the door and flopped down on the cot. It only occurred to him in the moment before he fully fell asleep that Orion had not followed him, and he was alone.

CHAPTER 20: STAND

Jason did not know what had happened to Dr. Chhaya or anyone else at the hospital; he had been ordered to leave, and he had left. He was assigned to one of the ships Keraun had brought with him to Phan. His crew consisted of a few of Keraun's soldiers as well as Major Miyasato and the others that had been under his command prior to Keraun's arrival, but there was a different feel to them now. None of them, not even Keraun's units, were looking forward to seeing Ametria, let alone landing on that planet, and Jason heard dark whispers and felt the crackle of tension wherever he went. He knew that he should do what he could to keep morale up, but he was having trouble with his own spirits. As the ship tore away from Phan, he did not try to shake off Dr. Chhaya's last few words, keeping them against his heart instead.

The man was right. It wasn't enough. None of it was.

And now he had to broadcast a memorial speech that demanded a call to action against a broadly defined group, and he had to disguise it as a remembrance of the dead. A few hours earlier, Keraun had transmitted to him a copy of the speech that the admirals expected to hear. Jason read it over three times without seeing the words. The fourth time he forced himself to focus, but it made him sick to his stomach and he had to look away.

Major Miyasato approached him not long after that, and found him chewing on the words during a rehearsal, trying to force them out and just giving up in disgust instead. "If you're ready," the major said after a particularly snarled sentence came to a crashing end, "I managed to get a video exchange with your sister approved."

"Great," Jason said, looking back at the speech. "Thank you."

"They only approved it for today, Captain."

Jason threw a hard glance at her. "Today?"

"I'm sorry, but it's the best I could do."

"No, I know," Jason said, "and I appreciate that. It's just…" He looked at the speech again. "Well, we need to slow the ship for the broadcast anyway," he muttered.

She nodded. "They want it monitored," she continued, "and they think it would be better if it happened before the war announcement."

"Which one?" Jason asked, brandishing the datapad with the speech Keraun had given him. "Theirs or mine?"

The major frowned. "I'm sorry?"

"This memorial speech I'm supposed to give," Jason said, not fully certain he could trust Miyasato but not caring at this point, either. "It's just propaganda in favor of a purge."

"You're kidding."

"I wish. Commander Keraun feels that we're fast approaching that point." He tossed the datapad down, suddenly unable to even touch it anymore.

There was a harsh silence from Miyasato.

Jason wondered if he had made a mistake. "The Seventh Sun is our enemy," he said quickly, "but a purge just… It feels wrong."

"Yes," Miyasato said, her voice small and quiet.

Jason looked at her, and waited.

"I met a lot of very interesting people as I was working my way through medical training," Miyasato said. "Not all of them were human." She gave Jason a pointed look. "I joined the Star

Federation because I wanted to do some good, but I'm starting to think that's actually impossible. Especially if we're going to war."

"You'd be surprised," Jason said quietly.

After a moment, the major asked if Jason was ready to speak with his sister. He nodded, and she turned to leave.

"What's your story?" Jason said, calling her back. "You keep looking at me like you know something. It's making me paranoid."

Miyasato smiled. "Let's just say I'm very glad that my rank isn't high enough to warrant inspection of my personal life."

"What happens if you get promoted?"

She hesitated, looking at Jason sidelong. "I'm a good surgeon," she finally said, "An excellent one. But I'm very careful not to be the best."

"Remind me not to come to you for any more medical treatment."

She smiled again. "For you, Captain, I would risk a promotion."

"I appreciate that."

Shortly after Miyasato left, a soldier walked in and gave Jason a crisp salute. He led Jason to the ship's communication terminal and accessed the band that connected the ship to Sciyat. Once the connection had been established, the soldier stepped aside and stood at attention, not facing Jason but clearly making his presence in the room felt.

Jason ignored him and focused instead on the holographic projection of his sister brought up by the communication terminal. Within seconds, Jason was smiling. He had not realized how much he had missed Ranae until now.

She looked much the same as he remembered, though she was wearing her hair differently. She used to wear it as a dense cloud of black curls reaching to her shoulder, but it had been cropped short now. Jason decided that he liked it. It allowed the natural roundness of her face to show more, and her smile seemed broader, fuller, and happier. Outside of that, Ranae had the same wide nose, proud forehead, and strong cheekbones that had decorated her face in perfect balance ever since her teenage years. She held herself with graceful ease, and beamed at Jason when the connection fully synched up.

"Hey, Baby Jay!"

Jason groaned. "Thirty-two years old and I'm still Baby Jay?"

"You'll be Baby Jay when you're eighty," Ranae said, grinning wickedly.

"Which means you'd be, what, just shy of ninety?"

"And always old enough to think of you as my baby brother," she shot back, and laughed with him.

Behind her, Jason saw what looked like the interior of a residential home lit by bright sunlight. It took a moment, but he finally recognized the living room from his last visit to Sciyat, when his extended leave had granted him time to visit his family and stay with Ranae, Tomás, and their two children, Maria and Andre. With a jolt, Jason realized that had been almost five years ago. The room was much as he remembered it: clean, warm and friendly, and tastefully decked out with small sparks of color. The Sciyati police officer standing almost, but not quite, out of sight was painfully out of place in that room.

"I'm sorry we don't get to talk much," Jason said, focusing on his sister again.

"Don't be," Ranae said. "I know you don't have a lot of time for these things. We're pretty busy on our end, too." She paused to massage one of her temples with her fingertips. Her dark brown skin pulled taught under the motion, tugging her large, round eye out of shape. "We have a huge project right now, and we're behind as it is." She sighed, dropped her hand, and blinked to clear her vision. She smiled then, broad and white, the skin around her dark eyes crinkling exactly the way it had for as long as Jason could remember. "But everything moves slow on Sciyat. Sometimes I wonder if we're on a planet or a giant ball of molasses."

"I hear Sciyat is about as sweet these days."

"Oh, it is," Ranae said, rolling her eyes, "But when it

comes to work, everything just feels sticky."

Jason grinned. "So where are Tomás and the kids?"

"Tom went into the office, and I'll head there myself later today. Maria and Andre are in school. I'll tell them you say hello."

"Do they even remember me?"

"Of course they do. They may not see you much but they know you." Ranae sighed again, but she was smiling. "You should see them. They're almost teenagers now, and they're absolutely horrible. You remember how Tomás was teaching them Earthborn Spanish when they were younger? They picked that up before I could even blink. Next thing I knew, they were switching in and out of it whenever they didn't want me to know what they were up to."

"You should learn it yourself. Imagine their faces when you jump into the conversation."

"I've been trying." The good humor slipped off Ranae's face. "Between Galunvo and the Sciyati dialects, I don't think there's much room left for another language. I catch most of what they're saying these days, but with Tom's mother helping them, they're getting too quick for me."

"How is Mamá Ramirez?"

"Same as ever," Ranae said, rolling her eyes again, this time in disgust. "Between me and Tomás, I don't know who's sicker of hearing her say that she absolutely loves the kids, but *just* wishes her son had picked a lighter wife."

"Oh, Ranae," Jason said, adapting a false tone of preaching sympathy, "don't you know we're past all that in this day and age?"

His sister snorted. "You and I both know that we never moved past that. We just found something that we hated more."

Jason nodded, the false humor slipping away.

Ranae shifted forward a little. "Speaking of which," she said slowly, "we've heard some things about the Star Federation and this… new threat."

Jason sensed the sudden flare of tension through the

soldier in the room with him.

"I can't talk about that," Jason said. "Sorry."

The soldier relaxed a little.

"I understand," Ranae said. "It's just… scary, you know?"

"Yeah," Jason said. "I know."

Ranae looked at him in silence for a moment. Then she raised her hand and brought it towards the camera. She did not touch it, and Jason realized that she was reaching for the projection of his face. He could see her fingers running along what must have been his cheek. "Be careful out there," she said, her voice thick with sadness.

"I will," he promised, and tried to imagine his sister's hand brushing against his skin, warm and familiar. He wondered if he would ever be able to hug her again. Regular leave would not grant him enough time to travel all the way to Sciyat and then back to wherever he'd be stationed now that he was under Keraun's command and restricted to the areas surrounding the Andromeda Reach. He had to survive to see his next extended leave if he wanted to visit Ranae again. He tried not to dwell on that.

They talked for a little while longer about things going on in Ranae's life. Major milestones and minor frustrations, plans for upcoming birthdays and visits from the Ramirez family for holidays. Jason liked to hear these things. They were always so different from the experiences he had with the Star Federation, but they did not talk about those things. They never did.

Jason did want to tell Ranae, to talk to her as he could talk to no one else. He wanted to tell her that he had seen Neo-Andromedans in action firsthand. He wanted to tell her that he had to give a memorial speech that had been drained of all heart. He wanted to tell her that he had watched someone's brother die. But he was a soldier, first and foremost, and he could not tell a civilian any of those things.

After a while, they said their goodbyes, said that they loved each other, and Jason let the soldier disconnect the terminal. Jason knew the soldier would send transcripts of the entire conversation back to the Star Federation space station, but there was nothing to worry about this time. At least, not as far as that conversation went.

Back in his private quarters, Jason picked up the memorial speech and read it through again, but he knew that he could not say these words. He kept thinking about how he had not been able to stop Keraun from killing Aven, or maybe how he had not tried to stop him. Then he thought about Ranae, and how she would feel if his name came back to her as a casualty of war.

"Stand and Protect," he whispered.

A while later, Jason stepped out of his private quarters, returned to the communication terminal, and broadcasted his memorial speech back to the Star Federation space station as he had been ordered to do. He said some of the words Keraun had given him, and attributed the attack at Ametria to the Neo-Andromedan group known as the Seventh Sun. The rest of the speech was his own. He asked the galaxy to remember those that had fallen in the attack, but to never forget that retaliation should not come at the cost of the lives of the innocent.

"We know our enemy," Jason concluded. "We know where our focus must lie. And we know that we cannot lash out in broad strokes, for if we do so, we fail to uphold the key goal of the Star Federation. We fail to protect."

It wasn't the most eloquent speech Jason could have written, but he felt far better after saying it. He knew it would piss off Keraun and possibly some of the admirals, but he did not care. Major Miyasato had warned him to stay on the fleet commander's good side, but that had felt too much like the wrong side.

CHAPTER 21: SAFETY

Min was exhausted. She had barely gotten any sleep the night before, but still had been prepared for two big, tense meetings between her and the company's primary investors, both concerning the fate of the dealership and their partnership with the manufacturers after the latest renegade raid on a shipment, before the Star Feds had scrambled her schedule. The headaches Flynn's shady attacks and painful interview slanders had brought on were nothing compared to the tension Min felt crackling up and down her spine as she watched Star Federation soldiers prowl around the dealership, scanning cruisers, probing inventory logs, interrogating employees, and combing security footage. The Star Federation had arrived far sooner than expected, long before the Justice Keepers had come to claim the truth. Without full confirmation of Mezoran amnesty, the Star Feds could not be turned away, and Min could not shake the feeling that maybe, just maybe, she and her brother had overextended their reach.

Deshi had known what to expect, but Min's easy-going younger brother had slowly slipped into a nervous silence as the Star Federation presence thickened. He now stood next to her in her office, hands clasped tight behind his back and fighting down dry swallows as they watched a lieutenant seated at Min's desk run through the company's data.

Min brushed her shoulder lightly against his, her fresh, crimson sash curling a little with the movement. "Be calm," she murmured to him in Terra-Six Chinese. She was reasonably certain that none of the Star Federation soldiers present at their dealership could understand the dialect, but she could not bring herself to risk speaking above a whisper. She was glad she had kept her voice low when a soldier glanced at her, but he returned her polite smile easily enough and went back to sweeping her office for hidden objects. He was a little rougher than he should have been with the delicate paintings hanging from the walls, and Min had to speak up.

"Please be careful with those," she said, keeping her voice as non-confrontational as possible. In spite of that, there was a quick crackle of tension as several pairs of eyes snapped to her. "They have sentimental value," Min quickly explained. "Our father painted them."

The soldier inspecting the paintings said nothing, but he did handle them more gingerly from then on, much to Min's relief. They were the only two paintings that had survived from Terra-Six, and Min often liked to look at them and remember her father's stern, quiet concentration as he had run his brush over the thin paper. He had pretended not to notice whenever his children had paused to watch the paint bloom, but Min had caught him smiling almost every time, and he had told her once that it was important that they keep their passions alive. Even with soldiers crawling around her dealership, Min was glad that she had followed his advice.

"Clean," the soldier inspecting the paintings announced a few minutes later in Galunvo.

The lieutenant nodded from behind the desk, frowning at the data readouts, but she finally finished reading, stood up, and came to thank Min and Deshi for their cooperation. She was a short, stocky woman with light brown skin, a round face, black hair drawn back into a bun, and a stern but polite manner in a brisk sort of way. "We'll be clearing out now. Thank you for your time, Executive Fang," the lieutenant said to Min.

"It was no trouble," Min replied, though it actually had been a great deal of trouble to redistribute the stolen shuttle's signature before sending it off-world to be gutted, wash the dealership of all traces of Lissa's presence, edit the security footage, and leave enough suspicious evidence to condemn Flynn's dealership and exonerate theirs in the eyes of the Star Federation. It had not been an easy night, and Min worried that they had forgotten something.

The Justice Keepers would be leery of all of that activity, but as long as she and Deshi explained the full truth, Min knew that she could count on support and exoneration in the Mezoran justice system. If the Star Feds found enough evidence to arrest her and Deshi before the Mezorans arrived, however, they would never even see the chance to take refuge under Mezoran law.

"I only wish we knew what you were searching for," Min continued to the lieutenant. "We could have helped you look."

The lieutenant shook her head. "Classified information, but you don't need to worry. Our team should be nearly finished outside as well."

Min nodded and with a gentle nudge, she managed to steer her brother out of the office. They walked with the lieutenant and her small team back to the showroom where they found a few other soldiers waiting.

This group had been left to interrogate the employees— none of which had been present the night before when Lissa, Ashburn, and the arkins had shown up, Deshi had ensured— and scan the room for evidence, though now that their task was complete, most of them had grouped around the sky cruiser display, studying the wicked Wind Cutter model. It glowed in the spotlight cast over the pedestal, cleaner and brighter than the sunlight filtering through the windows, and the cruiser held the soldiers' attention captive.

The lieutenant cleared her throat, and the soldiers sprang back from the sky cruisers, snapping to attention with guilt and glee sparking in their eyes.

"At ease," the lieutenant grumbled, though without any real anger, and the soldiers relaxed. One stepped forward to quietly relay their findings to the lieutenant. Their sweep of the showroom had come up clean, and the outside team had similar results.

"All right, we're done here," the lieutenant said once the soldier had finished.

Min let her breath out in slow relief, and she saw Deshi unclench his hands as the tension melted out of his shoulders.

"Send a report to Commander Anderson," the lieutenant continued. "Let her know that we're—"

"Not quite finished," a woman's voice cut in.

Min turned to see a blonde, pale-skinned woman stalking towards them across the showroom floor. Her uniform was the same ashen gray as the other soldiers', but Min caught the golden flash of a fleet commander insignia pinned over the woman's heart.

Shit, Min thought, but she forced herself to keep her polite composure.

The mirth melted away from the soldiers as the fleet commander approached, and their hands and feet glided back into the formal Star Federation salute. The lieutenant snapped to attention, and rang out a greeting to the fleet commander.

"Status report?" the fleet commander demanded as she stepped up to the lieutenant.

"Everything's clean," the lieutenant said.

"Of course it is," the fleet commander muttered, eyeing Min up and down. "You the owner?"

"Chief executive officer," Min returned.

The fleet officer's expression said that that was close enough. She glanced around the showroom, taking in the holographic displays of starships and the gleaming, rotating sky cruisers. She seemed distinctly unimpressed. "I heard you have quite a rivalry with another dealership," the fleet commander said.

Min smiled. "That's the price of success."

The fleet commander's brown eyes narrowed. "It may

interest you to know, then, that the owner of that dealership was found dead less than six sidereal hours ago."

Min's smile dissolved. Fleet Commander Anderson was looking for a reaction, and only a very specific one would keep Min and her brother out of Star Federation custody long enough for the Justice Keepers to arrive.

They should have been here by now, Min realized, feeling a small surge of panic in her chest, but she had to keep calm and play along with Anderson until the Mezorans came.

Min made herself stare blankly at the commander for a moment before throwing a bewildered glance at her brother. She was relieved to see Deshi looking stunned, though she was not certain if that was the result of his acting or the appearance of the fleet commander. "How?" Min asked Anderson.

"Shot," the fleet commander said simply. "Local authorities said there was nothing they could do for him by the time they'd found him."

"I'm saddened to hear that," Min lied. "We were far from friends, but…" She let the thought trail away unfinished.

Anderson studied her closely. "How far?"

Out of the corner of her eye, Min saw the large doors that led out to the sky cruiser landing pad slip open, and two Mezorans stalked into the security chamber. Min felt a wild wash of relief, but she kept her focus on Anderson, and forced herself to frown. "I'm sorry?"

The fleet commander considered her for a long moment, and in spite of herself, Min shifted uncomfortably under her stare. She could see the fleet commander taking in the signs of her exhaustion and weighing them carefully.

"The Star Federation is in pursuit of a fugitive," Anderson finally said. "We traced him to this location."

Min shook her head and feigned mild confusion. "I'm sorry, Commander, but other than your soldiers, we haven't seen anything out of the ordinary here."

"Nothing?"

"No."

Anderson rocked back on her heels and tilted her head

thoughtfully, but her eyes remained hard and glaring. "I'm so tired of people hiding things from me," the fleet commander growled.

The doors connecting the security chamber to the showroom rolled open, and the Mezorans stepped through. One was the expected Justice Keeper, the other a higher-ranking and more dangerous Truth Seeker. Min quickly took in the colors of their sashes: black with two horizontal white stripes for the Truth Seeker, and solid white for the Justice Keeper.

That was not good. The Truth Seeker knew that there were lies to be rooted out, and the Justice Keeper was ready to act if necessary. Still, Min was relieved to see them; she and Deshi were beyond the grasp of the Star Federation now.

Focusing back on Anderson, Min offered the most pleasant smile she could. "We hide nothing on Mezora," she said easily, but the fleet commander's narrowed eyes told her that that had been the wrong thing to say.

As the Mezorans drew closer, Anderson barked out orders for her soldiers to start another sweep of the dealership, this time under her direct supervision. She swung away from Min to face the oncoming Mezorans, and she did not balk when they slowed to a halt in front of her, towering over her. Though they both wore breathing masks to shield their lungs against the oxygen in the dealership's modified air, Min could plainly see their agitation.

The Truth Seeker curled itself into a tight crouch, studying Anderson intently. Its secondary arms were folded out of sight behind the primary two, though Min heard a distinct thrumming noise as the Mezoran breathed; it was the equivalent of a human snorting in disgust.

The Justice Keeper cast a slow glance around the room as the Star Federation soldiers scurried back to their tasks, its secondary arms breaking away from its chest and tracing the paths of activity. The light caught on the venom that tipped the secondary digits. Though all Mezorans' secondary arms secreted venom, they usually kept them drawn so close to their chests for both safety and social courtesy that Min had never seen the milky venom in person before. The toxins were unique to each individual Mezoran, and served as something of a fingerprint for their species, but only the Justice Keepers were permitted to use their venom to carry out registered and approved kills. This Justice Keeper was tense all over, ready to spring into action and lash out with its toxic fingers if the Truth Seeker so much as blinked at it.

Min spread her hands in greeting and made to step forward, but Anderson shot her a cold glare. "You stay put," the fleet commander growled before facing the Truth Seeker again. "This is the site of a Star Federation investigation. You are interfering. Leave now."

The Justice Keeper snapped its attention to the fleet commander and made a harsh hissing noise.

Anderson did not flinch. "We were granted approval to carry out our investigation and make an arrest." She gestured at Min and Deshi. "These two are coming with us."

Min felt a sudden harsh grip on her arms, and her hands were pulled behind her back. Laser cuffs clapped down around her wrists, and from Deshi's burst of outrage, she knew they had done the same to her brother, but she kept her eyes trained on the Truth Seeker.

"We have authority here," Anderson growled. "Stand down."

The Truth Seeker uncurled slightly from its crouch. "The arrest," it droned in Galunvo, voice thickened by the breathing mask and a heavy accent, "was to be only under absolute evidence." It cocked its head and blinked lazily at the fleet commander. "This one finds absolute evidence?"

"We have what we need," Anderson said, not missing a beat. "The Fang siblings are under Star Federation arrest."

"This one finds absolute evidence?" the Truth Seeker demanded again.

"Yes," Anderson snapped. "We—"

"Lying." The Truth Seeker rocked its weight on to its primary arms. "This one is lying."

Min had to fight down giddy giggles of relief. The arrogance of the Star Federation knew no bounds, but it would hit an unmovable wall on Mezora, as Anderson was discovering now. Justice Keepers that were chosen to be elevated to the rank of Truth Seekers underwent elite training to teach them how to pick up even the faintest signs of falsehoods, and each individual Truth Seeker specialized in interactions with a single species. This one had been trained to detect human lies. It would not have come to speak with Min and Deshi otherwise.

"Our evidence is—" Anderson began.

"Lying," the Truth Seeker droned, and the Justice Keeper turned its venom towards the fleet commander.

"We found—"

"Lying."

"There was data to—"

"Lying."

Tremors of anger rippled through Anderson. "We traced the signature of a stolen shuttle to a rival dealership, and though there's no evidence to support it, I believe the Fangs rerouted the signature to throw off the Star Federation's efforts and delay us until they could be granted full amnesty under Mezoran law."

"Truth," the Truth Seeker said, almost smugly.

The Justice Keeper relaxed, almost reluctantly.

"We know that—"

"Lying."

Anderson took a deep breath. "I suspect," she said deliberately, and with no interruption from the Truth Seeker, plunged ahead, "that the Fangs struck up some sort of deal with a fugitive that the Star Federation is currently pursuing, probably trading the stolen shuttle and possibly the assassination of Christopher Flynn for a fresh starship."

"Believed truth," the Truth Seeker said, turning a quizzical look on Min. "Confirm or deny."

"Confirm, but there are hidden truths within the truth," Min said, switching into one of the Mezoran dialects.

Anderson twisted a sharp glance back at Min, but there was no flicker of understanding in her eyes. Just panicked confusion.

Good, Min thought. *The Star Feds have even less knowledge of Mezora than I had hoped.*

With the Truth Seeker's attention riveted on her, Min explained the full story, leaving out nothing, not even Lissa's criminal record as the Shadow and the knowledge of Lance Ashburn's desertion of the Star Federation. These were not crimes that Mezoran law would have recognized. Bounty hunting was not so far removed from the tasks of Justice Keepers, and Ashburn's actions meant nothing outside of Star Federation territory. As far as the Mezorans were concerned, he was nothing more than a coincidental bystander.

The Truth Seeker agreed, and declared that the Star Federation had no jurisdiction over this incident. It was isolated to Mezora, and it fell wholly under Mezoran law.

"No fucking way!" Anderson spat when this was announced in Galunvo. "This is a Star Federation case and you have no authority over it!"

"Untruth," the Truth Seeker said icily.

"Lying," Anderson hissed, "and you know it."

Min felt herself go cold. Respectfully disputing the affirmed truth as an "untruth" was generally harmless and socially acceptable. But directly accusing a Truth Seeker of lying was a capital crime on Mezora.

The Star Feds know nothing, she reminded herself. *Absolutely nothing.*

The Truth Seeker turned to the Justice Keeper.

Exhausted and exasperated, Min was ready to let this play out to her advantage, but Deshi was of a different mindset. Min saw her brother take a step forward, preparing to speak in an attempt to diffuse the situation, but the soldier holding him yanked him back. The movement caught the attention of another soldier, and he stepped forward to help restrain Deshi, but Min's brother twisted out of their grasp and jumped in front of Anderson.

"That one does not—" was all he managed to get out before two soldiers tackled him to the ground and a third came up to help as Anderson stepped back.

That was the moment when the Justice Keeper made its strike. The venomous limb shot out, piercing the air where Anderson's face had been only a moment earlier, and cut open the cheek of the soldier who had come forward to help restrain Deshi.

The soldier froze, and in the stunned silence, Min watched the blood seep out of the wound, dribbling in dark red drops down the soldier's face to stain the gray fabric of his uniform. With a jolt, Min recognized the solider as the one who had been checking her father's paintings back in her office. He raised his hand to touch the blood in the same slow, cautious way he had touched the paintings after she had asked him to be careful. He looked hard at the red smear on his fingertips, then his eyes slipped out of focus, his body spasmed, and he collapsed on the ground. Min watched in frozen horror as foam began to seep through his lips, but Deshi immediately began to struggle on the ground.

"Innocent!" he shouted. "That one was innocent!"

The Truth Seeker looked at the dying soldier without remorse. "Truth," it said, and made a twisting gesture to the Justice Keeper.

The Justice Keeper pushed its breathing mask up, revealing a long, rounded snout with sharp jutting teeth. It picked up the poisoned soldier with its primary limbs, gripping him firmly against the spasms, and raked its pointed tongue over the wound once, twice, three times. Its tongue was almost as rough as the rest of its scaly body, and the licks left raw, red marks on the soldier's graying skin. The Justice Keeper lay the soldier on the floor again, and all watched as the spasms slowly subsided into shivers.

"That one lives," the Truth Seeker said after a moment, and then looked at Anderson once again. "That one dies."

A wave of real fear washed over Anderson as her eyes snapped up from the poisoned soldier to the Truth Seeker.

180

"What?" The Justice Keeper advanced towards her, and she stumbled back. "You can't—"

Min tore out of the soldier's grip and threw herself in front of Anderson. "Please, that one does not understand the offense," she said in the Mezoran dialect. "That one would not have said such things otherwise."

The Justice Keeper paused and looked to the Truth Seeker, who considered Min for a long moment. "Do you take responsibility for that one?" it asked her, still in the Mezoran language.

"I do not," Min said. "I only know that that one," she jerked her head towards Anderson, "is from the Star Federation, and is therefore ignorant and stupid."

The Truth Seeker made a deep thrumming noise. "That does not excuse that one from punishment."

"I agree," Min said, "but I respectfully encourage exile over death."

The Truth Seeker gave another deep thrum, but said in Galunvo, "The Star Federation leaves Mezora, or the Star Federation dies." It fixed a flat stare on Anderson. "That one chooses for all."

The fleet commander's eyes flickered over the poisoned soldier, still shivering on the ground. Two of his comrades hunched over him, trying to confirm that he would actually survive. Anderson looked at the anxious faces of the rest of her soldiers, then at Deshi, and then finally at Min. Her gaze was so harsh that Min feared the fleet commander would actually refuse the chance and condemn herself and her squadron to death. Anderson's soldiers would have to kill the two Mezorans to get past them, and if by some miracle they succeeded in striking one of the Mezorans' very few vulnerable spots, the Star Feds would never make it off-planet. The Mezoran council had approved their presence, but Min knew that the Justice Keepers had kept a very close watch over Anderson and her soldiers from the moment they had entered the atmosphere. Mezora would not look kindly on an outsider lashing out against their customs, and attacking a Seeker-

Keeper team would whip up the wrath of the entire planet.

Anderson looked ready to take that challenge.

But then, her voice quietly angry, the fleet commander said, "The Star Federation leaves."

The cuffs were removed from Min's and Deshi's wrists, and they were left in their dealership with the two Mezorans. The Star Feds quickly filed out of the dealership in two neat lines, save for the soldiers who had hoisted up their poisoned fellow and carried him outside. They headed directly for their shuttles and filtered in, but before Anderson boarded, she shot one long, dangerous look at Min through the thick glass of the airlock that divided the showroom, security screening room, and landing pad from each other. Then she, too, slipped inside the shuttle, and the bulky, familiar crafts closed.

While the soldiers had been leaving the dealership, Deshi had led the Truth Seeker to a private communication terminal so it could file a report and mark this Star Federation squad as unwelcome on Mezora. Deshi rejoined Min as the thrusters of the shuttles blazed to life, and with the Justice Keeper watching them closely, they moved to the bank of windows that made up a wall of the showroom and followed the paths of the shuttles as they lifted off of the landing pad, rose into the sky, and carried Fleet Commander Anderson and her soldiers out of their lives.

Min and Deshi stood shoulder-to-shoulder looking at the sky and the pink clouds long after the shuttles had disappeared, waiting for the Truth Seeker to return and ask any other questions it might have.

"Do you think we did the right thing, helping Lissa like that?" Min asked her brother in Terra-Six Chinese as the Truth Seeker returned and called for them.

"Absolutely," Deshi said without hesitation.

"Good," Min said, turning away from the window. "So do I."

CHAPTER 22: RELEASE

Lissa and Ashburn spent a few sidereal days going over the new starship, getting to know the systems and the minor quirks of the ship. It was a beautiful craft, state-of-the-art with fast, clean systems and a good amount of speed buried in the thrusters. It used energy very efficiently, far better than most other starships Lissa had seen in its size class. It would be capable of sustaining faster-than-light travel for healthy distances, and looked to Lissa like it could outrun all but the specialized starship designs. It had a more basic weapons system, nothing truly spectacular or powerful by way of pulse cannons, but the shields were strong and the ship responded to the lightest touch on the controls, gliding and turning effortlessly.

They put in to port on a lonely, quiet little planet not far from Mezora, stocked their supplies, bought and traded for new clothing, and then coasted back out into space. No one came after them. No Star Feds or Seventh Sun agents. They were blissfully and peacefully alone.

They were also painfully and anxiously alone with each other.

Ashburn did not say much in the days following the visit to Mezora. He kept cool and civil but always distant, and Lissa noticed that he was paying less and less attention to where the enerpulse weapons came to rest onboard the starship. She knew that wasn't a sign of trust. He was growing apathetic, and not far beyond that lay resentment and betrayal. He had left everything behind when he had deserted the Star Federation, but he had not come after her with nothing to lose. That was rapidly changing.

Lissa kept a close eye on Ashburn as he drifted through the ship. He kept himself on a different schedule than her, sleeping while she worked to translate the datapad from Daanhymn and oversaw their course of travel, then coming to take over the controls whenever the first yawn escaped her.

The ship had automated systems and did not need constant supervision, but she suspected that Ashburn already knew that.

Between Ashburn's cold distance and the snarled coding of the datapad, frustration nibbled at the edges of Lissa's mind, and she found herself losing her grip on reality.

The void between the stars was an unforgiving place to be stranded, and in the empty space, the whispers found their way back to Lissa's ears. Her sleep became troubled, her dreams bright with life, too much life that needed to be snuffed out, and twice she woke to her own screams, the collar tight around her throat. Blade was with her for those shattered dreams, amber eyes shining in the dark, but if Ashburn heard her screams, he did not let it show.

Finally, Lissa woke from a particularly bad nightmare, bathed in cold sweat. She slipped out of her quarters, into the washroom, and tried to rinse away the faces that danced before her. There had been the usual appearances of the Daanhymn overseer and the other Awakening workers that she had killed, and the Phantom had drifted in this time, inviting her to hunt with him before he had turned on her and tried to slit her throat. Rosonno had been there as well, pulling her away from the light and towards an icy death, whispering words that had no real meaning but carried so much weight that Lissa had felt pain beneath them. None of that had haunted her as much as

Aven's presence had.

In her nightmare, Aven had not been Awake. His eyes had been clear and sharp, as they had been before his sickness. He had been strong and healthy, his skin unbleached by illness, but fear had wrapped itself around him, and he had tugged Lissa desperately after him as he fled the scene of his first bounty kill. In the nightmare, he had been shouting at her over his shoulder, but in reality, he had only been mumbling, and the words had not made sense. Then Min's screams had pierced the night, and suddenly, the hoarse whispers of, "I killed him. We can't stay. I shot him. I killed him…" had solidified into merciless sense, both in the dream and in the memory.

Onboard the new starship, years and light-years away from that moment, Lissa splashed water on her face and tried to untether herself from the past, but she had never succeeded before, and did not expect to now.

Welcome to the fight for me Little Light.

Water ran over Lissa's skin, dripping off her nose and chin, and she shivered. She raised her head and looked at herself in the polished glass mirror of the starship's washroom. Like all glass that went into starship manufacturing, this bit was allegedly unbreakable, but as Lissa stared at her reflection, she wanted to test that claim more than ever.

She saw her own eyes, hard metallic silver and so unlike the eyes of any natural living thing, rimmed with crazed exhaustion. She saw the cold, gaunt lines and angles of her face, stripped of all fat by years of hard travel and strictly rationed food, made all the more severe by the determined set of her jaw permanently etched into her face by time spent bounty hunting. She saw the black collar around her throat, studded with seven little white stars, and how easily that one, tiny thing made her no different from a Seventh Sun agent.

Lissa raised her hand to the cold mirror, and covered her reflection. Shaking, she dropped her head, and her hand curled into a fist. A small, tight cry slipped out of her, and she hit the mirror. Pain laced through her hand, but the mirror and Lissa's reflection remained unbroken.

A small whine sounded from the open door of the washroom. Blade stood in the threshold, Orion just behind her and craning his neck to see over her head.

Lissa held their stares for a moment, then moved away from the mirror and nudged the arkins away from the door. She stepped into the hallway and crouched next to Blade, letting the black arkin press her head into Lissa's shoulder. Orion nuzzled into Lissa's outstretched hand, and blew a soft puff of warm air against her arm.

"I can't do this," she whispered.

"Probably not."

Lissa looked up sharply to see Ashburn standing a few paces away, arms folded and a deep frown on his face. His blond-brown hair was messy and in need of washing, there was a thick layer of stubble scraping over his jaw, and the dark rings around his eyes were so out of place against the square shape of his face. He looked almost as bad as she felt, and she realized that he must have been sleeping about as well as she had.

"Neither of us can," he said. He reached up to rub the back of his neck, and Lissa noticed that he did not seem to feel any pain from his enerpulse wound anymore. "We don't trust each other."

"No."

"And how could we?" He gave a heavy sigh. "I was a Star Federation soldier and you... Well, the only person you could ever trust is lying in a hospital."

Lissa hesitated, then slowly shook her head. "I haven't been able to trust Aven for a long time. He protected me from a lot of bad things, but he also ruined a lot of the good ones." She stood and faced Ashburn. "We stopped trusting each other after what happened with the Fangs." She considered him for a minute, balking at the thought of revealing more about her past, but she could feel the tether loosening. "Do you still want to know about them?"

After a long, slow pause, Ashburn nodded.

So Lissa told him. She told him more than she had meant

to, but once she started talking, she felt something release its hold on her heart, and each word made her feel a little lighter.

She spoke of her and Aven's escape from the Seventh Sun's main base, how their caretaker Asanra had put them onboard a ship with fleeing uncollared Neo-Andromedans, and how Asanra had been killed in helping them. She told Ashburn about the dark whispers shared among the uncollared, all far older than she and Aven had been, about their reluctance to keep children with them and their decision to dump them before they became trouble.

She gave a bitter laugh then. "I was thirteen at the time. Aven was fifteen. And the things we saw on the Seventh Sun base put us far away from childhood."

Ashburn listened silently as she recounted the two years she and Aven had spent alone after the uncollared had thrown them off, learning how to steal in order to stay alive. She had been a better thief than her brother, smaller and quieter, but Aven had finally found legitimate work, though he had not realized that Terra-Six was a human colony until it was too late. But by then, they had learned to keep their heads down and their eyes low, and were lucky that they had been born without streaks or flecks of color in their irises. So they had gone to Terra-Six, and signed up for work on a spice farm. The family that owned it had emigrated to Terra-Six from another human colony, and was part of the first generation of settlers on the fresh planet. That family, the Fangs, had been distant but polite towards Aven and Lissa and the few others that had signed on to assist with the farming machinery, but as time passed, Lissa grew closer with the two older Fang children.

"Min was my age. She was fiercely loyal to her family and respected her father's wish that she contribute to the farm and help it grow, but in her free time, she was at the ground port studying starships, and she took apart any scrap parts she could get her hands on. She was good at it," Lissa remembered, "really good, but she always found new ways to put things back together. She made them better. It was like she could breathe life into metal." Lissa put her hand on the wall of the starship.

"I can almost feel her in this ship's design. She must have had a hand in it somewhere." Lissa smiled sadly. "It might have even been one of her projects in spare time. And she gave it to us."

She fell into pensive silence then, but Ashburn pulled her back out. "What about the older brother? Deshi?"

Lissa shook her head, jolting out of her reverie. "Jian, not Deshi." She pulled her hand away from the wall. "Deshi was the younger one. He was a sweet boy, but Jian… He was Aven's age. He and I were very close. Closer than we should have been, but we didn't care at that point. It's hard to care when you're enjoying each other."

Aven had cared, however. He had spent years learning how not to anger humans, and one day, he had pulled Lissa aside and hissed a warning to her, reminding her that they were not human, and her relationships were putting them in danger. Lissa had not trusted Aven to understand that Min and Jian and even their father Renshu already knew that they were Neo-Andromedan but simply did not care, and so she had not told him. He had found out anyway not long after, during a mild confrontation that had spun wildly out of control, and that had led Aven to make his first kill. Then he had grabbed Lissa and fled.

"We learned afterwards that there was a small bounty on Renshu's head. He had gotten involved with some black market dealers a few years earlier. It was a way to make a little more money and keep his family out of poverty when a blight had hit and most of their crops were destroyed. He was almost done with that partnership and running a completely clean business when Aven shot him. I guess those dealers didn't like that he was pulling out, so they put out the bounty." Her mouth twisted bitterly. "The reward was so small there almost wasn't any real threat to it. It should have expired before anyone made a serious effort to pursue it. But that didn't save Renshu from bad coincidences, and Aven told me that we had to run. So we ran. Afterwards, Aven claimed the money, we used it to get off Terra-Six, and things went on from there."

Ashburn said nothing.

"From what I understand," Lissa continued, "Min, Jian, and Deshi tried to keep the spice farm, but some rival caught wind of their father's death. He started causing a lot of trouble and they were forced to sell. They somehow made it to Mezora, and Min set up a starship repair shop with her brothers' help, and they worked their way up from there. Totally clean, totally honest, right up until I walked in and traded them a bounty contract for a starship."

"What about Jian?" Ashburn asked gently. "We didn't meet him."

"Deshi said he'd gone to head up their new dealership in another city. He also said something about a wife and a new baby, but that's not something I need to know." She looked off. "That's Jian's life now, and I'm not a part of it."

Ashburn was frowning again when she looked back at him.

"What did you expect?" she asked. "There was nothing for Jian and me. I think we both knew that, even from the start."

"Didn't you ever want to see him again?"

"I did see him, once. It was a few years after Aven and I had fled Terra-Six. This was… about five years ago now. Almost six. The Fangs still had their repair shop, and I ended up on Mezora looking for exactly what they were offering. I needed some maintenance work done on the starship Aven had bought for us. *Lightwave*, it was called. Aven picked the name.

"It was just wild luck that I ended up on Mezora, in the same city the Fangs had landed in, and Jian recognized me on the street." She sighed. "They all knew that I had nothing to do with their father's death. I was *with them* when we heard the enerpulse shot. They knew. But they still hated me. Even Jian. But he hated me a little less than the others, enough for us to spend a couple of nights together." She shrugged. "In the end, though, I was still Neo-Andromedan, and I couldn't sacrifice that for him."

"I thought he didn't care?"

"There's a difference between not caring and respecting.

Min and Deshi understood that. Jian did not. He wanted me to stay on Mezora. He said that if I cut myself off from Aven, Min and Deshi might be able to forgive me, and I suppose he was right, wasn't he? But back then, I couldn't do it. I wouldn't. So I left Mezora, and I went to pick up Aven on Banth."

After a long moment, Ashburn asked, "Do you regret it?"

Lissa shook her head. "The only thing I regret was not leaving sooner. Jian was... wonderful. He was smart and strong, loving and loyal, but he always wanted me to be something I could not."

"And what was that?"

"Human."

A thick silence settled over them. They had sunk to the floor by this point, sitting with their backs pressed against the walls of the hallway, facing each other. The arkins lay next to them, pressed up against their legs and dozing quietly, but Ashburn disturbed their rest by standing. He extended his hand to Lissa. She hesitated, then took his hand and let him pull her to her feet.

"On Mezora, when we were hunting, you told me to stop forgetting that you are not human. It's not that I keep forgetting. It's that I don't fully understand what you're capable of, and that scares me a little." His gaze drifted to the collar around her throat. "I don't understand what a lot of Neo-Andromedans are capable of." He looked her in the eye again. "But I still want to help. I wish you'd let me."

Lissa held his gaze for a silent moment. "I've been on my own for a very long time."

"I know. And maybe you don't have to tell me everything, but you did promise me the truth back on Ametria. So, going forward, at least we'll have that."

She nodded.

"You should probably try to get some rest." Ashburn took a step away from her. "We have a lot to do." He turned away.

"Lance," Lissa said, calling him back. "Thank you. For getting me off of Daanhymn. And for keeping Blade safe."

He nodded. "Of course."

Lissa turned away, and drifted back to her sleeping quarters. She slipped inside, slid back under the blanket, and though her sleep was still plagued by dreams and nightmares, she was no longer alone in them.

CHAPTER 23: PREPARATIONS

Lance was still wary of Lissa, and he knew that she felt the same way towards him, but as the days slipped away in the wake of her trusting him enough to reveal something of her past, the tension leaked out of the ship. Lance adjusted his schedule to overlap with hers a bit more, though he did not like the idea of fully relying on the automated navigation system during the small time window in which they both slept. He did not think that the system would fail, but if something came screaming out of the depths of space, hungry for their blood, he would prefer someone to be at the controls.

To fill the lonely hours when Lissa was asleep and he was not, Lance studied the systems of the starship. Most were fairly typical, such as the navigation and defense systems, and though they were different from Star Federation design, he figured them out easily enough. Others were more complex, like the ship's cloaking system. Most ships used heat sinks to lay down lighter trails, or erase them completely for a short time and disappear from the radars, but this one had a special overdrive feature that pumped out a trail energized beyond the infrared and visible levels of the spectrum when the ship traveled at high speeds. It burned almost twice as much energy as the ship normally would whenever it was used, but unlike the heat sinks, it had no hard limit other than the life of the ship's power cells, and most tracking systems were not designed to look for signatures in that spectrum. Lance recalled the brownout at Ametria, however, and was glad that the overdrive feature was optional.

Lance became intimately familiar with the ship, right down to the tiny quirk of a two-second delay between shutting off the tracking display and the moment the display actually vanished. That was the only noticeable flaw that he found. The ship was sturdy, fast, and so far reliable, and there wasn't much to occupy his mind once he'd grown weary of learning the ins and outs of the systems.

He did, however, stumble upon the navigation sphere he had taken from Aven's room, tucked into a pocket of his clothing and forgotten. For a brief moment, Lance considered giving it to Lissa, but discarded the idea almost as soon as it had come to him. The navi-sphere had been important enough to Aven to hold a secure place in his memory, and even though Lance had not been able to get the thing to work again, he knew that the little black sphere marked a deeper connection between Lissa and her brother. If he gave Lissa the navi-sphere, the thing was bound to trigger bad memories. Even though she had finally opened up to him about the Fangs and seemed like she was beginning to trust him, Lance would not fall into a false sense of security so easily. He knew that he was an auxiliary member of this hunting team, easily disposable if he pushed too hard or stepped too far the wrong way. So, he tucked the broken navi-sphere away in his personal quarters, hidden from sight, and tried to busy himself with other thoughts. But there was only so much solitude that he could take.

Conditioned to the constant murmur of activity onboard Star Federation vessels, Lance felt the silence of the tiny starship like a weight chained around his chest, and not even Orion and Blade provided much relief from that. The time he had spent on the shuttle had been dulled by painkillers and stims. This aloneness was sharp and painful. Finally unable to take it any more, he shifted his sleeping patterns and spent a few hours each sidereal day sitting next to Lissa as she worked to translate and decode the datapad from Daanhymn.

They did not talk much beyond adjustments to their course and mild promises to find a safe planet to let the arkins out to stretch their wings and legs, but even with the wariness and the thick layer of caution coating every interaction, Lance was grateful for the company, and he had the feeling that Lissa was, too. Gradually, she started to relax more and more around him, and one day, after a few harmless questions about food and other supplies on the ship, he felt brave enough to ask something more personal, though he had decided to keep the conversation away from Aven for the time being. When he asked her how she had met Blade, however, she replied without hesitation that she had found the arkin a few months after Aven had uprooted her from Terra-Six.

Lissa said that she had been trying to settle into the rhythm of Aven's new life as a bounty hunter, and one day while Aven prepared for a hunt, she had been out buying supplies and provisions. She had been on her way back to their ship when she had seen the very young Blade digging through some garbage.

"I had to throw her nearly half of the food I'd bought before I could get anywhere near her, but she was so stuffed by that point that she was half-asleep and didn't even want to move. I took her with me, cleaned her up, kept her fed, and she decided to stay." Lissa glanced up from the datapad and looked at Blade. The black arkin sprawled on the floor and snored. "Aven wasn't too happy about that, but I couldn't take being alone with him anymore. I wanted someone else around."

There was a small silence after that.

Lissa broke it by asking about Orion's origins, and Lance sat staring for a long time at the enerpulse wound burned into the gray arkin's left flank before answering. It was an old wound, and the fur had grown back a long time ago, but the enerpulse shot had left its mark and every time Lance looked at the dark patch, he remembered the way the arkin's scorched fur and flesh had smelled.

"I killed the man responsible for that scar a long time ago," Lance finally said aloud. "His name was Red Jack."

Lissa said nothing, but there was no mistaking the sharp interest in her eyes as she put the datapad down and swiveled around in her seat to fully face him.

Lance almost turned away, unnerved by her keen attention and his reveal of something so personal, but he was reluctant to lose the fragile trust that was slowly building up between them. And the past was the past. It was harmless enough to dredge it all up. One measured word at a time, he began to tell the tale behind Orion's scar, but his voice gained momentum as he went on, and to his surprise, Lance found himself recounting the story in full.

"Red Jack" had been the self-given name of a vicious gang leader terrorizing the far-flung Earth colony Terra-Two. Lance had run with that gang for less than two years, and in spite of their open hatred for a Star Fed brat like him, Lance had desperately wanted to join them, and feel like he belonged somewhere outside of the life he had been bred for.

Both of Lance's parents had been Star Federation officers, but he had no real ties to either of them. They had conceived him, his mother had given birth to him, and then they had left him to be raised by the Star Federation alongside a bunch of children just like him. Lance had spent his entire early life on the main Star Federation space station. He did not remember either of his parents ever visiting him. If they had, he did not remember what they had looked like. He did not know if they were even still alive. He had never felt the urge to check. But he had felt the burning need to run away, and just after his sixteenth birthday, he had stowed away on an outgoing supply ship, only to be discovered and thrown out on Terra-Two, the nearest port planet. He had spent a few hours wandering the city he'd been dumped in and avoided police forces that were not the least bit interested in him before crossing paths with the Red Runners.

When Lance had first seen Red Jack's Runners, he had sensed their danger, but he had also felt their closeness, their bonds. He had hungered for that, and done everything he could to worm his way into their ranks. Now that long years had bled into the space between his days with the Runners and the present moment, Lance often felt disgusted at the memory of wanting to officially join that gang, but Red Jack had done him the greatest favor, and scoffed at his request.

"You're pathetic," Red Jack had said. He been standing next to a cage, Lance recalled. He had started dabbling in breeding arkins for pit fights, and when Lance had asked to undergo initiation, he had approached Red Jack in the arkin holding room. Tiny growls and the warm, heavy smell of animal droppings had filled the air, but Red Jack with his piercing dark eyes and dyed red hair and sharp grins and fatal gestures had drowned out all else.

"Worthless." Red Jack had unlatched the cage next to him, stuck his long, thick arm inside, and pulled a small gray arkin out by the scruff of its neck. It had flapped its frail little wings and swiped at Red Jack with its paw, but there was no strength behind the motion.

"Weak." Red Jack had thrown the little creature at Lance, and Lance had just managed to catch it and pull it close before it could squirm out of his grasp. "Just like that thing."

Lance had looked down at the little arkin cradled in his arms, and the arkin had looked back up at him, yellow eyes bright against the black mask of fur.

"Runt of the litter," Red Jack had continued. "Not fit for fighting, or for living." He had started towards Lance, slowly. "That's what happens with arkins. The weakest only gets weaker, and its brothers and sisters will sense that, and kill it themselves. They know that there's only room for the strong." He had closed the rest of the distance, and held out an enerpulse pistol to Lance. "You want to survive, golden boy? You want to be strong? You want to run with Red Jack?" Red Jack waved the barrel of the pistol over the young arkin. "You want to join? Kill this."

And Lance had considered taking the enerpulse pistol and blasting the little creature into death, but the arkin had been looking at him and its stare had been impossible to ignore.

"I can't," Lance had whispered, and taken a step back.

Red Jack had smirked, raised the enerpulse pistol, and fired.

Lance had managed to turn out of the line of the shot, but the energy pulse had scraped the little arkin's back leg, and the creature had screamed and screamed as Lance had fled, not daring to look back but hearing Red Jack's laughter ring in his ears, and the sound had stayed with him for a long time.

A few sidereal years later, Lance had the Star Federation insignia and the rank badge of a lieutenant stitched on the left breast of his uniform, just over his heart. He remembered being acutely aware of that badge as he held had Red Jack at gunpoint. He had disarmed the gang leader with ease, and cornered him in the very same room that Red Jack had ordered him to shoot Orion in. Cages that held young arkins bred for pit fights had stood all around the room, a little rusty for their age but too familiar all the same, and the arkins within had howled when Orion had entered the room. The large gray arkin had silenced them with a roar. It had been hard to say who had cowered more, those arkins or Red Jack.

With the gang leader pinned against the wall and his enerpulse pistol lying useless on the far side of the room, Lance had looked into Red Jack's eyes and seen real fear. A fear so tangible and familiar that Lance almost had not pulled the trigger.

Almost.

As Lance recalled, his superior officer Jason Stone had seemed to recognize the revenge killing for what it was, but the higher ups had decided to promote Lance even with that warning. Lance had played by the rules after that, and been the prime example of a perfect Star Federation soldier worthy of the leadership ranks. And Orion had stayed with him, an arkin the color of the Star Federation, save for that patch of dark gray that marred his left flank.

When he finished reliving the past, Lance turned to face Lissa. He had never shared the full story with anyone before, but somehow, a Neo-Andromedan bounty hunter seemed like the best person to tell.

"I suppose," she finally said after a long silence, her gaze intense but not harsh, "it was always easier for you to walk away from the Star Federation than it should have been."

Lance shrugged. "Once a Star Fed, forever a Star Fed, right?"

Lissa shook her head. "I'm not so sure you ever were a Star Fed to begin with."

"I suppose that's good," he murmured, remembering what she had said on Mezora. "Means I should be a little easier to trust."

She looked at him for a long time. "It means you're unpredictable." But she gave no indication of whether or not that was a good thing.

Lissa unraveled the Daanhymn datapad soon after that spoken flood of memories. It had taken a long time due to Lissa's rusted Neo-Andromedan language skills, but the moment finally came when Lance felt a tap on his shoulder, and Lissa showed him a log of recent information exchanges stored on the datapad. She pulled four planet names out of the log: Ametria, Daanhymn, Jetune, and Daraax Beta.

"And you think there are bases at Jetune and Daraax Beta?" Lance asked. Both planets were inhabitable, but he no longer considered that a problem for the Seventh Sun.

"The Daanhymn base sent most of its data to Jetune," Lissa replied, pointing to a large chunk of the log. "There's probably another Awakening station there, but something's going on at Daraax Beta. I haven't fully translated all of this yet, but the last transmission from the Daanhymn base went to the Daraaxi system." She shifted on her feet, and began to massage her left shoulder. "I'm pretty sure that one had to do with me."

Lance took a close look at the translated time stamp on the log. "That last one went through just before I got to

Daanhymn. It might have been some sort of emergency transmission. A relay to superiors telling them about the compromise of the base."

Lissa frowned. "You think?"

"The Daanhymn base seemed pretty underdeveloped. It was cannibalized from the remains of a human colony, and didn't look like it had the best technology." Lance's mouth curved into a grim smile. "Or security, past the flowers, but those were terrifying on their own."

Lissa's smile was a bit more genuine, but it lasted only a moment. "Daraax Beta housing a superior base makes sense, but I'd like to finish translating the transmissions before we go charging over there."

"That's probably a good idea, but if you had to guess, what do you think we could expect to find there?"

"I really don't know," she admitted. "But whatever it is, it will probably be guarded by more than just flowers."

"Small, fluffy animals, maybe?"

Lissa gave him a hard look, and Lance had to laugh. It felt wonderful after the stress and tension of the previous days and he let it roll through him freely, but Lissa only frowned and shook her head before focusing on the datapad again.

"These are the only planet names I've been able to find," she said, bringing Lance back out of the delirious bout. "But even if I had more of this translated, I don't think we should start in the Daraaxi system."

"So Jetune, then." Lance considered this for a moment, seriousness sweeping back in. "Are you sure you want to start with an Awakening base?" he asked gently. "I mean, after what happened..." He left the thought unfinished.

Lissa sank down into the seat next to his, perched on the edge, and leaned forward. She rubbed her shoulder, not meeting his eye. "It's either Jetune or Daraax Beta. We have to start somewhere, and those are our options."

"But are you sure you're ready?"

She looked at him then, without malice but without any warmth, either. "You can't waste time in a hunt. You have to keep moving."

Lance met her gaze levelly. "Mistakes are made when you rush."

"I've been careful my whole life. Always planning out my next move and checking over my shoulder, but that didn't keep me safe. The Seventh Sun still found me. So did the Star Federation. Maybe it's time to make some mistakes, and show that I'm not afraid to make them."

"All right then," Lance said after a small pause. "To Jetune." He turned to the controls, ready to enter the coordinates, but hesitated. "We're going to need warmer clothes."

Lissa agreed, and they put into port at a lush, lonely little planet not far from their drift location. They landed without trouble, disguised themselves with hologram projectors, bought a little more food from a small village nestled in the foothills of a huge mountain range, and traded for some heavy, fur-lined outerwear and specialized thermal innerwear.

When they got back to the ship, they let the arkins out to hunt in a deserted field of tall grass, though Blade could not make it off the ground. Lissa watched the arkin struggle for a few minutes before she gave up and settled for running, her wings tucked in against her sides. Orion glided over her for a short while, tracing out the thick path she cut through the grass, then dropped down and ran beside her. Even limited to running, the arkins caught several small creatures, and devoured them greedily. When they had finished eating, Blade shot out of the tall grass into a patch of dry soil, unfurled her wings and tried to take off once again, but only threw up small clouds of dirt. She gave a frustrated roar, and sauntered back to where Lance and Lissa sat waiting on the crest of a small hill.

"She's supposed to make a full recovery," Lance said quietly as the arkin approached. "Maybe if she rests the wing a little longer."

Lissa shook her head and pushed herself to her feet. "Some things just don't heal."

CHAPTER 24: RAID

The winds of Jetune were dry and bitter cold, drowning Lance in wild rushes of thin air as they fought to flood through even the smallest gap in his thick clothing and soak his skin with a deadly chill. The heavy, fur-lined clothes held up.

The coat Lance wore hung down to his knees, fastened securely but fitting loose around his shoulders for mobility. The outer layer of fabric blocked the worst of the wind, and the brown-gray fur of the interior shielded him from the rest. The large hood extended low over his brow, and the sleeves were long, stopping just shy of his knuckles. He wore thick gloves and pants as well as sturdy boots, and under all that was the secondary layer of lighter thermal wear. The thermal wear was thinner and tighter, but it kept in his body heat and protected him from the cold. A breathing mask from the starship was fitted over his head, closing off the wind from his face and sending more air to his lungs than the atmosphere ever would have, wind or no wind.

Lissa's clothing was almost identical to his, the only difference being that her coat was more gray than brown and camouflaged better with Jetune's flat, cracked crust, not that there was anything to hide from. She kept pace with him as they trekked over the frozen, dead land, pausing occasionally to check her navigation sphere. The first time she pulled the navi-sphere out, Lance went cold with shock, but he reminded himself that the broken one was still hidden away in his private quarters. He had checked before they had set out for the base. Out on Jetune's barren surface, he bit down on his surprise and watched in silence as Lissa checked their position and adjusted their course.

They had found the coordinates of the Jetune base embedded within the datapad from Daanhymn. Those communication logs had held more than just transcripts of correspondences, and Lissa had managed to pry the extra information out of them on the way to Jetune. They had landed the starship a comfortable distance away from the base before setting out on foot. The air was too cold and too thin for the arkins, and Lance and Lissa had agreed that they should remain on the ship. Orion had made his displeasure with the decision known, grunting and sighing as Lance and Lissa had dressed for the weather, but Blade had only stared at them in total silence. After her failed flight attempt, she had been sullen and distant even from Lissa.

"I'm worried about her," Lissa had said as she and Lance had stepped out of the airlock, but there had been nothing to do except begin the long, lonely walk to the base.

Jetune was not a large planet and both Lance and Lissa were more than capable of crossing the distance between the ship and the base, but the unyielding wind and the flat, barren land stretched the walk into eternity. Lance and Lissa stopped three times to rest and huddle together on the ground, their backs to the wind and their shoulders pressed together, trying to steal some spare warmth from each other.

"We're nearly there," Lissa said as they crouched on the ground the third time.

Lance wiggled his toes, feeling the chill in his feet, and glanced up. Jetune's weak, distant sun hung halfway between the horizon and the peak of its arc, but days were long on Jetune and there were still plenty of hours of daylight. That did not deter a few stars from shining near a horizon that was more black than blue.

"I have to admit," he said, hearing the distortion of his own voice through the breathing mask, "the Seventh Sun amazes me. I can't believe where they've managed to build, and how they've operated under the Star Federation's radar for so long." He frowned at the frozen ground. "They've finally begun to scare me, and I know that probably doesn't mean much to you, but I've seen battles lost before they started because fear got a foothold." Lance pressed his knuckle into the unyielding ground. It was almost the same shade of gray as the uniforms of Star Federation soldiers. "Fear is dangerous when you're about to face your enemies."

"Not as dangerous as forgetting to respect them," Lissa murmured. She stood. "Are you ready?"

Lance nodded, took Lissa's extended hand, and let her help him to his feet.

They reached the base not long after. They tried to stay low, moving slowly, but with Jetune's flat surface, there was not much to hide behind or blend with. Lissa's coat was at least close to the color of the ground, and Lance stayed behind her and tried to make himself as small as possible. They crouched as they drew near, ultimately dropping on to their bellies and crawling a short distance, but Lissa slowed to a halt well away from the base. Lance settled next to her, watching the base and trying to pick out what had made her pause.

The base itself consisted of three close, squat, geometric buildings, hexagonal or maybe octagonal in structure. Lance couldn't tell the shape for certain, but the roofs were low to combat the undying winds. There were no windows, no overhanging structures or other elements that would have given the weather purchase, though the largest building had a giant, horizontal access door.

"The one on the left looks like it might be a ship hanger," Lance said. "If they had one on Daanhymn, there's probably one here, and that's the only building big enough to house a ship."

Lissa gave a small, sharp nod, barely registering under the

large hood. "I don't know what's in the one on the right, but whatever it is, it's nothing essential."

"How do you know?"

"There's frost buildup around the door. It doesn't get much use."

Lance squinted, but could not make that detail out. *She's not human,* he reminded himself.

Focusing on the last building, Lance and Lissa remained still for a long time, watching and waiting. Nothing came or went from the base, and there were no signs of life at all.

"Do you think it's abandoned?" Lance asked. "If they knew we were coming, they might have pulled out."

"If they knew we were coming," Lissa returned, "we never would have made it this far." She never looked away from the base.

"There's no reason for them to be hanging around outside," he said, "but I'd expect something. Maintenance work, security checks, *something.*"

"I know," Lissa said, and he heard the hard edge in her voice. She glanced over her shoulder at him, her face half-hidden by the fold of the hood. "It's an Awakening base. If they're all busy inside, then maybe…"

"Maybe," Lance agreed. "Are you ready?" He kept his voice calm, but he felt his nerves start to shake. If there was an Awakening going on, he wasn't sure if he was ready to face that, let alone if Lissa should, but they were too far in to walk away now. They had to move.

And Lissa moved. She stood, and brazenly walked the remaining distance to the base. Lance ran after her and fell into step beside her. No alarms sounded. Nothing shot at them, no one came tearing out of the base brandishing weapons and promising death, nothing moved.

"They really didn't expect anyone to find them here," Lance murmured as they stepped up to the entrance of the center building. "They're completely—"

Lissa touched the access panel, and a harsh beam of light washed over her. She went stiff, and Lance felt panic race up his spine, but the light found and focused on Lissa's throat. It lingered there for a moment, shining off the hard edge of her respirator mask and the soft lining of her hood before snapping off. The access panel beeped twice, and the door hissed open.

Lance exchanged a stunned look with Lissa, but understanding bloomed in her eyes. She reached up to press her hand against her neck, but the thick coat blocked her reaching fingertips. "The collar," she said, her voice small and tight. "It scans for collars."

"Then I guess it was good that you…" He let the thought die, a little disgusted with himself for even thinking it, but Lissa gave him a piercing stare all the same. He swallowed and looked back at her. She was breathing hard, and the stiffness had not gone out of her.

"We will get it off," he promised.

She stepped past him into the dim interior of the base without a word.

As the door shut behind them, cutting off the wind and the light, Lance pulled off his hood and respirator mask. It was much warmer inside the base, and he peeled off his gloves and shrugged out of his coat as his eyes adjusted. Lissa did the same next to him, letting hers fall to the floor as she whipped out her enerpulse pistol and held it at the ready. Lance drew his, and they stood for a tense minute, waiting.

They heard nothing, but they did not relax.

They were in a small, rectangular room lined with lockers. All of them were closed but not sealed, and on a quick inspection, Lance found that they held outerwear similar to what he and Lissa had worn. They found an empty locker and stuffed their coats inside, reluctant to leave anything out for a Seventh Sun agent to stumble upon.

Lance knew that they'd never survive without those coats if they were forced back outside, but he doubted that they would live that long if they were caught. As he moved through the inner door, the quiet emptiness of the base closed around him, and his skin crawled.

The next room was larger, trapezoidal in shape with shallow hallways leading off two of the smaller sides. Directly across from Lance and Lissa was a long, solid wall with three large doors set in it, all closed. The room itself was deserted, and Lance moved further in, glancing down each of the halls. There was still not a soul to be seen, just more doors and empty rooms: living quarters and storage spaces, from the looks of them.

"Something's not right," Lance whispered.

Lissa held up her hand. Her eyes were fixed on one of the closed doors, and she stood with her head slightly cocked, listening intently.

Lance heard it then, too. A low thrum of power, pulsing with a steady rhythm. It was faint, but definitely present at the lower edges of his hearing, and he placed the source somewhere behind the closed door that Lissa had fixated on.

Wordlessly, Lance swept the barrel of his enerpulse pistol in a wide arc as he and Lissa moved towards the door, scanning for a threat. None materialized. He turned back just as Lissa touched the panel next to the door, and it opened smoothly for them.

Beyond the threshold, the room was the largest one yet, and it was alive with noise. The pulsating power thrummed louder, setting a steady rolling beat beneath the sharp exchange of voices. There was a large glass chamber set in the middle of the room, containing an Awakening machine much sleeker and sturdier than the one on Daanhymn. Power thrummed along the feed cables and pulsed into the machine, and Neo-Andromedans stood all around the glass chamber, working the controls and calling out observations and instructions to each other.

One Neo-Andromedan stood back from the others, making a slow circle around the room and peering at data readings over the others' shoulders. He was the one to see Lance and Lissa first. He glanced their way as he moved around the room, paused, glanced at them again, tensed, and stumbled backwards into another Neo-Andromedan, his mouth wide with shock.

Lance felt rather than saw the moment when Lissa's control shattered. Almost in unison with her, Lance raised his enerpulse pistol, and opened fire. The movement was almost mechanical for him, and he felt grimly detached from the action as he fell into the rhythm of the attack. He had to be. Neo-Andromedans looked far too human, and Lance had to focus on their metallic eyes and the collars around their throats. Targeting those pieces instead of their wholes made it easier to pull the trigger whenever he saw a Nandro's face, and the bigger struggle became preserving his vision against the light of the enerpulse shots.

He must have killed at least half a dozen Nandros before the chaos in the room began to shift, and the Seventh Sun agents found their feet and began to run. Lance chased two around to the far side of the glass Awakening chamber. He hit one square in the back of the head with an enerpulse shot, but the other escaped him. As he went after the fleeing agent, Lance saw at least two more slip out of the room, but before he could run after them, he was suddenly face-to-face with another Nandro, and this one had managed to draw a weapon. He refocused his aim, squeezed the trigger, and—

"LANCE!"

—and he swung the barrel of the pistol away from Lissa, and the shot sailed just wide of her. He came to a grinding halt, face-to-face with her.

Lance stood frozen for what felt like a long time. He and Lissa were both breathing hard in the suddenly lifeless room, eyes locked in desperate horror. Silver eyes against his green. Metallic eyes that had registered as Neo-Andromedan first and foremost, followed sharply by the Seventh Sun collar around her throat. He could not find the words to fill the silence.

What he did find was a flash of movement over Lissa's shoulder, and he lunged around her. His next shot missed, landing just above the crawling Seventh Sun agent, and she rolled on to her back and threw her hands up in surrender, screaming something in a language that he could not understand. He stepped closer to the agent, his pistol at the ready, but before he could take the final shot, Lissa said, "Wait."

Her voice was soft and distant, but Lance forced himself to pause. The Seventh Sun agent squirmed on the ground, but she gradually grew still and dropped her voice down a few levels.

Lance gave the agent a hard, cold stare, but snuck one quick glance over his shoulder at Lissa. She was standing in front of the glass chamber, outlined by the glow of the power, staring at the Awakening machine. Her pistol was lowered at her side, but Lance saw the tense rise and fall of her shoulders as she breathed.

"Turn it off," she said, her voice cutting across the thrum of the machine.

The Seventh Sun agent squirmed again, spitting out more incoherent words.

"Turn it *off*?" Lissa screamed, rounding on the agent. In two quick steps, she was standing over the agent. She bent down, grabbed the agent by the arm, tugged her to her feet, and flung her towards the ring of controls. "Get them *out*! TURN IT OFF!"

The agent bounced off the control panel. She threw up her hands again, her voice growing desperate and hysterical now.

Lissa started towards her, but Lance reached out and caught her wrist. She rounded on him, and he saw the harsh light creeping back into her eyes.

"Don't," he began, holding her wrist tight, but he never got any further.

There was the sudden buzz of an alarm, and Lance looked over to see the Seventh Sun agent hit something on the control panel before diving forward and sprinting towards the door. His enerpulse shot just missed her. Then the glass chamber in the center of the room dropped with shocking speed into the floor, and the Awakening machine split open.

The Neo-Andromedan that stepped out was shaking on his feet. He was thin and short, with strawberry-blond hair and skin the color of cream. He wore a garment similar to the one Lissa had been wearing on Daanhymn, and around his throat was a thin black collar studded with seven white stars.

The Neo-Andromedan took a steadier step forward. He raised his head. His eyes—rose gold flecked with green—fell on Lance and Lissa. They burned with Awakened light as they darted first to Lissa's throat, then to Lance's collarless neck. His bright gaze fixed hungrily on Lance's face. Then he was in the air, his mouth twisted into a hungry snarl, eyes burning and clawed hands reaching, ready to strangle.

Lance stumbled back, pulling his weapon up, but in the split second before the Awakened Neo-Andromedan slammed into him, he knew that he would not get the barrel up fast enough.

One quick shot blazed forth from Lissa's weapon, burning into the Awakened Neo-Andromedan's body, and he fell heavily against Lance, driving him to the ground, but Lance rolled out from under him, springing back to his feet and fixing his weapon on the Nandro in the same motion. The Awakened did not move.

"You all right?" Lissa asked, her voice tight and dry.

Lance nodded, eyes still on the body.

After a motionless minute, Lance moved forward. Gingerly, he prodded the fallen Neo-Andromedan with the toe of his boot, confirming that his life was truly gone. Lissa's enerpulse shot had burned clean through his skin, revealing bone, but Lance left the Neo-Andromedan facedown, sparing himself and Lissa the worst of the view. The smell of scorched flesh crawled into Lance's nose, and he stepped away from the corpse, but now that he had slowed down and looked, he saw that there were corpses all around him. He ran a hand over his mouth as he turned in a slow circle, taking in the carnage. The sight turned his stomach, but he was too battle-hardened to be sick beyond that. Then he turned back to Lissa and felt his heart drop.

She was staring down at the fallen Awakened Neo-Andromedan, one hand gripping her enerpulse pistol, the other at her throat, scratching and pulling at the collar. The light was out of her eyes, and with it, most of her energy. She did not look shocked or horrified. Just very tired, and maybe a little sad.

"Could we have helped him?" Lance asked quietly.

After a long moment, Lissa shook her head. She began scratching harder at the collar.

Lance stepped in front of her, and took her hand away. "I promise you, we'll get it off."

Lissa grimaced and pulled away. Her eyes circled the room, lingering over each body. "This wasn't like a hunt," she said.

"No," Lance agreed, looking around with her. "It wasn't."

Lance and Lissa quickly moved out of the Awakening room. They kept their weapons at the ready, but they met no one as they moved through the base. The building was once again deserted, any survivors having already fled, but Lance kept himself alert and watched the shadows. Now that the Awakening machine was off, the interior of the base was considerably brighter. The light revealed clean, orderly hallways and rooms, but everyone who had worked there was either dead or gone, and with the paths clear, Lance and Lissa found the central computer easily enough. Lance stood guard while Lissa accessed the system. With the Awakening going on at the time of the attack, it had been left unencrypted and unguarded, and Lissa freely copied information on to the fresh datapad she had brought from the ship.

When she was finished, she secured the datapad to her belt, then reached up to touch her collar, but stopped herself and forced her hand back down.

They made their way back out of the base and found their belongings in the small entrance chamber where they had left them, though a few of the lockers now gaped open and empty. Outside, Lance and Lissa saw that the largest building had been accessed, and whatever had been inside was gone now. They shifted their attention to the final building, the one with the frost around the access door. The access panel scanned Lissa's collar, cracked the frozen seal to let them in, and offered up to them three land cruisers and a cache of wildly mismatched clothing and personal items. Lance wondered if they had once belonged to Awakening candidates, but thought better of sharing that idea. Lissa stood looking at the shelves for a long time, as if she was trying to etch these things into her mind, these lost fragments of someone else's life. He didn't ask, and she did not say.

They powered up two of the land cruisers, and rode them back to the starship, gliding low over the flat land. They found the ship and the arkins unharmed, and Lance took the helm for the take off. It was not long before they had left Jetune and the Seventh Sun's base behind, along with all the kills and the hard light in the eyes of the Awakened Neo-Andromedan. They left everything behind.

Lance glanced at Lissa, sitting quietly next to him with the datapad on her lap and her hand on Blade's head and her gaze lost somewhere in the distance, and saw the collar around her throat.

Almost everything, he thought.

CHAPTER 25: IMPACT

Rosonno did not remember how he had come to the little green planet, but it was beautiful and peaceful, like a well-kept secret. He stood not far from the edge of a cliff, grass pushing into his small, bare feet. There was a settlement not far behind him, he knew, full of Neo-Andromedans living quiet, tranquil lives, and he needed to return there soon, but as he stood watching the sun disappear below the horizon and the sky give way from bright fire to a night the color of a bruise, something felt wrong. Something nibbled on the back of his mind, and try as he might, he could not calm that mental itch. He looked up at the emerging stars, and frowned when he saw that a small cluster of them was moving.

Then he remembered.

Someone had let the secret of the Neo-Andromedan colony out.

The moving stars turned into Star Federation ships, and they ripped open the sky and screamed over the planet, raining down pulse cannon fire as they purged world of Neo-Andromedan life. Rosonno heard himself crying as he ran back home, the ground tearing at his feet, but white fire fell upon the world and burned it all away. And he could only stand there, watching the chaos, listening to the screams, while the

Star Federation insignia hung in the sky.

Rosonno squeezed his eyes shut, and when he opened them again, he was in his private quarters aboard his starship, breathing hard as the last traces of the burning world lifted from his vision. His dreams were often intertwined with memories, as that one had been, and they were often of that night, one of the few he remembered from his youth.

The Andromedan War had already ended by that time, but the purge had continued, and despite the Star Federation's best efforts, Rosonno and a few other Neo-Andromedans had slipped through the cracks and made their way back to the abandoned base the Andromedans had left beyond the outskirts of the galaxy. They had found new life there, but they had never forgotten the smell of that burning night, and the sounds of the screams.

Rosonno did not like to sleep.

As he sat up, the lights came up in his room, bathing everything in a soft glow. His cot was immaculate, not a wrinkle in the blanket. He had fallen asleep at his desk, bent over his work, datapads spread out before him. Rosonno pinched the bridge of his nose, and blinked away the bleariness of sleep. He took a deep breath and let it out slowly.

Soon, he thought. *Very soon.*

Rosonno straightened out the datapads on his desk, back into neat lines, and rose from his seat to stretch. As he worked the twinge out of the muscles of his neck, his eyes fell on the communication terminal. A light was flashing blue.

When Rosonno accepted the transmission, hologram projections of Tyrath and Ereko flickered into focus.

"*There* you are," Tyrath sighed, and after the customary greetings, she told him that the Jetune base had gone dark without pausing for breath. "We have an evac report, but we're getting mixed stories from the survivors."

"Survivors?" Rosonno asked, his heart pinching tight.

"There was an attack," Tyrath said, and Rosonno noticed the dark circles forming under her eyes.

She forwarded the evacuation report to him, and Rosonno

glanced through it. The base had been infiltrated, most of the agents gunned down by unknown assailants.

"There's no number," Rosonno noted. "How many attackers were there?"

"That's the problem," Tyrath said. "Some of the survivors say two, and others are swearing it was ten. They're too frantic to give a solid story, and there's no record of the attack outside of their memories. We have to wait for them to calm down, and then hope they can sort out the details."

"And while you're doing that," Ereko cut in, gaunt face twisting with disgust, "we're wasting time." He was reading something, Rosonno saw, only paying half attention as his gold-shot gunmetal eyes ran over the lines with alarming speed, but half of his focus was evidently enough. "We don't know who this was, but we are nearly in position and the loss of the Jetune facility does not matter."

Anger cut across Tyrath's thin face. "After what happened on Daanhymn and at Ametria, I fail to see how this does not matter."

Rosonno went cold at Tyrath's words. *It can't be her,* he told himself. *She has to be dead by now. The Star Federation landed on Daanhymn. They would have found her if she had not starved.*

But those thoughts rang hollow, and Rosonno felt that unreachable itch at the back of his mind again.

"I meant," Ereko drawled, not deigning to look up from whatever he was reading, "that we no longer needed Jetune to supply Awakened for the first strike."

"But—"

Ereko droned over Tyrath's protests. "As for Ametria, we always knew we were at risk of losing that base in particular. We've already swept the wreckage and just have a final salvage team performing one more run before the Star Feds move in to pick it over, whenever that may be. And Daanhymn has not turned out a usable Awakened in years. It was barely a base to begin with. We have all of the Awakened we need for now, and plenty more in stasis. Those that have been allotted to the first strike are on their way to me as we speak. Everything will be ready in a few days."

There was a hard silence.

"You may be ready," Tyrath said quietly, "but I think we should delay the first strike."

"That is not your decision to make," Ereko fired back, finally engaging Tyrath completely. "First Lit Arrevessa and I have been planning for this for a long time, and we are so close, too close to throw away all of our preparations and slink back into the darkness. It's time to blaze forth."

"But what about these attacks? We cannot ignore them."

"No," Ereko agreed, "but we can't let them throw off our operations either. We proceed as planned." First Lit Ereko disconnected shortly thereafter, leaving Rosonno and Tyrath to trouble themselves alone.

"Ros," Tyrath said after a long silence. "Do you think that Arrilissa…?"

"No," Rosonno said, managing to sound more convinced that he felt. "She couldn't have made it off of Daanhymn." He brushed a wrinkle out of his sleeve. "Right?"

"Right," Tyrath said slowly. "I'm worried about this, though. I sent a scout team back to check the base, and their scans revealed that whoever attacked Jetune just left afterwards. There's no one there anymore."

"Then it's not the Star Feds."

The Star Federation would have left behind a team to search the base and dig through the computer systems, not pull back and leave it all behind.

Tyrath agreed. "There's something else, too." She frowned and shut her eyes, and the dark circles looked deeper. "Whoever attacked the base did not force entry, and they didn't hack their way in, either."

"One of our own did this?"

Tyrath grimaced. "Someone with a collar did."

"Has Sekorvo been told?"

Tyrath nodded. "I spoke to him first. He's already tapping his network, listening for the more dangerous dissenters. He says that if he finds any, he's sending them to the nearest

Awakening facility." She sighed heavily, and her loose clothing fluttered with the motion of her chest. "I'm worried, Ros. Things are not happening according to plan."

"No," Rosonno agreed. "Someone is being... unpredictable."

Tyrath frowned for a long, silent moment. Then she opened her mouth, ready to tell him something, but slowly swallowed the thought and simply said goodbye instead, leaving Rosonno alone with his work and his fears.

She has to be dead, he told himself. *She has to be.*

CHAPTER 26: RED

Ametria burned before the starship, red and angry and all too eager to swallow up lives. Jason took a long look at the visual display of the planet as his ship made its final approach, and felt his skin crawl.

This was the second time he was traveling to this planet, and he had barely scraped away with his life the first time. He did not want to push his luck.

The salvage team shared his wariness; they had arrived almost half a sidereal day earlier, but they had made no move to descend to the surface and begin the recovery efforts. They wanted overhead support, and for all his fear, Jason could not bring himself to send in soldiers without going down himself. So he had shaken off the tremors and donned a fighter pilot's suit, promising to lead the support fleet in and keep the Ametrian wildlife at bay.

Major Miyasato came to see him shortly after that announcement, and had not hesitated to let him know that she thought that his idea was a stupid one. "What happens if you die down there? Did you stop to think that, with you gone, we'd be transferred to the command of one of Keraun's captains?"

"They're capable soldiers."

"They're assholes."

Jason rounded on her. "If I hear you say that again, Major, I will have your rations cut for three days."

Miyasato pursed her lips but said nothing.

He did not try to soften the edge in his voice. "Morale is bad enough without one of my junior officers talking like that."

"I understand, sir," she said, "but you going out with the fighter fleet is putting a few people on edge."

"I can't bring myself to order someone to do anything that I wouldn't do myself," Jason said.

"A noble thought," Miyasato returned, "but one that's likely to get you killed."

Jason went back to straightening out his fighter pilot suit.

"We're all under stress with this assignment," Miyasato said, "but Captain, you in particular have been... on edge."

Jason busied himself with his helmet, pointedly avoiding her eye but very aware of her scrutiny.

"I heard about what happened on Phan," the major continued gently, "what Keraun did to the Neo-Andromedan."

"I couldn't stop him," Jason muttered.

"I don't think anyone could have."

Jason frowned and sighed heavily, but before he could say anything else, his personal communicator came alive, and a soldier grimly informed him that they had just picked up activity around the remains of the destroyed Seventh Sun base.

"On the surface?" Jason asked.

"No. There are five small ships picking through the wreckage that's still in orbit. They're not hostile yet, but they're definitely Nandros."

Shit.

Jason tucked his helmet under his arm and headed for the fighter bay, Miyasato trailing after him, but she peeled off quickly and rushed for the medical bay.

"Have you found signs of a larger ship anywhere?" Jason said into his communicator.

"No, sir, just the small ones. One of them looks like that

driller from the reports on the assault of the *Argonaught IV*, but it's sitting in the heart of the debris field and looks like it's engaged with the wreckage. We're not sure if they're trying to lie low or if they just have no idea that we're here."

Jason told the soldier to keep a close watch on the Neo-Andromedan ships, and keep him informed of any changes in behavior. He hurried to the fighter bay.

After what had happened last time, all ships moving towards Ametria had approached with their cloaks on, though the salvage team had to be pushing the limits of their systems by now, and with Neo-Andromedan activity around the base wreckage, danger was looming over their heads. Only the Seventh Sun would have returned to Ametria to probe the wrecked base, and if they caught sight of the Star Federation team, there would be carnage; salvagers were not equipped for battle.

Jason chewed on that thought.

On the other hand, if the Seventh Sun had not expected the Star Federation to return, a small salvage team was probably all they themselves would have sent to Ametria. A team probably as unarmed as the Star Federation one he was rushing to defend.

You are a soldier, he reminded himself, *and we are at war.*

No matter what kind of ships were picking through the wreckage, they were Seventh Sun ships, of that he could be certain. But as he crossed the fighter bay and climbed into the cockpit of his hellhound, there was a knot in his stomach. Hostile ships he would have to engage and bring down. Unarmed ones...

The cockpit of the hellhound hissed closed around him, and the fighter came alive when he touched the controls. Power coursed through the fighter, and the hellhound shivered with anticipation, eagerly awaiting the moment it could lift off and surge into space, but Jason made the hellhound wait until the entire fleet was ready, and the maintenance teams had retreated into the safety of the side control room as they prepared to release the fleet into the void.

When he was given the all clear, Jason gently brought the hellhound up, raised the landing gear, and sent the fighter in an easy glide out into the endless night. The fleet formed up around him, and he signaled the main starship.

"Any signs of additional ships?" he asked the control room.

"No, Captain," the soldier informed him. "Just the five, including the driller."

Jason heard the strain on the final word, and knew that his soldiers were afraid. Their training would kick in when the time came, but he worried that the time might come too soon in some of their eyes. If one of them cracked under pressure, the whole operation would dissolve into chaos.

"Let us get in close," Jason told the control room. "Then send a transmission to the Neo-Andromedans. Inform them that they have the opportunity to surrender peacefully."

There was a tense pause, and the silence roared in Jason's ears.

"And if they don't surrender peacefully, Captain?"

Jason took a deep breath, and hardened his resolve. "Then we do not try to take prisoners."

"Yes, sir."

With the salvage team retreating out of harm's way and the main ship standing by, Jason led his fighter fleet in a silent glide towards the wreckage of the Seventh Sun base. He had the three teams take three separate paths of approach, bringing his own team down low towards Ametria's southern pole and then angling back up towards the debris field. The red planet loomed menacingly on Jason's left as he sent his hellhound prowling towards the wreckage, and in the light of the dying star that was Ametria's sun, Jason had a clear view of the glinting remains of the base. The debris field arced towards Ametria, falling ever closer to the surface as gravity slowly claimed the carnage, red light burning on the snarled, twisted surfaces of the wreckage.

As his team drew closer, Jason saw the winking hulls of three of the Seventh Sun ships as they flitted through the field.

There were no changes in behavior as the Star Federation fleet closed in, and Jason kept a watchful eye for any signs of hidden ships waiting to spring a trap.

He found none, and before long, there was a dramatic shift in the behavior of the Seventh Sun ships as the warning transmission from the main Star Federation ship rang out. Jason saw the three mobile ships overshoot the field, and drift a little further out into space than they had been doing previously. They doubled back almost immediately, seeking refuge among the wreckage, but before long, they emerged in a slow, cautious glide with the other two ships in tow. One was the driller, Jason saw, and the other looked like a supply transport. The first three ships were scouts. Other than the armored driller, none of them would have held up in combat, and he doubted that any of them were armed with more than a basic pulse cannon, if they even had that.

The voice of the soldier in the control room came over the fighter fleet communication line. "The Nandros have agreed to surrender."

Jason let out a hard sigh of relief, and he heard more than one soldier laugh with giddy triumph. "Second and third fighter teams will escort the enemy ships in one by one, starting with the driller," Jason told his soldiers. "First team will take the salvage crew to Ametria under my command once the driller has been secured."

Shepherding the captured Neo-Andromedan ships into the main starship went far smoother than Jason had even dared to hope. They cooperated fully, and their crews were taken to the brig without trouble. The soldiers in the control room kept Jason updated on the movements of the prisoners, and by the time he and his fighter team had escorted the salvagers to the Ametrian surface, all of the captives were secure.

"They're very quiet," Major Miyasato reported over the communication link, "even the ones that speak Galunvo, but I think some of them might be willing to talk, given more time. We'll want a consultant for that, but they're very cooperative so far, and it seems promising."

"I can't believe we caught them!" a voice cracked in the background as Miyasato's report cut out, and the thing that had tightened around Jason's heart on Phan finally loosened its grip, and he could breathe easier.

The salvage efforts of the *Argonaught IV*, however, were another matter entirely.

A number of beasts had begun to nest within the hull of the ship, and those had to be cleared out before the salvage team could get anywhere. There were a few unpleasant surprises when a rogue animal came shrieking out of the dark interior, having made its way inside through open doors and ruined ventilation systems, but caged inside his hellhound, there was nothing Jason could do about that; the salvage team was on their own inside the halls of the crashed starship. They were armed and prepared to deal with such incidents, but it was still a tense, dangerous operation. More than once, enerpulse shots and shouting hammered out over the communication line.

Outside of the hull, Jason focused on keeping the wildlife at bay. The smaller creatures were easy enough to scare off with one or two quick shots from enerpulse cannons, and Jason directed the fleet without much trouble until an Ametrian bull came lumbering over the horizon, caught sight of the activity around the dead starship, and loped towards them.

Jason left most of the fighters in reserve at the crash sight, but took several members of the team towards the bull. Harrying the beast demanded a large amount of improvised flying, and there was a heart wrenching moment when two fighters almost clipped each other when they both went in to dive at the bull and fire off their pulse cannons. They managed to swerve away from each other, but the bull's horns scraped one of the fighters, and the craft went down. The pilot managed to eject before impact and walk away from the crash, but walking turned to running when the bull went after her. Jason sent his fighter screaming after the bull, took careful aim, and let the hellhound bark. The Ametrian finally went down, and the stranded pilot hitched a ride back to the crash site in one of the larger fighters that had come down from the ship.

Two more bulls showed up before the salvage team had finished their work, but they were more interested in the carcass of the fallen Ametrian than anything else, and pulse cannons turned them away whenever they started creeping too close.

Finally, the salvage team emerged from the depths of the crashed ship, data and hard drives in hand. They boarded their drop ship, and Jason led them away from Ametria's burning red surface, back into the cool, dark eternal night that was space. The fighter team reentered the bay of the main ship, and as Jason climbed out of the cockpit of his hellhound, his soldiers gathered around him, cheering lightly, and the more familiar ones clapped their hands against his.

They had captured the enemy ships and successfully led the salvage efforts without a single fatality. The prisoners were calm and cooperating, and the necessary data had been secured for analysis. It had been a good day. That changed the moment Jason stepped out of the fighter bay.

The Neo-Andromedan prisoners marched past him and the rest of the fighter pilots in a grim line, hands bound behind their backs with laser cuffs, and their eyes covered with makeshift blindfolds.

"What the hell is going on?" Jason demanded from the first soldier he saw.

The soldier shifted uncomfortably. "A report was sent to Fleet Commander Keraun." The soldier cast a pained and pitying look over the marching prisoners. "He ordered us to transfer the prisoners to the salvage ships."

"Why?"

"The salvagers are supposed to relay the prisoners back to him. He wants to handle their interrogations personally."

Jason took a long look at the Neo-Andromedans as they filed past him. Rage burned in his gut. "Why did you blindfold them?"

"Commander Keraun ordered us to, sir," the soldier said,

dropping her voice low.

The rage boiled over.

"This is unacceptable. Hold them on this ship until I say otherwise," Jason ordered. Turning away from the soldier, he pulled out his personal communicator. "Prepare a long-range transmission," he snapped to the soldiers in the control room. "I need to speak with Fleet Commander Keraun. Now."

The communication terminal was ready for Jason when he arrived, but Keraun was not. The Hyrunian kept him waiting an irritatingly long time, and by the time he accepted the transmission, Jason's face was burning, his dark brown skin flushed with anger.

"Is there a reason the Nandros are still on your ship, Captain Stone?" Keraun clicked out. He had that bored, unimpressed air about him again, undercut by the permanent glare.

"Yes," Jason growled. "They are my prisoners. They surrendered peacefully to me and do not deserve this kind of treatment."

Keraun's permanent glare somehow deepened, and his voice snapped on the hard syllables more than it clicked. "Your actions put your soldiers in jeopardy. If that had been a trap, your fleet would have been decimated, and you would have doomed the entire mission to failure."

"But it wasn't," Jason said, fighting to keep his voice under control, "and I *knew* that it wasn't."

"Then you *know* that what you did goes against Star Federation policies."

"Your purge has not been officially initiated, Commander," Jason reminded him. "I acted as the situation demanded, and gave the enemy the chance to surrender peacefully, *which they did.* And now you want them blindfolded, crammed into salvage holds, and brought back to you? You have no right to treat these people this way."

Keraun's eyes glittered. "May I remind you, Captain, that you are under my command? Or do I need to bring you before the admiralty board and teach you that the hard way?"

Jason bit down on his words, but his hands balled into fists at his side.

The Hyrunian's glare returned to its normal intensity, and he shifted smugly. "As your commanding officer, I order you to send the Nandros to me, and that's the end of it. As for you," Keraun's putrid yellow eyes glittered, "you are needed on Yuna. There was apparently some sort of incident there a while ago. Nandros are believed to be involved. See to it."

Keraun cut the transmission with that, leaving Jason standing in silence, shaking with frustrated rage.

CHAPTER 27: PRESSURE

After the humiliation on Mezora, Erica had thrown herself into tracking down the stolen shuttle, barely eating and sleeping even less as she had poured over data alongside her soldiers, and after a few too many and far too long sidereal days, she had managed to tease out the stolen shuttle's signature once again. It had blazed a fresh trail all the way from Mezora to a tiny backwater planet in the next system over, but Erica had known that was a cold lead long before the team she'd sent out had reported back. It was no surprise when the report stated that the stolen shuttle must have been destroyed on that planet, all traces gone and dead-ending in the middle of nowhere. There had been no further signs of Ashburn anywhere, not even a scrap of fur from his beast, Orion.

Somewhere in the empty places between the stars, Ashburn had slipped away.

Lieutenant Mohanty and the other officers under Erica's command had redoubled their efforts to find him, but even with the official announcement of war in place, Erica could not exert her power to act on her hunch and return to Mezora to go after the Fangs. She knew that they had kept something from her, but Mezora had declared its independence from the Star Federation long ago, and the Fangs were officially beyond her reach. Any attempts to arrest or even question them further would do nothing more than damage the Star Federation, and Erica knew that her position as a fleet commander was not fully secure.

The start of the new war and Keraun's concentrated activities in the Andromedan Reach had confirmed her suspicions: her promotion had been a formality, a way to fill the need for a human fleet commander, but she was not expected to accomplish anything. They had given most of Ashburn's old territory to Keraun and were letting him deal with the Nandro threat. From what she understood, he was taking a very aggressive approach, sending many of his soldiers to Ametria for salvage efforts while he and a few chosen squadrons hunted down and rooted out smaller pockets of Nandros reported to be hiding within larger civilizations, though he had yet to make a live capture. His activity reeked of purge efforts, despite no fleet commanders co-signing his petition as of yet. And she—a fresh promotion and untested in the eyes of the admirals, prior service record as a captain be damned—had been given authority over the calmest part of the galaxy.

And in spite of that, she had lost Ashburn.

The admirals would not forgive failure this early in her time as a fleet commander.

Anger rolling up and down her spine, she stood in the control room of her starship, spine straight and hands clasped tight behind her back, watching the soldiers before her without really seeing them. She kept thinking about the Fangs and that infuriating Truth Keeper or whatever they were called on Mezora. And the way that other one had poisoned Private Kolosov…

He was in the infirmary, still recovering, but he had stabilized and was only plagued by low fevers and mild shaking fits now. The medics were keeping a close watch over him, but he would live.

Erica could not forget the sound of his choking breath and the sight of the foam on his lips. That would have been her if

Kolosov hadn't stepped in front of her by chance. She had botched cooperation efforts with the Mezorans, and almost died for it, but what had really set the fire in her heart was that she knew beyond any doubt that the Fangs had been hiding something. She had seen that immediately.

She had read once that Mezorans were incapable of lying, and that they wore those idiotic sashes to bare their intentions for the whole galaxy to see, provided you understood the bizarre color-coding system. The Fangs were not Mezorans.

Humans can lie, Erica's mind thundered.

The Fang dealership had been just a little too clean during the Star Federation's search, and Flynn's had been just a little too messy. The shuttle's signature had been strongest at the Flynn dealership, of course, but something didn't quite match up.

The evidence pointed to Ashburn striking up some sort of deal with Flynn, only to turn around and blast him with an enerpulse pistol, but that was too cold-blooded for Ashburn, and for any kind of deal to have been struck up between the men, there must have been some sort of preexisting connection. It was widely known that Ashburn had spent a few years of his youth outside of the Star Federation, dabbling in illegal activities ranging from gang membership to who even knew what, but Mezoran white-collar businessmen would have been beyond him at that point. Erica supposed that it was vaguely possible for the two men to have met years ago, but even then, Ashburn had been busy working his way up to the rank of fleet commander. Why would he have kept up with outdated acquaintances? When would he even have *met* Flynn? Ashburn's assigned territories had been far, far away from Mezora, even before he had been a fleet commander.

I'm missing something, Erica knew. *Something that the Fangs wouldn't say. Maybe even that Jason wouldn't say.*

Thinking back to him, Erica felt the rage go cold. More secrets, more lies, more expectations that had been impossible to meet. Worse yet, expectations that had never even been discussed with her. He had simply wanted something, and expected her to want it, too.

You should have given me the chance to say no.

But he hadn't, and now there was nothing left between them, and Erica had a new rank and a load of power that she was afraid to use. One wrong step, and it would all be taken away.

The anger turned hot again, and unable to stand the heat, Erica forced herself to move. She stalked out of the control room and tore off to her private quarters, ignoring the soldiers she met on the way. They all jumped out of her way and snapped to attention until she had passed, but she could feel their eyes on her back. Her skin itched and crawled under their gazes, and when the door to her room closed behind her, it brought a dizzying wave of relief, followed quickly by a wash of shame.

As a fleet commander, Erica's private quarters were larger and a bit more luxurious than those of other officers, though not by much. Still, the extra space, added desk and hover chair, silkier lighting, and softer, plusher cot made the room feel like a palace. Erica felt like an intruder.

She leaned heavily against the door, drew in a deep breath, and tried to clear her mind. Thoughts and doubts buzzed across her brain, but they slowly died away until nothing remained but one solid, clear seed of determination.

Find what you're missing, she told herself. *You know it's there. You just have to pick it out.*

Erica pushed herself away from the door, and moved to the desk. She sorted and picked up two datapads and three hologram projectors resting on the surface, but did not sit. Instead, she took them to her cot. As a captain, she had not had a desk to work at, and sitting on the cot with her back against the wall and legs tucked under her, she was able to focus better.

Activating the data pads, Erica ran through all the information on the mission, tracing Ashburn's movements backwards from his escape from the starship all the way back to the day he had briefed Erica and the other officers on the assassination of Captain Coleman. He had been the perfect image of a fleet commander that day, entirely devoted to the mission and the Star Federation, and determined to bring down the bounty hunter Shadow. Then the Ametria incident had occurred, and Ashburn had not acted the way protocol dictated when facing Nandros, and then that whole mess with Backélo had come to light and the very foundations of Star Federation oaths had been shaken.

How far could betrayal reach? How long could it live in secrecy before it came roaring out of hiding?

Erica tossed one of the hologram projectors into the air. It sprang to life as it fell, halting to hover in midair and bring up a copy of the security feed from the day Ashburn had escaped the Star Federation. For the hundredth time, Erica watched Jason enter the room and speak with Ashburn. Once again, she noted the way Jason kept his back to the visual, even ducking his head low when he began pacing, making his lips hard to make out. Without the audio, there was no way to tell what he was saying, and he blocked Ashburn's face for the most part as well.

"I know you let him go," Erica muttered as she watched the recording.

She wondered how much of Ashburn's helplessness was feigned. He had not even been able to dress himself, and yet he had somehow managed to get the jump on Captain Jason Stone? She still didn't believe Jason's story, but if Ashburn was a true traitor, she supposed it was possible that he had been faking. And yet, after seizing the tranquilizer from the medical dispenser and shooting it into Jason's arm, Ashburn's dizzy reeling looked genuine enough, and he nearly fell as he stumbled from the room.

From there, Erica watched Ashburn slog his way to the room that held his arkin as well as the black one recovered from Phan. She hadn't paid much attention to this before, writing the black beast off as a coincidence, much like the other officers had, but this time, she found herself frowning. The black beast was suspected to be the Shadow's arkin, though the bounty hunter had long since disappeared and it was unknown how exactly Ashburn had come to acquire the beast. That was another piece of information Erica had failed to acquire prior to losing Ashburn. All that Erica and the other Star Federation officers knew was that Orion had been strangely attached to the black. Ashburn, on the other hand, had not shown any real interest in the animal. Erica had just assumed that he'd taken the black arkin as a means of appeasing Orion, for the gray had refused to go anywhere without the black one.

Erica waved her hand to pause the recording, staring hard at Ashburn and the two arkins. She wondered if there had been more reason to take the black arkin than just to steady Orion.

She tossed a second projector in front of her, bringing up the images of Christopher Flynn's body, all picked out of news broadcasts. The Mezorans had refused to cooperate, and with access to the official investigation files blocked, Erica's soldiers had scrounged up what they could from the public media transmission waves in the wake of the kill. Still, the images the Star Federation had managed to find in the public sphere were surprisingly detailed and graphic.

The corpse was not a pretty sight, blackened and burned by the white-hot killing shot, but Erica looked closely. Mezoran Justice Keepers had determined that the shot had come from a distance, possibly even from an elevation, though there were no ledges or perches in the area where anyone could have set up a sniper's nest. It was a mysterious kill, but all agreed that it had been a cold, precise one.

Erica absently traced out a circle on her knee with her nail, barely feeling the pattern as she studied Flynn's corpse.

Too cold, too precise.

Still tracing the circle, Erica threw the final projector in front of her, bringing up the recording of Coleman's assassination. She had requested a copy of this video from the Intelligence Unit for no other reason than to have it on hand, but as she watched the captain's death play out again, she wondered how she had missed the importance before.

Ashburn had not killed Flynn. He had not taken the black arkin for no reason. He was with the Shadow, and had been ever since the Ametria incident.

Maybe even before that, Erica realized.

He must have rendezvoused with the Shadow at Daanhymn after escaping the Star Federation. Jason's claims that the Seventh Sun was too extreme for the Shadow rang through Erica's memory, but the Shadow was a cold, hardened hunter, and she was a Nandro. Erica knew that Jason was wrong. So very, very wrong. And Ashburn had allied with the Nandro hunter.

Based on what the salvage team had found on Daanhymn, the building there had indisputably been a Seventh Sun structure. Ashburn had lured the Star Federation there, and then the Seventh Sun had blown the base, killing a few soldiers and any leads they would have found on the Nandro organization. The shuffle on Mezora was still cloudy, but the last wisps of doubt had blown away. Erica was certain that Lance Ashburn had betrayed the Star Federation, and with it, the entire human race. With Ashburn firmly tying himself to the Shadow and the Seventh Sun and undoubtedly leaking terrifying amounts of information to them, Erica knew she needed to sort out her next move fast, before an atrocity came, but it turned out to be too late for that.

As Erica rose from her cot, her personal communicator burst to life, and a soldier informed her that they had received a distress call from Sciyat. Civilians were under attack.

Erica's heart dropped. She had family on Sciyat.

CHAPTER 28: SYNCHRONIZED

The slaughter on Jetune had not been in vain. Lissa needed to connect a few threads of information, but she quickly found what she was looking for. More advanced than the Daanhymn base, the Jetune facility had enjoyed a better success rate with its Awakening candidates. Most of the successfully Awakened had been sent to the Daraaxi system, but recent orders had requested that the next wave be sent to Sciyat, a peaceful world not far from Jetune.

"That can't be a base," Lance said after Lissa had relayed the information. "I know the Sun's built in some impossible places, but this has to be past their limits."

"I don't think they're building," Lissa said, inching back a little from him. She saw that he noticed the retreat, but Jetune had left its mark on both of them and he said nothing. "I think they're getting ready to destroy," she added.

"No, that's impossible." His glance was sharp with disbelief, but horror was creeping in at the edges. "The Sciyati settlements would've noticed a fleet moving in to attack them."

"I didn't say they needed a fleet," she returned. "All they wanted were a few Awakened."

He frowned. "I know they're dangerous, but the Awakened can't possibly do *that* much damage. It's a colony."

"A colony of civilians and a symbol of peace. And you've already seen what one Awakened can do against a dreadnaught full of trained soldiers."

"I have?"

Lissa lightly scratched at the collar, feeling the studs of the stars beneath her nails. "The ambush at Ametria, with your *Argonaught* and Montag's *Resolution*, involved an Awakened Neo-Andromedan."

Lance started violently. "Which one?"

"You know him as the Phantom."

He lost his breath for a moment and just looked at her blankly. "But he's a bounty hunter," he offered when his voice finally returned.

"He's more than that." Lissa looked off. "I think they use bounties as an excuse to send him out for harder targets. There's a… deeper satisfaction when the Awakened have to work for their kills."

A small silence played out.

"I'm sure they collect the bounties," Lissa hurried on, "just because they can, but they have to be feeding him other lives in between hunts. He wouldn't have lasted this long otherwise."

"How long is 'this long'?"

For a moment, the Phantom's Awakened eyes danced across Lissa's vision, wild with hunger. She heard his steady breathing and could almost feel the strain of her own muscles, the ghosted remnant of a fight. Then there was the twinkling flash of a knife blade across the Phantom's face, and his howls of pain and anger echoed out of reality and back into memory.

"At least three years," Lissa said. "But probably longer."

She felt Lance's eyes on her face.

"How do you know?" he asked.

Lissa took a slow, deep breath. She regretted opening up to him as much as she had prior to the Jetune attack, but what was one more glimpse into her past? "We tangled over a target, once. He got there first. I shouldn't have gone anywhere near him but I was desperate at that point. That made me reckless. I somehow caught him by surprise and I think that's the only reason I got out of there alive." She glanced away and began to rub her left shoulder. "You can always see it when they're gone. It's in their eyes. Nothing left except… light."

Welcome to the fight for me Little Light.

Lissa shifted uncomfortably, then forced herself to walk towards Lance and take a seat next to him at the controls, turning a thought over on her tongue before finally deciding to give it to her voice. "Did any of them make it out of the Ametria ambush? From Montag's crew?"

Out of the corner of her eye, she saw Lance studying her. "Just one," he said. "Myrikanj the Yukarian."

She nodded. She had not expected anything more.

Lance shifted them away from the past. "How long ago did whoever's on Sciyat ask for the Awakened? Does it say in the data?"

Lissa checked for the timestamps. "It was a while ago. They've had the time to send successful candidates. I don't know how many have gone."

"Do you think the Sun would have sent any Awakened from other places?"

Lissa realized that she had started scratching at the collar again, and she dropped her hand. "I don't know," she admitted. She reached for the ship's controls and brought up a galactic map. "Jetune was probably the closest base to Sciyat." She pointed to the vague locations of the two worlds. "I don't think they would've built anywhere near Earth and the Terra colonies, and even Sciyat is too far into Star Federation space for them to go unnoticed for long."

"Do you really think they'd move against that world?"

"It would send a message," Lissa murmured, "and not just to the Star Federation."

Lance lapsed into thought, frowning at the map, but he finally gave a resigned sigh. "I don't want to believe it, but I can see them trying it." He glanced at her. "You know, the Sciyat team was probably keeping close contact with Jetune. If they don't know already that we've hit that base, they're going to find out soon."

Lissa nodded, and felt her hand wandering up towards her neck again. To distract herself, she flexed her fingers, but that felt eerily familiar and sent a tremor down her spine. She shook herself. "We'd better move fast."

Lance turned to the controls, hesitated, and turned back. "Are you sure you're ready?"

"We can't waste time," Lissa said.

"I know," he said, each word slow and careful, "but this is hurting you."

Lissa looked at him, and thought back to the way he had looked inside the Jetune base, wholly submerged in the heat of battle. She remembered his eyes registering her metallic ones and then the collar around her throat as he moved to pull the trigger. His state had not been so different from an Awakening, but instead of heartbeats, he had seen just one more Neo-Andromedan.

"Does that really matter?" she asked.

"Yes."

Lissa held his frank, open stare for a long moment. She thought she saw genuine concern there, but she wasn't certain if it was for her, or for her capacity to guide him through the Seventh Sun and help him cripple the organization from within.

Probably the latter, she thought.

Regardless, Lissa set a course to Sciyat, and then spent the journey resting. She managed to convince Lance to do the same, but they both agreed to take manual control for the last leg of the trip. When the time came, they slipped back into their seats at the controls, watching peaceful little Sciyat draw closer.

As Lance brought their speed down and set them on a course to coast, Lissa grew more and more certain that the Seventh Sun would want to strike this world.

Hanging in a quiet part of the galaxy, Sciyat was a small moon orbiting a much larger, gaseous planet, but it had the atmosphere for paradise, and the civilization that had sprung up was a serene one. Discovered on the heels of the

Andromedan War, Sciyat swiftly became the pinnacle of peace and cooperation, with species from all over the galaxy making up its population. Humans especially wanted to bite into something sweet after the bitter war, and they flocked to the planet, ready for serenity. The Star Federation kept a loose watch over the world, but the galaxy understood and respected the colony's significance, as did the Seventh Sun.

Unleashed on Sciyat, the Awakened would rip through the settlements and maybe even slake their hunger long before help could arrive from the Star Federation.

Lance seemed hyper-aware of the distance between Sciyat and its sources of support. He grew antsy as they drew closer to the world, and tried to calm himself by stretching and loosening his muscles before the touchdown, but he kept throwing nervous glances at the tracking system.

Lissa could not blame him. One human, one Neo-Andromedan, and two arkins were the only line of defense between Sciyat and a massacre. They both knew it, but while he was busy praying that they would get there in time, she was just hoping that Sciyat and the Star Feds would appreciate the effort.

As they made the final approach, Lance stood next to Lissa, one hand resting on the back of her seat, and the other on the control panel supporting his weight as he leaned forward. With her, he watched deep green and blue Sciyat swell across the tracking display, its giant parent planet burning yellow-green behind it. Most of Sciyat's settlements were concentrated on one side of the lunar world with a few pockmarks of civilization blooming across the rest of the surface.

"Where do you expect to find them?" Lance asked.

"Somewhere near the main settlements, but far enough to be out of the action when the time comes." She passed the datapad to him. "There were coordinates for a drop point in the last exchange between Sciyat and Jetune. I'm hoping they're somewhere around there."

"Only one drop point?" He studied the datapad for a

moment. "Is that really enough?"

"Maybe from Jetune," Lissa said. "I think you were right. They're probably not waiting on Awakened from just one base."

She felt Lance tense next to her. "Will taking out whoever's overseeing this operation stop all this?"

"It might."

"And if it doesn't?"

"Then there isn't much we can do."

He shot upright. "We have to do *some*thing."

"All we can do," Lissa said, glancing up at him and keeping her voice as calm as possible, "is run."

Lance looked back at her in grim silence.

"We're not guardians," she reminded him softly. "We're not saviors. We don't have an army. We only have us." She faced the controls again, but was acutely aware of him standing directly behind her, in a prime attack position. She fought off a shiver. "And we have our limits."

After a moment, Lance sank down into his seat, his grip hard on the edges of the datapad. Out of the corner of her eye, Lissa watched him struggle with the weight of those limits. For an instant, Ashburn the Star Fed returned, and with him came the refusal to believe that there was anything beyond his reach. Then he shook himself, and the last residual traces of his military rank were washed away by acceptance. With a resigned sigh, he put down the datapad and began to work the controls. "We can't fly in blind," he said. "We need to scan for some sign of the Seventh Sun." He shot her a pointed look. "And I don't think we're going to run into problems this time."

Lissa winced a little at the memory of the Ametria crash, but she knew he was right. Sciyat was not Ametria, and thanks to the Fangs, they now had a ship that could hide itself.

Min had given them the most advanced ship Lissa had ever seen. It wasn't built for heavy battle, more of a scouter than a fighter, but with the speed and the cloaking system combined with the reach and stealth of the ship's tracking signals, detection and dogfights were more than avoidable. A perfect ship for hunting.

Lissa and Lance worked together to sift through the data that poured in from the scans of Sciyat's surface. They had input a command for returns on areas with low power levels in hopes of narrowing their search, and were rewarded with a few buildings set up in more remote areas, mostly residential units. There were land and sky cruisers in these areas, but they managed to disentangle readings of a few starship signatures as well. Most of these were grounded close to the residential structures, but a few had touched down in unsettled areas, and these were the ones Lance and Lissa lingered over, going over each ship carefully before moving on to the next. They brought up visual displays, searching for some telltale sign on ship after ship, until Lance suddenly grabbed Lissa's arm and pointed at one of the images.

"It's that one," he breathed.

The starship in question sat near the center of a large clearing near the edge of a forest. There was a small cluster of homes not far from the location, too close for anyone's comfort, let alone covert Seventh Sun operations, but Lissa considered the vessel all the same. It was roughly triangular in shape with a shining white hull, a stark contrast against the green and brown ground beneath it.

"That looks like a human ship," she said.

"It's not," Lance said with solid certainty. "It's supposed to look like one of the old Earth designs, but humans never put airlocks there."

Lissa looked closer. The aerial view offered by the visual display revealed that there was nothing fancy about the ship, and it looked to be of an older, clunky design, but it was in decent condition and nothing seemed out of place. "What about the airlock?"

"It's too far back. Human designers always put airlocks in the middle for balance."

She frowned. It looked to be in the right place to her, but she was not an expert on airlock regulations for human-built starships. Then again, a lot of humans did have a keen thirst for symmetry. "Are you sure about this?"

"If there's one thing I learned as a Star Fed, it's how to tell when a guilty ship is trying to look innocent."

Lissa hoped that he was right.

As they headed for the area, they flew low and kept the scanners up, and the system began to pick up activity around the ship. There were people working on or near the ship, though Lissa could not tell how many there were for certain. If they were Seventh Sun agents, numbers did not matter. They all had to go.

After a few more minutes, Lissa gave Lance control of the ship and rose from her seat. "I need to take Orion," she said. "Blade can't fly."

Lance frowned at her and half-rose from his seat. "I should take him. I know how he flies."

"No, I need you on the ship," she said, turning away. "I trust you with the weapons systems more than myself. Hit them from the sky and give me room to work, but try not to damage the Sun's ship. I need to get in there and see if I can find anything."

"Lissa," he said, but when she turned back to him, there were no challenges in his eyes. "Be careful," he said.

She nodded, and called for Orion as she started for the airlock. The gray arkin hesitated long enough for Lance to gesture for him to go, then he scrambled after Lissa. Blade tried to follow, but Lissa bent over the arkin and whispered, "Not this time."

Blade whined when Lissa and Orion left the room without her, but she did stay, her bad wing hanging awkwardly off her side.

At the airlock, Lissa drew her enerpulse pistol and swung on to Orion's back. He unfurled his wings, letting her lay flat and loop her arm around his thick neck. He was larger than Blade, and even just standing still, Lissa could feel the flex of his muscles beneath her. Lissa moved a little further up on the arkin's back, adjusting to meet his natural balance, but not quite synching up the way she could with Blade.

Please heal, Blade, Lissa thought. *I need you.*

Lance's voice cracked over the ship's communication system. "Lissa, I have faces on the visuals. I can't tell who the leader is, but everyone down there has those black collars. I can see them."

Lissa swallowed past her own collar.

"I'm going to take out as many as I can," Lance continued, "then I'll open the outer airlock for you. I'll be firing freely so watch yourself when you move in, but that should give you some cover. I'm going to have to swing over the clearing and come in to land so I can't stay long, but I should give you time to get in close. Brace yourself for speed reduction." There was a small pause. "Safe flight, you two."

Lissa opened the ship's inner airlock and steered Orion inside. She moved the arkin to the forward wall, and he hissed and threw up his paw to push against it when the ship began to hemorrhage speed. They fought against the pressure, and then had to wait as the ship's pulse cannon fired off. Even on Orion's back, Lissa could feel the power coursing through the ship as the weapons deployed, and she bent lower against the arkin's neck, waiting.

Finally, Lance's voice rang out again. "Opening outer airlock in three... two... one..."

With a roar, the wind came charging into the airlock, buffeting Orion and scooping against his wings. He growled and pulled his wings in tighter, then surged forward and leaped out of the airlock. He let himself fall, then snapped his wings out and pulled into an easy glide.

Lissa was not prepared for the movement. It was not how Blade would have launched, and the difference jolted through her, but she recovered and bent low over Orion's back.

Lance had managed to slow the ship as much as he could, almost to the point of hovering, and was raining down shots on the ground near the white starship, cratering and scorching the soil. There were what looked like the burned remains of a few Seventh Sun agents, but there were still at least five live ones running around, trying to dodge the pulse cannons. One managed to get behind the ship and take off for the forest.

Lissa angled Orion towards the fleeing Seventh Sun agent, sailed in a wide arc around the concentration of Lance's fire, brought the arkin down low, and fired off a shot at the agent. Orion's rhythm threw her a little, and her shot hit low, burning into the agent's lower back. He went sprawling, and as Orion climbed back into the sky, Lissa glimpsed the agony on his face. Over her shoulder, she watched him drag himself towards the forest, collapse, try again, collapse again, and lay still.

Check him last, Lissa thought, but Orion grunted and pulled up short as an energy pulse from a rifle shot past him, and Lissa had to turn her attention back to the other agents.

She let Orion climb higher as she surveyed the scene again. It looked like there was only one agent left, the one who had fired at Orion, but he slipped under the belly of the Seventh Sun's starship and disappeared from sight.

Lance had already let up on the pulse cannon. He was struggling to keep the ship in place. The craft was rocking back and forth, trying to do what it had been built for and launch itself in a burst of speed. He needed to let it go, and after another short battle with the thrusters, he did just that. He let the ship streak over the clearing, but turned in a wide arc to come back it in for a landing. Lissa could not wait for that.

"All right, Orion," she said, raising her voice over the wind, and the arkin's ears twitched back towards her. "Bring it down, low and fast."

Orion grunted, twisted in the air, tucked in his wings, and dove towards the ground. Lissa huddled down against his neck, wind whipping her face and stinging her eyes. She could feel the drag against her clothes, but the ground rushed up to meet them at a dizzying speed all the same.

Lissa forced herself to keep her eyes open. If she had been riding Blade, she would have saved her vision, and let the arkin pull up when she needed to. She did not trust Orion to do the same, and sure enough, he pulled up a little sooner than she had anticipated.

As they shot towards the Seventh Sun's ship, Lissa urged

him closer to the ground, and tried to pick out the form of the agent crouched underneath.

Orion groaned a little, and Lissa felt him shift as he made to pull up and fly over the ship, but she leaned forward again and pushed his head back towards the ground. "Keep low," she shouted. "Hold steady."

Orion grunted but allowed himself to slip closer to the ground, wings spread in a hard, fast glide.

The wind ripped tears from Lissa's eyes, but she forced herself to keep them open. She saw the agent rise and turn towards Orion. She saw him raise an enerpulse rifle and take aim. Lissa threw up her own weapon, lined up the shot, waited for the extra shudder of Orion's flight pattern, and fired.

This time, she hit her target, and the Seventh Sun agent went down hard.

Orion shot under the belly of the ship, wingtips barely clearing the craft's hard-surface landing gear. He burst out of the shadow of the ship back out into the bright sunlight, Lissa clinging to his back. The arkin yipped in triumph, but Lissa only felt cold understanding.

This was easy. This was familiar. This was something she could do, and do very well.

Then there was a sharp pain at her neck, the world slipped out of focus, and she did not remember falling.

CHAPTER 29: BROKEN

The moment Lance had the starship on the ground, he leapt out of his seat and ran to the airlock. He dove out of the ship, paused long enough to sweep the area with the barrel of his enerpulse pistol, confirmed that there was no movement, and then sprinted to where Lissa lay. Orion came down out of the sky before Lance got there, crouching protectively next to her still form. Lance saw her move a little when the arkin nuzzled her, and relief flooded through him, but he kept running. He skidded to a halt when he reached her and dropped to his knees, pistol falling to the ground beside him.

Lissa had not fallen far, but it had been enough to stun her, and Lance quickly checked for broken bones. He did not find any, but he didn't trust himself to make a definite diagnosis, and from the way Lissa was looking beyond him rather than at him, he knew that there was something wrong that he could not help with.

"Can you hear me?" Lance asked, moving into Lissa's direct line of sight.

Lissa gave one very light, very slow nod.

"What happened? Did he throw you?"

Lissa shook her head very slowly. "Collar," she rasped out, reaching up to gently touch her neck. She was breathing hard, and Lance could see the unsteadiness of her vision, but he wasn't sure if that was from the fall or from whatever the collar had done to her.

She stayed on the ground for a few more moments, but began to shift a little. Lance helped her rise into a sitting position, warning her to go slow. She was focusing beyond him again, but this time, Orion glanced in the same direction, bared his fangs, and loosed a deep growl.

Lance looked up and saw two Seventh Sun agents moving out from under the white starship. They did not look like they had been involved in the initial fray, and must have been inside the ship when Lance had opened fire with the pulse cannon. Looking at them now, he thought that he understood why.

One of the agents was a woman. She was tall, thick and hard with muscle, with a square set to her jaw and a harsh light in her copper-colored eyes. She moved with a deliberate grace, surprisingly quick and sure-footed for her build, and she kept the barrel of her enerpulse rifle trained on Lance and Lissa. She was a private guard. Lance was certain of that.

Next to her, the man looked awkward and unimpressive. He was shorter than the guard, and heavier on his feet, but there was a bright spark behind his gunmetal eyes, and he considered Lance and Lissa the way he might have deliberated the best way to dispose of hazardous waste. He was the authority here. There was no mistaking that. In a low voice, the man said something to the woman in a language that Lance could not understand, and she shifted her hold on her weapon.

Behind the agents, Lance saw a shadow stir in the open airlock of the blue-gray starship and streak towards them, low and fast.

"Let's see now," the man said in Galunvo, loud and clear this time, staring directly at Lance. There was no shock, no fear, just the mild disgust of being forced to handle trash. "Ashburn, isn't it? The Star Federation officer. The one we ambushed at Ametria." He folded his arms over his chest, letting his eyes fall on Lissa, though there was no spark of recognition. "And you've conscripted one of our own, I see."

245

Lance felt Lissa tense, and he tightened his grip on her shoulder.

The man tossed his hand dismissively, vaguely gesturing at his fallen comrades and the destroyed ground. "This ultimately will not matter." He glanced at the woman, ready to say more, but caught movement out of the corner of his eye and turned to face it. He yelped in surprise, and took a step back.

Shadow-colored Blade pounced. She slammed into the shoulders of the man, tackling him into the dirt. She bounded off of him, twisted, sprang off the ground and came down hard on the man again. With a throaty growl, she closed her jaws over the arm he threw up to defend himself, and dragged him away.

Orion ran after them.

The final Seventh Sun agent watched for a stunned moment, her mouth open and her grip on her weapon slack. Then the hard set of anger flooded back in, and she swung the barrel of her rifle towards the arkins.

Lissa moved. She grabbed the enerpulse pistol Lance had dropped, whipped the barrel up, and fired.

The shot was wide, and only grazed the agent, but it was enough to throw her off balance. She howled and gripped her injured shoulder, but only for a moment. Hissing through the pain, she refocused back on Lance and Lissa, but Lance had already closed his hand over the enerpulse pistol and refocused the aim, and one quick shot was all that was needed.

By the time Lance had gotten Lissa to her feet, supporting most of her weight as he had on Daanhymn, the man had stopped screaming and the arkins were trotting back across the clearing, both of them stained with red. Lance tried not to focus on that as he helped Lissa back to their starship.

"We need... the data," she panted as they passed the Seventh Sun's ship.

"I know," he told her. "I'll take care of it."

Lissa shook her head. "You can't... read it."

"Neither can you in this state."

"Still better... than you."

Lance had to admit to himself that she had a point. He did not like the idea of her pushing herself after being drugged with what he could only hope were non-fatal tranquilizers, but he did not fight her on the issue and instead helped her into the Seventh Sun's ship.

Lance sent the arkins ahead of them, scouting for signs of life, but there was no one else on the ship, and they moved through the craft without any trouble past the difficulty of navigating the interior. The hull may have mimicked a human design, but the internal layout was anything but. They found the crew quarters where Lance had expected to find the control room, and the control room where a galley would have been on another ship.

After Lance helped her across the control room, Lissa sank gratefully into a seat. Under her bleary guidance, Lance accessed the main computer, rounded up as much data as he could, and transmitted it all to their starship. Then he wiped that transmission from the memory of the Seventh Sun's ship, helped Lissa to her feet, and steered her back outside.

She was a little steadier after the rest, Lance noticed, but was still having trouble focusing. In spite of that, she insisted on sitting with him in the control room and helping him make sure that all the data had come through. By the time they had finished, her eyes had slipped closed. With a panicked jolt, Lance checked her vitals, but was relieved to find that she was only sleeping. Lance carried her back to her room. He laid her gently on her cot and stood looking down at her for a long time.

Twice now, he had seen the Seventh Sun wipe away Lissa's strength and reduce the fast, deadly bounty hunter to something exhausted and vulnerable. If he wasn't afraid of the Seventh Sun now, then he knew that he was a fool. And yet, twice now, he had seen Lissa fight back.

She had been right earlier when she had said that they had their limits. But if he had to pick someone to test those limits alongside him, he would have chosen Lissa every time. But for now, he left her to sleep off whatever sedative the Seventh

Sun's collar had injected into her bloodstream. He could do nothing for her beyond that. He left her door open and the arkins to watch over her.

Back in the control room, Lance brought the ship off the ground, and pointed the craft away from Sciyat's surface and back out into space. They had nearly cleared the atmosphere when six starships came streaking towards the world, and from the visual display the tracking system gave him, Lance saw that those ships were unlike any design he had seen before, and yet there was an eerie familiarity to them. It eventually occurred to him that they resembled the fighter fleet that had attacked his soldiers at Ametria. Then he knew what they were, who was piloting them, and what they carried.

He considered sending a warning message to someone on Sciyat, but that would have hindered his and Lissa's escape, and given the Star Federation something to track. He and Lissa couldn't afford that, not while their trail was still unknown and they could stealth their way to safety.

He realized with a cold jolt that he was thinking like a hunter now, a thought pattern that the Star Federation should have driven out of him a long time ago. A true Star Fed would have turned the ship around and surrendered, would have gone after the Seventh Sun drop ships and opened fire on them and died in the battle, would have sent word back to Sciyat and revealed the blue-gray ship's location and signature, would have done anything except what Lance did. He angled the ship out into space, and put on speed.

We're not saviors, he remembered. *We don't have an army. We only have us.*

And all they could do was run.

CHAPTER 30: FALLEN

Rosonno was mulling over the latest file First Lit Sekorvo had sent to him regarding a potential Awakening candidate when a small, sharp surge of pain pricked at his throat. His hand shot to his neck reflexively, but in the instant before his fingertips hit the hard collar, he realized what that pain meant. Knowing was easier than accepting, however.

Slowly, Rosonno rose from his seat in his private quarters onboard his starship, turned away from the thin desk and his work, and stepped into the small washroom. He took a deep breath before glancing in the mirror, but he saw the change in his collar immediately.

One of the seven stars was no longer white, but dark red. It greedily drank in the light.

It had been agreed among the First Lit that they and they alone should know immediately when one of the Seventh Sun's leaders had fallen. Their collars were specially outfitted to monitor their heart rates, and when a First Lit's life stopped pulsing, the other collars pricked the remaining First Lit, and filled a star with their blood.

On Rosonno's collar, the third star from the right had turned deep red.

Tyrath, Rosonno thought with a small surge of panic, but

then he realized that his reflection had confused him. Tyrath's star was third from the left. Ereko's was the red one on the right.

His blood had spilled, and he was gone.

Rosonno stood looking at his collar for a long time. His own star was next to Ereko's, bright and white and full of life. First Lit Arrevessa's was on the other side of the dead one, right in the middle of the collar, and Tyrath's was the next one over. Then came Sekorvo and Niradessa, and Zeran was all the way back on the other end, next to Rosonno's star.

Rosonno had thought that he would be prepared to see a drop of red somewhere along the line of white, but that red was just too deep and too mesmerizing to be anything but unnerving. He swallowed, and the stars bobbed up and down, the red one glaring hard at him.

Be rational, Rosonno told himself, and he forced his feet to take him back into his quarters.

His work lay on his desk, organized into neat piles and carefully arranged to make access to data as quick and easy as possible. The floors were clean, the blanket on his bed was folded into tight, crisp lines, and everything was lit by a bright wash of pure, beautiful light. The light caressed the soft fabrics of his clothing and gleamed off the hard surfaces of his workspace, but it came into conflict at the communication terminal set into the corner of Rosonno's room, struggling to hold its own against the flashing red light that told him that the other First Lit wanted to talk. All six of them.

Five, he corrected himself, and for the first time, the collar around his throat felt just a little too tight.

Rosonno touched the communication terminal, and five holograms materialized before him. When he had spoken to Tyrath, the single hologram had projected her in her full height, but with all of the First Lit in conference, Rosonno was offered only cropped views of their faces and shoulders. He had never liked this feature of the communication terminals; it was difficult to see telling facial ticks and fidgeting hands were always obscured, though with Ereko gone, the holograms were a little larger, and it was a little bit easier to read the moods of the other First Lit as they rushed through the customary greeting.

Niradessa was openly distressed, eyes darting in wild patterns as she glanced from face to face on her own terminal.

Zeran looked nervous, as though he expected his own heart to give out and fill another star with blood.

Sekorvo seethed with silent rage and his jaw was tight, almost as if trying to cage a scream within his body.

Tyrath was confused, and her hand kept slipping up to touch the red star on her own collar.

Arrevessa was the only calm one, stoic and silent with her fingers steepled before her mouth, not looking at any of the other First Lit, but simply frowning lightly at something Rosonno could not see.

"Was it the Star Federation?" Niradessa demanded the moment the greetings had concluded. "Did they learn too much from Daanhymn?"

"No," Zeran cut in, his voice fluty and almost breathless. "There was no intel on the first strike to be gathered from the Daanhymn facility. They would never have known where to find Ereko. Or any of us." He shook his black hair out of his eyes and licked his thin lips. At that moment, his mouth was uncomfortably red against his fair skin. "Hopefully," he added under his breath.

Arrevessa's silver eyes shifted up for a moment, beautifully bright against her dark tawny brown skin, but she said nothing and allowed her gaze to slip away again.

"Even if they somehow did find out," Tyrath put in, dropping her hand away from her collar with a strong gesture of finality, "Ereko had already called for several Awakened, and their drop ships would have reached the upper atmosphere of Sciyat at the time of his death. The first strike should be underway." Her brows slashed into a deep frown. "Unless those ships were intercepted?"

"They've reached their destination and completed the drop," Arrevessa said. She did not speak loudly, but so seldom were her interjections that they always rang with severity, and silenced followed her voice. "Our sleeper agents helped them breach the skies without trouble. The Awakened are on the surface, and the first strike has officially begun." She shifted a little in her seat, and brushed her fingers thoughtfully against her chin. "The Star Federation did not know. We may proceed as planned."

"But who killed Ereko?" Sekorvo demanded, folding his arms over his broad chest with an odd, coiling motion. His jaw came back to the square, firm set as soon as he finished speaking, clenched so tight that Rosonno could see the outline of his jaw hinge underneath his bronze skin. His nose slashed in a hard line down his face, and his eyes burned hot copper chipped with icy blue under his heavy brow.

Not for the first time, Rosonno thought that Sekorvo's eyes looked like they yearned to be touched by the light of an Awakening, and if it wasn't for his duties as a First Lit, the man might have eagerly stepped into a machine. Perhaps the Seventh Sun could use an Awakened First Lit in the future, but not today.

"Do you think someone just found him?" Niradessa asked. "Just saw what he was and killed him?"

"That is a possibility every Neo-Andromedan has always lived with," Zeran quipped, a bit too eager to latch on to any explanation.

"I suppose that's true," Rosonno said. "And ever since the Star Feds went public with the Ametria attack, galactic media has been buzzing all over the return of the Neo-Andromedan."

"As if we'd ever left," Niradessa grumbled, pushing golden wisps of her hair out of her eyes.

"Panics like the ones that sparked during the Andromedan War are bound to resurface," Rosonno continued. "But we've always known that. The Star Feds could initiate a purge, and that will fully ignite civilian hostilities. The pattern will be exactly the same as it was during the war. We knew that going in. All of us did."

"So you really think Ereko was killed by hostile civilians?"

Tyrath asked.

"No," Arrevessa cut in before Rosonno could respond. She shifted her gaze back to the communication terminal, and her eyes gleamed with something unfathomable. "I doubt that he does."

Rosonno did not know how to respond, so he only waited for Arrevessa to continue. She did so by reaching for something outside of her hologram projection, and then a small light on the communication terminal flashed green. Rosonno accepted the incoming transmission, and a recording of Ereko flared into focus, pushing the hologram projections of the First Lit off to the sides.

The recording was a communication transmission Ereko had sent to Arrevessa, and it showed him talking through the final preparations his scout team had made for the attack on Sciyat, rattling their activities off with clinical boredom as he prepared his ship to leave the surface. Arrevessa's voice cut in to ask a question, and Ereko responded with the same flat tone. When the shouting started, he did not seem to hear it, and it was only when the heavy, booming fire of an enerpulse cannon sounded that his words slipped into silence, and he looked over his shoulder. He stood like that for a long time, listening to the sounds of a battle that never should have found him, frozen until an agent suddenly appeared to tell him that a single starship had attacked, and that someone on an arkin had jumped out of the airlock of said starship.

Rosonno's grip on his communication terminal slipped, and he saw Tyrath jerk up sharply.

The recording showed that First Lit Ereko did not ask questions. He only stepped away from the computer terminal, and he did not come back. Instead, a man and a woman came to the terminal in his place a few minutes later, and Rosonno felt his heart stop.

"That's all you need to see," Arrevessa said, cutting across the audio, and the First Lit closed the recording. "They took data from the ship, how much and what kind I cannot say, but they have it now." She shifted in her seat, facing her communication terminal squarely, silver eyes burning bright. "Are they angry civilians, First Lit Rosonno?"

"No," he said, and his breath scraped through his throat.

"That's Arrilissa," Sekorvo cut in, "isn't it?"

Rosonno nodded, not trusting himself to speak.

"And Fleet Commander Lance Ashburn," Niradessa added. "So Arrilissa has defected to humans?"

"I think Ashburn defected to her," Arrevessa said, and there was a briskness to her now, a need to get through the business at hand as quickly as possible. "My people caught wind that he'd been expelled from the Star Federation and declared a Beta not too long ago. They thought he'd just snapped under the strain we put on him and cut and run on his own, but it looks like he met up with Lissa somewhere."

"Daanhymn," Rosonno said weakly. "He must have picked her up from Daanhymn."

"And the last time they were together," Arrevessa said quietly, "the Ametria base was destroyed. Now, one of the First Lit is dead, and we have to assume that our safety has been compromised."

There was a heavy silence.

"What do we do now?" Niradessa finally asked, her voice husky with uncertainty.

Arrevessa considered this for a long time. "We proceed as planned." Rosonno shook his head, and two of the First Lit began to voice their disapproval, but Arrevessa held up her hand. "It is far too late to step back. We need to watch the Star Federation. We track their movements, and when the time is right, we attack. We have come too far to do anything less. We owe it to ourselves and to our people, whether they wear the collar or not.

"Lissa and Ashburn pose a problem, yes, but we can prepare for them now. If they wish to hunt us, let them come. There is a chance our next strike will scare them away for good, but if not…" She steepled her fingers once again and settled her eyes on one of the projections before her, and Rosonno's skin crawled; he knew she was looking at him.

"You're our expert on Lissa, First Lit Rosonno. Do you know how to handle her this time?"

Rosonno swallowed hard, and felt the grip of the collar around his throat, usually so comforting but now tight and heavy with the weight of a dead star. "I know how to kill her."

"Then do it," Arrevessa said, "before she causes any more trouble."

Rosonno nodded stiffly, and one by one, the First Lit disconnected. Tyrath was the last to go, lingering just a moment longer and on the verge of saying something, but then she, too, flickered out of sight.

There was a hard lump in Rosonno's throat, and his breath was raging through his lungs, but he tried to stay calm. He tried, and he failed. With an angry shout, he lurched away from the communication terminal, found his work desk, and raked his arm over the surface, sending the neat array of datapads arcing through the air and clattering to the floor. He slammed his fists on the desk, breathing hard, and squeezed his eyes shut.

She wasn't supposed to survive Daanhymn, his mind screamed, and the thought echoed back over and over again inside his skull. *She shouldn't be alive.*

But she was, and now she threatened everything.

Rosonno tried to tell himself that she was just one person, and it did not matter if she had one rogue Star Fed with her, but he found no comfort there. He knew that the Seventh Sun was prepared to deal with armies. They were ready to take on the Star Federation and meet them head-on, and they were ready to avenge those wrongs committed during the Andromedan War. But they were not ready to be hunted. For all of Arrevessa's calm certainty, Rosonno knew that the First Lit would not survive the hunting game, and he knew that if Lissa found them, she would kill them.

The Seventh Sun had to find her first.

Straightening up and catching his breath, Rosonno smoothed back his hair and brushed a few wrinkles out of his clothes. He picked his datapads up off the floor, rearranged them into neat, straight lines on his desk, and then stepped back to his communication terminal. He reached out to Syreth's control team, and gave them their latest and quite possibly final assignment, though he did not tell them that.

CHAPTER 31: PROMISE

The battle on Sciyat raged for the better part of a sidereal day, and the Star Federation suffered a shameful number of casualties given the size of the opposing Nandro force. Losses on the civilian side were much higher, and once the threat was neutralized, Erica found herself anxiously waiting for the list of names of the dead alongside her soldiers.

A peaceful, idyllic world deep within Star Federation territory, Nandros never should have set foot on Sciyat, and yet they had come. From what Erica understood, there had been a small wave of drop ships that had let loose demonic Nandros in the most heavily populated settlements. There had not been a lot of them, five or six per drop ship, but they had ripped through the civilian population and crippled the Sciyati police force before the Star Federation had even caught wind of the attack.

When the first wave of soldiers had arrived, they had buffed up the defensive lines and beaten back most of the Nandros, even killing a few, but there were some Nandros that had not been accounted for, and they had wormed their way past the defensive lines to continue feeding their bloodlust.

By the time Erica had arrived, most of the surviving civilians in the targeted settlements had been evacuated off-planet, and the grounded soldiers were holding strong in the cities, though they had seemed confused.

"We have a couple of Nandros that keep coming back to pick at the lines," a major had informed Erica, "but it's like some of the others just switched off. We got a report from the next city over that said they found two Nandros sitting dazed in the middle of a bunch of bodies, like they had no idea what they were doing there."

"Were those Nandros taken alive?"

The major had shaken his head. "Too risky. You should've seen what they were doing before they shorted out."

But Erica got an idea of it when one of the Nandros came back to harass the soldiers. It did not stand a chance against the line of enerpulse fire, but the way it moved was otherworldly. It was too fast and too fluid, spinning and dodging around shots, weaving closer, ever closer to the soldiers, until one shot landed between its blazing, metallic eyes, burning away the flesh and dropping the body with a solid *thud*.

After that, Erica had led the soldiers on a cautious offensive, and though another Nandro got the jump on them, they successfully fended it off, and reclaimed the streets.

Now, Erica was receiving the "all clear" message from the other targeted cities, and she focused on directing the fresh waves of soldiers to either take up guard posts in the untouched settlements or assist with the cleanup efforts in the damaged ones. Slowly, the list of casualties was growing, and unable to bear the suspense, Erica put out a special inquiry after her sisters and their families. The news that they were all alive and well was a welcome relief, and Erica could concentrate on the tasks at hand more easily.

She sent a transmission to the Star Federation space station, informing the admiralty board that the Nandro threat had been subdued, and Sciyat was secure once again. Though she spoke the words with confidence, they rang hollow in Erica's ears.

They should never have come here, she kept thinking. *Not here.*

Peaceful, beautiful Sciyat. Far under the wings of the Star Federation. Home to countless retired officers and many military families. It was the last place the Nandros should have attacked, and yet it was the first.

And that battle had reminded Erica and her soldiers that for all their training and experience, they were still vulnerable because those that they fought to protect could still be hurt.

Erica forced herself to concentrate on the recovery efforts, making sure that the evacuees were safe. There was not a large amount of destruction in cities themselves—just a few damaged areas from light pulse cannon fire that the Nandro drop ships had loosed upon arrival and departure—and once the soldiers were certain that the Nandros were really gone and the unstable buildings had all been closed off, they allowed the civilians to return. Erica ordered a firm Star Federation presence to remain, however. She did not trust the Nandros to stay in hiding for long, and she would not take any chances.

Of course, what she did not expect was the broadcast from the Seventh Sun.

They took over the news wavebands, cutting out the video and releasing only an audio message, but that was more than enough to terrify the population of Sciyat all over again.

"Sciyat was only the beginning," the broadcast scraped out in perfect Galunvo. "We will rise above the darkness that the rest of the galaxy tried to drown us in. We will walk free of the shadows, and blaze forth with new life. Our light is strong and unbroken, and we will outshine all else. We will make the galaxy pay for the suffering thrust upon the Neo-Andromedan race. We are the Seventh Sun, and we will avenge our fallen. We will destroy the Star Federation. Nothing can stand against us, and nothing can outrun our light. We will burn on, or we will drown you in the dark."

The broadcast ended, leaving grim, bewildered silence in its wake.

"Find out where that came from," Erica ordered once she'd found her voice again. "Trace it as far as you can." She turned to a new soldier. "Send a message to the Daanhymn

259

salvage team. Tell them to double down on their efforts. I want information, and I want it now." Another new soldier. "Contact the main station, tell the Intelligence Unit that we need a full team on Nandro language translation. Relay everything we have on the Nandros back to them immediately."

With sharp salutes, the soldiers jumped to their respective tasks, and Erica went back to overseeing the rehabilitation of the lunar world and trying to keep the civilian population under control. Hysterics were breaking out, and though Erica could not blame them, she knew that scared, frantic civilians could lead to riots, and they could not afford that. Martial law was put into effect, and an eerie quiet descended on Sciyat as the first night of the curfew settled in.

Erica listened to reports coming in from around the lunar world. Most of the patrols had no trouble with their sectors, and said that all was quiet, but a few had needed to deal with rebellious individuals and a few small but very vocal groups demanding more information on the Nandros and the Star Federation's plans for them. The soldiers had taken care of the trouble easily enough, but Erica did not like disturbances coming so early.

She could almost smell the fear of the Sciyati population, rank and thick on the wind, but more than anything, she felt how heavy the world was with life.

Late that night, alone in the private quarters that had been set up for her in an embassy building on Sciyat's surface, Erica sat on her cot, exhaustion seeping into her bones and a headache beating behind her eyes. *All these people,* she thought as she massaged her temples, *and all the ones out among the stars. We have to protect them all. We have to stand firm. We have to.*

But they could not do that if they did not go on the offensive. The Star Federation had officially declared war, but that was not enough.

Rising, Erica moved to the communication terminal that had been set up for her. Activating it, she sent a quick broadcast to the main space station, informing the admiralty board that she was co-authorizing a purge of Neo-Andromedans. She was informed that she was the sixth fleet commander to co-sign Keraun's petition that day, and though that was more than was needed, Erica was glad to know that she was not alone.

She fell asleep that night comfortable in the knowledge that she had done the right thing, and would be able to serve the galaxy far better now that she and the rest of the Star Federation could strike at the Nandros aggressively.

Stand and Protect, she thought as her eyes slipped closed.

CHAPTER 32: MIRAGE

Yuna was dead. There was no other way to describe it.

Jason had never been to the planet before, but he had heard of a world covered in rolling sand dunes, peeping rock formations, and one bitter, toxic oasis that life stubbornly clung to, refusing to die no matter how harsh the conditions became. The Yunis had learned to tame the oasis, to separate life from death in the water and keep themselves alive. That was over now.

Standing on a deserted, private starship port that jutted over a deep, crumbling valley that had once been filled with water, Jason looked down and wondered what this world had truly been like before the oasis had died.

The wind was hot and relentless, picking up sprays of fine, white gold sand and sending small clouds tumbling and falling into the valley. At the very bottom of the pit was a small, acrid pool, but that had shrunk visibly since Jason's arrival, and sand was slowly piling into it. Already, the desert was filling the void, repairing the scar left behind by the Seventh Sun.

"Water killers," one of the few remaining Yunis had told Jason when he had arrived. The Yuni had been an old, frail man, barely able to walk but more than able to cut and sear with words. "They tried to take the planet, and when we fought back, they turned on our heart." The old man went on to describe what he called the rain of white fire.

Most of the visitors to Yuna had simply turned tail and fled after regaining control over the main ground port, but some had stayed to pick another fight. A few Seventh Sun starships had converged on the city, blasting into oblivion those that had tried to stand against them, while agents on the ground had slipped a machine into the oasis, and it had eaten the water. The Seventh Sun had stayed to nurture it along, and then slipped away when there was no hope of recovering the oasis, long before the Star Federation had arrived.

"They did something to accelerate the surface evaporation of the water," a lieutenant had confirmed to Jason. "But that wouldn't have been enough to drain the oasis this fast. We think they really did send some sort of machine into the water, and that it dived down and somehow redirected the flow of the underground spring feeding the oasis."

"That's a hell of a thing to do," Jason had muttered back. "How were there no distress calls until now?"

The lieutenant had shifted uneasily. "There are reports of distress calls from Yuna dating back almost a full sidereal month," he had said, his voice low. "With the territory reassignment, there's been some... delays."

"We begged for help," the old Yuni man had cut in, glaring at Jason from underneath his protective scarf. "We prayed for you star guardians to answer our calls, but you never came." His expression was unfathomable, concealed by the fabric wrapped around his face to keep out the sand, but his eyes were dark, glittering, and angry.

"We're here now," Jason had said.

"Too late," the old Yuni had spat. "Nothing to do now. When we realized you weren't coming, those of us who could leave, did. The rest of us will die with our heart. We will be worn away by the sands, buried and forgotten until the winds see fit to dig us back up."

Jason had put out an order to evacuate the planet and get as many Yuni civilians to safety as possible, but that old man and a few other Yunis, a good number of them elderly, refused to go. When the soldiers had been on the brink of force, the Yunis had stepped out of the city and melted into the desert. The soldiers had not found them. Jason had called off the search and let them go, focusing as much as he could on the remaining survivors of the population.

Major Miyasato and the other medical officers had done what they could, providing rations of clean water where it was most needed and doing their best to ease suffering where it would have gone to waste.

"This is so hard," Jason overheard a medic say to Miyasato after a particular Yuni had succumbed to death after a long, drawn-out fight.

"This is war," Miyasato had returned grimly. "Nothing about it is supposed to be easy."

Jason felt the true sting of those words a short while later when word of the attack on Sciyat reached them. An attack of that magnitude was enough to warrant the knowledge of all Star Federation soldiers, but outside of the briefing passed along by another one of Keraun's captains, most of the information came from news broadcasts picked up during the long, midday hours when the soldiers rested and waited out the worst of the glaring heat of Yuna's sun. The soldiers stood and sat huddled around the communication terminals, listening with joyless faces to the news, and while a lot of them were having a hard time believing that a few Neo-Andromedans had caused so much damage, they spoke with pain and confusion strung tight across their voices.

Jason listened to the reports with his soldiers, and said nothing.

He knew that he wasn't the only Star Fed with family on Sciyat, but his rank had allowed for an immediate inquiry after his family. Ranae, Tomás, and their children were all alive, though Tomás had been badly injured by stray enerpulse fire at the beginning of the attack. His condition had stabilized quickly, however, and he was expected to make a full recovery. Many, many others had not been as fortunate. Slowly but surely, names were being matched to faces on the casualties list.

Jason watched the heavy toll this took on his soldiers, but he received his own stinging slap when the media suddenly turned on him. They brought up his memorial speech, juxtaposed the audio with images from Sciyat, and ripped him apart.

"What is wrong with this man?" one broadcaster snapped, his face a rigid mask of anger. "He wants us to put ourselves and our families in danger because he thinks there are a few innocent Nandros hiding somewhere out there?" He shook his head disgustedly. "I think not!"

One of the soldiers switched the frequency to a less aggressive broadcast, but all of Jason's subordinates suddenly had a very hard time looking at him, and the ones that had transferred over from Keraun's squads glared at him with open hostility.

Finally unable to stand any more, Jason slipped back outside into Yuna's blinding, blazing heat. He had donned a pair of goggles and wrapped his face and head with protective scarves, shielding himself against the worst of the sun and sand, but he still felt dry and scratchy as he walked through the skeletal city, the hot winds cutting across the quiet with breathy, mischievous whistles.

Back at the private starship port overhanging the remains of the oasis, Jason stood on the flat, hard surface, feeling the wind tug and play with the loose ends of his scarves. His mouth was dry and his tongue felt swollen, and even with the scarf over his nose and mouth, each breath had a gritty feel. He had a container of fresh water with him, and he was acutely aware of its weight in his hand, but he couldn't bring himself to drink.

Instead, he had a wild, desperate urge to take his water and all the water that had come with the Star Federation and dump it into the oasis. Pure, fresh water to replace the bitter, toxic water the Seventh Sun had destroyed. But he knew that was a stupid fantasy. He could dump all the water he wanted to into

Yuna, but it would not have mattered. In the end, the pure water would have just mixed with the bad, muddling all the good intentions that had come with it and draining out all the same. All that would have left him with was no drinking water and a ruined throat.

Staring down at the oasis, Jason's thoughts drifted to Ashburn and the Shadow. He wondered where they were, if Ashburn had ever found her, if they were even still alive. He had heard nothing about them, and so he had to hope that they were out there, doing something, anything, but that did not stop him from wondering if he had done the right thing after all.

Good intentions swirling into a pool of toxicity, and being lost forever.

Wind whipping around him, Jason looked out across the dying oasis. The water had drained noticeably since his last visit, and heat shimmered through the air. It bent the light and made the buildings on the far side of the oasis dance and twist and finally disappear.

CHAPTER 33: TRUTH

Vinterra missed Daanhymn. It wasn't until the forced evacuation and relocation of her research team that she had actually labeled the planet "home", but the more she thought about it, the more Daanhymn had felt like home. It was a foolish thought, she knew. Daanhymn was a dying world, and as the years ground on, it would have become more and more inhospitable, and she would have needed to leave it all the same. But at least she would have had the time to say goodbye. Now, instead of bittersweet farewells, forced abandonment punctured her heart, and she felt as though she were stranded in space. She was lost in the void, struggling to catch the shattered pieces of her life before they drifted too far away from her reaching fingertips.

The First Lit were making it all the harder to catch the shards.

After the evacuation, Vinterra, Haelin, and the surviving members of the Daanhymn team had been temporarily relocated to another outpost, but their new assignments had come racing in almost as soon as their starships had touched down, and right on the tails of those messages had come the individual conferences with First Lit Niradessa via the outpost's long-range communication terminal.

Vinterra did not know what First Lit Niradessa had told the other Daanhymn survivors, but her instructions to Vinterra had been perfectly clear: as far as anyone was concerned, Candidate Arrilissa had not survived the Awakening process, and the exposure of the Daanhymn base to the Star Feds was intentional. The Seventh Sun was leading the Star Federation into a trap, a preliminary distraction before the first strike. The Daanhymn teams, including her research assistants, were being reassigned, and to far better positions as reward for their hard work.

"And what about those who died by Lissa's hand?" Vinterra had asked.

First Lit Niradessa had smiled sadly, lines of regret neatly folding into her round, gentle face. Her golden hair was drawn up into a pile on the crown of her head, but a few wisps hung in loose curls against her pink skin, and her upturned eyes, silver shot through with green, were large and round with remorse. "Their deaths were tragic, but we must ensure they did not die in vain. The old truth will only bring panic and disorder. Our people believe that the dead had volunteered to stay behind and make it appear that the base had not been abandoned. They lured the Star Feds in further, and allowed our trap to catch its targets." The First Lit's eyes had held Vinterra's in a vice grip. "This is the truth of what happened on Daanhymn."

Vinterra had felt a thousand different protests rise to her tongue, but she had bitten them back. For all of Niradessa's sweet, tender showmanship, Vinterra had sensed a ruthless core, and she had not wanted to crack the First Lit open to find it.

"As for you," Niradessa had continued, and a little too much of the sadness had dripped out of the First Lit's eyes like water shaken from fingertips, "we have an opening on Daraax Beta. You'll be working directly under First Lit Tyrath, as per her request. She's very interested in the work that you did with the Daanhymn flowers and would like to apply that on a large scale to the Awakened in stasis." Niradessa had rolled her shoulders in a lazy shift of weight, and looked at Vinterra as though too much time had been wasted on her already. "If you decline this assignment, we may be hard-pressed to find other work for you."

Vinterra could not decide which sounded more unpleasant: working with the Awakened again, or a vague threat against disobedience. Ultimately, however, she had accepted the assignment.

In truth, Vinterra was ready to throw herself into any kind of work. She wanted to carry close her memories of Daanhymn, but she wanted to forget them, too. The sunsets, the flowers, the glowing pollen rising on the wind to dance with the stars across the night skies, those were the memories she wanted to keep. Everything else could be cast aside. Just as Haelin had done to her.

"Just go!" Vinterra had screamed when Haelin had come to say that she had been given the chance to serve the Seventh Sun far better than she ever could have on Daanhymn, and without another word, Haelin had gone.

Vinterra had cried for a long time, even after she had fled from her temporary quarters in the outpost, unable to stay in that room and feel the space Haelin had filled. She had hoped that the fresh air would help calm her, but she had kept looking at the ground and not seeing blue flowers and everything had just felt wrong. By the time she had dried her tears, Haelin's ship had left, and Vinterra had turned her focus to her new assignment, requesting data from Daraax Beta and trying to get an early grip on the tasks that awaited her.

First Lit Tyrath was enthusiastic about working with the few pollen samples from Daanhymn that remained, and wanted Vinterra to head the team that would create and introduce the new stabilizers to the in-stasis Awakened. The work promised to be long and complex, but Vinterra needed that now.

When her transport starship arrived at the outpost, Vinterra gathered up her few meager possessions and set out for her new life on Daraax Beta. It was a long journey across the galaxy, and Vinterra filled it with studying. She forged a mild friendship with another agent who was concerned about the amount of food—or lack thereof—that Vinterra was eating, and he took it upon himself to ensure that she ate something at least twice a day, even if they were light meals. He was openly friendly and seemed to tell good stories, but Vinterra had trouble listening and did not remember half of what he told her. He didn't seem to mind, but outside of mealtimes, he left her alone and sought out better company. When the ship reached Daraax Beta, he and Vinterra said a pleasant goodbye, and then never saw each other again as he went with the ship to the next destination, and she disembarked.

Daraax Beta was a grim world. It had an austere sort of beauty, with sweeping rock formations and oceans lapping toxic purple-blue beneath a dark sky, but life had never lived on this world, and never would have if the Seventh Sun had not shed its light upon the surface. If Vinterra wanted to walk outside, she needed a pressurized suit and a small team to go with her, for the danger of being lost to the silent wilderness was far too high for solitary journeys. Few agents ever went out on the land, and Vinterra quietly slipped into daily routines alongside them, spending most of her days inside the facility.

Built on a plain, the Daraax Beta building was as somber and unornamented as the world it stood on. It was only two stories tall on the surface, and at first glance seemed only twice the size of the Daanhymn base, but at the center, the Seventh Sun had drilled into the surface of the planet, and carved out a spiraling chamber that reached deep into the ground and held shadows firmly in its grasp. Lights ran all the way from the surface to the very bottom, but even with the few thousand Awakened held in stasis at Daarax Beta and the handful of others that were prowling the galaxy on special operations, there were not enough Awakened currently in existence to fill the chamber, and a solid pool of darkness sat at the base.

Vinterra did not think she could hate anything more than the screams of the Awakening trials, but at least those had been heavy with life. The bottom of the chamber was dead and empty, and whenever she had to descend to work on one of the Awakened, she did her very best not to look down.

The Awakened themselves were another spike of coldness in Vinterra's heart. Even if the holding chamber was not filled to capacity, there were still more Awakened here than she had ever seen in her life, and in her early days on Daraax Beta, shivers chased each other up and down her spine. Though they had their eyes shut, though they were locked in their individual pods, though they posed no real danger to her, Vinterra kept looking at their faces, and wondering how hot their eyes burned behind their closed lids. Eventually, she learned to look at the Awakened without seeing them, and just focus on the numbers the stasis pods spat out.

First Lit Tyrath drifted through the stasis facility like a dream vibrating on the edge of a nightmare. She was polite enough to the workers, Vinterra included, but there was no familiarity with her, and she expected nothing short of the best. She occasionally asked Vinterra how work on the pollen studies was going, and offered her access to whatever resources she required, though they needed to wait for the Star Feds to lose interest in Daanhynm before they could collect more pollen. When Vinterra asked for a special piece of equipment that needed to be imported from off-world, however, First Lit Tyrath personally delivered it to her within a single sidereal day.

"Don't be afraid to ask for anything else you might need," the First Lit told Vinterra as she handed over the package containing the delicate tool. "We need these Awakened ready for the main assault, and I need you to do everything you can to help them along."

"Of course," Vinterra nodded, and as the First Lit glided away, she turned back to her work.

She had found Haelin's note on the morning of her second day at Daraax Beta. It had taken her a few minutes to muster up the courage to read it, and then it had taken her even longer to blink away the tears that had blurred her vision. She had not yet calmed the anger that had sparked after the tears had gone. It now burned deep in her belly, and although she suppressed it, kept the flame down to a low flicker, she would not extinguish it.

The Seventh Sun had taken Haelin away, and put her in an Awakening machine. If Vinterra had been stationed anywhere else, she might never have learned Haelin's final fate, but on Daraax Beta, full access to the results of Awakening trials throughout the galaxy were at her fingertips. Vinterra dared not look up Haelin's results directly for fear of Tyrath or another agent realizing what she was doing, and the time it took to casually stumble upon the data from the base Haelin had been sent to was agony, but Vinterra did eventually learn that Haelin had been successfully Awakened, and survived long enough to be put into stasis.

Getting her transferred to Daraax Beta was all too simple. All Vinterra had to do was mark Haelin and a few other Awakened as good test subjects for the developing Daanhymn pollen drug, slip that list to one of her more disinterested colleagues, and watch as her list was approved in full. The marked Awakened were put en route to Daraax Beta shortly thereafter, and Vinterra settled in to wait as patiently as she could for Haelin's arrival.

Vinterra kept the knowledge of Haelin's transfer even closer to her heart than the memories of Daanhymn, letting it burn through her with hope. The time would come for her to let the flame rage into an inferno, but until that moment, she had to bide her time a little bit longer, and wait.

Until then, there was work to be done.

CHAPTER 34: SPEED

When Lissa woke, the memory of Sciyat was sharp and clear up to a point, but then it dissolved into a hazy blur. She did remember that the fight had been quick with most of the Seventh Sun's agents falling to the pulse cannons of the starship, and she had taken out one, maybe two, on her own, but the final one had fallen to a leaping shadow.

Lissa sat up, groaning with the effort. She waited for her head to clear, but there was a persistent dull throb at the back of her brain. She was exhausted, but hated the thought of going back to sleep.

The lights in the room came up as she moved, and she blinked against the brightness, glancing around to gather her bearings. She winced a little when she saw the wash of light gray around her, and when she reached up, her fingers brushed the collar, but it slowly dawned on her that she was in her private quarters onboard the starship. She could see the outline of the storage compartment sunk into the wall where she kept her spare clothing, and on the wall behind her was a projected display of their current galactic location, travel speed, and destination coordinates.

Most importantly of all, Blade lay next to Lissa's cot. She was dozing, but the moment Lissa swung her legs over the edge of the cot, the arkin's eyes slipped open and she pushed herself to her feet.

Lissa ran her hands over Blade's fur, remembering the leaping shadow. "I'm not leaving you behind again," she murmured.

Blade blinked at her.

"Leaping shadow," Lissa whispered.

Blade nuzzled into her fingers, and Lissa felt the dampness of the arkin's fur. A few hairs stuck to Lissa's skin when she pulled her hands away. Blade had been bathed recently.

Slowly, Lissa got to her feet. She was still in the traveler's clothes that she had worn on Sciyat, and there were streaks of dirt smashed into the fabric, but she had no desire to change just yet.

With Blade by her side, Lissa moved out of her quarters. She rinsed her face with cool water in the washroom, and found a few clumps of black and gray arkin hair that had not been washed away. They stuck to the floor and the walls, defying whatever effort had been put towards cleaning them. There was a strange comfort in seeing them. Tiny little frustrations that did not matter, but still made up the details of life outside the cycle of hunting and running and hunting again.

Lissa drifted to the control room after that, and found Lance sitting with Orion, slowly rubbing the arkin's ear and staring thoughtfully at nothing in particular. He did not realize Lissa had entered the room until she slipped into the seat next to his. Then he jumped a little and half-rose, but she waved him off.

"How do you feel?" he asked as he sank back down.

"Tired," she said. She stretched, winced, dropped her arms. "Sore."

"Thirsty?" he asked, reaching for a ration of water near his feet.

Lissa accepted the container gratefully.

"You went down pretty hard," Lance said, watching her sip the lukewarm water. "I found a mediscan to check for broken bones, and that came up negative, but I'm worried there might be something I overlooked."

"So, what? You're taking me to see a doctor?"

"I thought Dr. Chhaya might be able to help." He made a tentative gesture. "Especially with the collar. If that thing is pumping stuff into your bloodstream, it's not safe for either of us to try to take it off."

Even through the truth of that statement, Lissa saw the bigger danger. She tensed, wary of Lance all over again. "It's not safe for us to go back to Phan, either," she told him softly.

Lance grimaced and turned to the controls. "I think the Star Federation is going to be focusing their attention elsewhere for a while." He brought up one of the galaxy-wide broadcast bands on the communication system, and news reports filled the ship.

Whoever they had killed on Sciyat had not mattered in the end. The Seventh Sun's attack still came, and the reports mentioned particularly vicious Neo-Andromedans ripping through heavily populated areas. The attacks had targeted civilian-heavy spots, and by the time Star Federation support had arrived, a devastatingly large number of people were dead, and the Seventh Sun had not-so-quietly retreated back into space. They had left a message for the Star Federation. It was the first of two messages, this one recorded at the time of arrival.

"This is only the beginning," a visual recording of a Seventh Sun agent informed the galaxy, gesturing to the havoc wrought on Sciyat. "The Star Federation tried to purge us once, and they failed. Now, it's our turn. We will destroy the Star Federation, and then we will sweep across the galaxy until our light has touched every world, every race, and every life. We are the Seventh Sun, and we burn brighter than all." She grinned wickedly. "Welcome to the Light."

After that, the news broadcast centered on Star Federation retaliation, namely the official initiation of a purge by all but one of the Star Federation's ten fleet commanders. Two of the officers that had signed off were given special attention: Keraun, who had first initiated the purge, and Anderson, the

Star Federation's human fleet commander, who had fought tirelessly for Sciyat and then added her name to the list of signatures as soon as the lunar world had been secured. Lissa saw Lance stiffen at the names, but she did not want to ask about them just yet. Instead, she listened to the rest of the report in grim silence. The broadcast ended with a reminder to civilians that they were now obligated to report any and all Neo-Andromedan activity to authorities, though direct involvement in purge efforts was strongly discouraged.

"Discouraged," Lance said, switching off the broadcast. "But not punished." He gave Lissa a steady look. "We're going to have to watch our steps very carefully now."

She looked back at him, and felt her lips curve into a dry smile. "I've done that my whole life."

He considered her for a moment, then glanced towards the communication systems, but made no move to bring the news broadcast back up. "You were right about us needing to run," he said. "It was all we could do."

Lissa forced her dulled mind to focus on him for a moment. She saw the resigned hang of his head, and the slack, disappointed slant of his shoulders. This was not how he had looked on Ametria, or on Jetune, or on Mezora. This was different. This was safe. She reached out and touched his arm. "But that's not the only thing we will do."

Lance nodded, meeting her eye. He seemed to be struggling with a decision, but after a moment, resolve flashed across his face and he dug into his jacket pocket. He pulled out a small black ball and handed it to her. "I thought you might want this."

Lissa stared down at the navi-sphere. It was the one Aven had always carried, and the twin to the one secured to her belt.

"I'm sorry I didn't give it to you sooner," Lance said. "There was a lot going on and... I may have been a little afraid that you'd want to kill me when I handed it to you." He gave her a long, searching look, then added quietly, "He was alive when I saw him."

Lissa ran her thumb over the crack in the surface. "It's

broken."

"Yeah. He, uh, threw it at the wall. After I told him what happened to you."

She raised her head and looked Lance dead in the eye. Her voice was calm and quiet when she said, "That's not why he threw it."

Lance hesitated, and then shook his head. "No."

She looked at the navi-sphere again.

"Are you all right?" he asked after a long pause.

"I'm…" Lissa searched for the word, for the feeling, but there was no pain, no anger, not even any shock. "Relieved, I think," she finally said. "I always knew that if I ever held this again, it would probably mean that Aven wasn't alive anymore. But then, he hasn't really been alive for a long time." She leaned forward and put the navi-sphere on the control panel, resting it between a few raised buttons. It fractured the reflection of the light on its black surface, and Lissa knew with solid certainty that her brother was dead. The tether had been cut. "It's better this way. No one can touch him now. Not me, not the Star Federation, not the Seventh Sun." She looked back at Lance. "He outran the Light."

Lance held her gaze for a long time. "The Seventh Sun has some pretty grand ideas about themselves." He turned in his seat, taking her hand in his. She did not pull away. "Burning brightest of them all, and all those other comparisons to light."

"'Light touches everything,'" Lissa said, remembering words from a long time ago. "'Nothing is faster, nothing is concealed from it.'" She laughed suddenly, and was surprised by the firmness of the sound. "Starships have been faster than light for a long time."

Lance half-smiled, but the rest of him was taken over by something unfathomable. "It's not just starships." He looked her dead in the eye. "Shadows are faster, too."

Lissa said nothing.

After a moment, he released her hand. "It was just something that occurred to me." He turned back to the controls. "You should probably get some more rest. We've got a ways to go before we reach Phan. There's not much worth staying awake for."

Lissa studied him for a long moment, and it occurred to her that she was finally glad that he was there with her. She thought that, maybe, if it had come to it, she could have gone after the Seventh Sun alone, but she was grateful that she did not have to. "Shadows are faster than light?" she asked.

Lance glanced at her, and nodded.

Lissa stayed in the control room. There was data to be translated and locations to be found, hunts to be completed and enemies to be confronted, but for now, Lissa did not think about those things and gave herself over to exhaustion, relaxing for the first time in a very long time. She stayed and she watched Lance pilot the ship as it sprinted past the stars, plunging through the darkness and carrying them forward, always forward. And together, they outran the light.

ABOUT THE AUTHOR

K. N. Salustro is a writer from New Jersey
who loves outer space, dragons, and good stories.
When not at her day job, she runs an Etsy shop as a
plush artist, and makes art for her Society6
and Redbubble shops.

For updates, new content, and other news,
you can follow K. N. Salustro on:

Wordpress: https://knsalustro.wordpress.com/

Facebook: https://www.facebook.com/knsalustro/

Twitter: https://twitter.com/knsalustro

65220558R00176

Made in the USA
Charleston, SC
17 December 2016